The Lighthouse Keeper

Colin Youngman

The Works of Colin Youngman:

The Lighthouse Keeper (Ryan Jarrod Book 3)

The Girl On The Quay (Ryan Jarrod Book 2)

The Angel Falls (Ryan Jarrod Book 1)

The Doom Brae Witch

Alley Rat

DEAD Heat

Twists*

Incorporates:
DEAD Lines
Brittle Justice
The Refugee
A Fall Before Pride
Vicious Circle

All the above are also available separately

Colin Youngman

This is a work of fiction.

All characters and events are products of the author's imagination.

Whilst the majority of locations are real, some liberties have been taken with architectural design, precise geographic features, and timelines.

A SprintS Publication

Copyright 2020 © Colin Youngman

All rights reserved.

No part of this publication, paperback or e-book, may be reproduced, stored in a retrieval system, or transmitted, in any form or in any means – by written, electronic, mechanical, photocopying, recording or otherwise – without prior written permission of the author.

ISBN -13: 979-8-56904-564-8

The Lighthouse Keeper

DEDICATION

For Lewis.

'In order for the light to shine so brightly darkness must also be present.'

Francis Bacon

'We serial killers are your sons.
We are your husbands.
We are everywhere.'

Ted Bundy

CHAPTER ONE

'I was eight years old when I knew I was going to die. I don't mean die at some point; I mean die right there and then.

It was the smell I remember most. The smell of stale beer, cigarette smoke, and sex. Of course, I didn't know what sex smelt like. Not back then. But that's what it was. And it was the worst by far.

Apart from the stench, the other thing I remember were the calluses on his fingers as they squeezed me by the throat. They pushed my face down into the mattress. I could barely breathe. They kept on holding me while he forced my head into the frame of the old Z-bed until my neck wedged in it. I knew he was going to unfold the bed. I knew he was going to do it, and I knew it would break my neck.

That's when I knew I was going to die.

But I didn't.

When I looked up, the gun quivered in Mum's hand. She looked less alive than Uncle Jed even though he didn't have a head anymore. All that remained of it was the splatter of brains across the old mattress, against the wall, and over my face.

Strange thing is, it wasn't him I blamed. I still don't. I blame HER. It was her fault. She brought him into the house. Our house. My house.

Anyway, that's my story. You know everything now. I just thought you deserved an explanation, that's all.'

**

It wasn't yet dawn but Ryan Jarrod sat on a wooden bench, dressed in T-shirt and boxers, and breathed in the scent of pine and lavender.

The rear garden was like the house itself, small and modest, but it was his garden outside his house. That's what mattered.

Like most others in The Drive, it consisted of little more than a boxing-ring square of lawn bordered by privet and hawthorn, and the pine and lavender his senses feasted upon. Backing onto its rear fence, the gardens of The Crescent lay still as starlight.

Ryan cupped his hands behind his head and looked up at the pre-dawn sky. Life, he thought, was good.

He heard the French doors slide open. Hannah Graves, girlfriend and colleague, stepped through, a tray laden with toast, croissants, and a carafe of coffee in her hands. She sat next to him and he slid his arm around her shoulders.

'You're too good to me,' he said.

'I know.' She craned her neck and kissed him.

She buttered toast while he poured the coffee.

'Back to work for you tomorrow,' he said.

She bit into her toast, an index finger dabbing crumbs from her lips. 'I'm ready for it. Not used to time off. Besides, when I do get any, it reminds me of…well, you know.'

He did. Little over a year ago, an undercover mission had gone wrong. She had been abducted. It very nearly cost Hannah her life. Instead, the external damage was restricted to a deviated septum where her nose had been broken. Psychologically, though, she struggled and needed constant activity to keep her mind occupied and away from what-might-have-been.

Ryan tenderly touched the bend in her nose. 'I've been there, too, remember. I know what it's like.' Self-consciously, he sat on his fire-scarred hands.

She nestled her head against his shoulder.

'Why don't you move in? Permanent, like?' Ryan asked.

Hannah sighed. 'Not yet, Ry. Give it a while, yeah? You need to get used to having a place of your own first.'

What she didn't say was, the place creeped her out. Just a little, but enough to raise a few red flags in her head.

'Suppose. You spend most of your time here now, that's all I was thinking.'

'And it's a good thought. Hang onto it.'

They sat in silence as the sky glowed silver as frost yet warm as mother's milk.

'If you're sure you're going back to Jesmond,' he said, 'Why don't you pack your gear up while I'm at the station? It's going to be a scorcher today so how about a run down the coast tonight? A couple of pints in the Left Luggage Room, maybe grab a curry at Shampans? I'll need to book, of course.'

Ryan stood. Stretched until his back clicked. He tangled his fingers in Hannah's curls. 'I've got to get mesel sorted for me shift now but it's dead quiet at the minute so, unless all hell breaks loose, the DCI should be okay with me shooting off early. How does that sound?'

'Mmm,' she said through a mouthful of toast. 'It sounds good.'

It did, except he should have known better.

All hell WAS about to break loose.

**

Chelsea Birch turned her back on the bone-white dome of the Spanish City. She reached behind her, tightened the band around her hair, and breathed in the salinity of sea air.

She felt good. What's more, her fitness tracker told her that her pace was good, too. Chelsea set off back along the links, retracing her steps northbound.

The sky was clear and light, the prelude to sunrise, but streetlights still illuminated the promenade. They picked out the reflective, hallucinogenic whorls of mauve, lime green, and cerise adorning her black lycra running gear.

The sea to her right lay calm and tranquil, the A193 on her left quiet, the music from her headphones loud. George Ezra passed the musical baton to the Kaiser Chiefs as she crossed the Brierdene car park and veered right onto lush grass.

Chelsea checked her watch, dipped her head, and increased her pace; hair swinging behind her like the tail of a show pony.

The miniature golf course was hidden beneath a swirl of low mist which hung inches from the ground like a spirit. A lone greenkeeper tended to the turf and he acknowledged her wave with a salute as she jogged past.

The morning sky blushed pink as the sun peeked up at it from below the horizon. The day promised warmth yet, for now, she was grateful for the cool breeze generated by her pace.

She was on the cliff path, her gaze focused on the smooth dark water far below. She lowered the volume of her music so she could make out the sound of the tide, like the peaceful breathing of a sleeping child. It never failed to soothe her.

While Chelsea treated happiness as an unwelcome imposter, she at least felt cautiously content with life. It was the best it ever got for her, and she was comfortable that way. For once, she was the one in control and she liked the feeling. She afforded herself a smile. 'Let's face it,' she thought, 'After everything, I deserve it.'

Chelsea had completed three and a half of her five-mile route. Only her favourite stretch remained. She swung right, lengthened her stride across the deserted clifftop car park, and continued along the headland's downslope towards Curry's Point.

Ahead of her, the salt-washed white column of St Mary's Lighthouse, circled by screeching kittiwakes like riders on a carousel, emerged from a blue-white sea fret which softened the angularity of the distant Blyth wind turbines.

Chelsea had timed her run to suit the tides. The causeway to the lighthouse's island was exposed and accessible and, with the sounds of nature all around her, she hopped her way over puddles and algae and lichens towards St Mary's Island.

Her fingers sought out the volume control and her ears drowned in the warm tones of Pharrell Williams's 'Happy' as she squinted into the red petals of a blossoming sun.

Inexplicably, her vision darkened, then burst in a prism of white light. She was on her knees, a fiery explosion burning at the base of her skull where the man gripped her ponytail.

Her headphones somersaulted from her as the attacker pushed her forward, still holding her hair in a vice-like grip. He hauled her sideways. Filaments of her red mane tore from her scalp. Chelsea knew where he was dragging her. She felt the cold against her legs as he forced her from the causeway into the sea, the surface a blurred sparkle in the rising sun.

Seconds later, the water lapped at her thighs, cold and forbidding. She felt dizzy. Realised she'd stopped breathing. She opened her mouth to fill her lungs with oxygen, only for her throat to flood with thick saline as the man pressed her face beneath the waves.

She squirmed, managed to raise her face from the sea, and forced water from her lungs with an explosive cough.

The hand tightened its grip. Drove her head beneath the surface once more. Held her there. She twisted and kicked. Spots danced across her vision. The hand was relentless, crushing her head downwards so her face became encased in wet sand and debris, clogging her throat, grinding her gums until they bled.

Everything darkened. Chelsea's mind began to close down at the same time as her lungs exploded with pain. Her only reflex was to scream, and it was the scream which sealed her fate. Solid clumps of wet sand blocked her throat. There was only one thing left for Chelsea Birch; the spastic, reflexive kicks of death.

The man stood. He brushed sand and shells from his hands as he spoke to her.

'…I just thought you deserved an explanation, that's all,' he concluded.

He bent to retrieve her headphones from the causeway. Music still played, tinny and remote, but enough for him to recognise the song. The man chuckled.

It was Talking Heads.

Psycho Killer.

CHAPTER TWO

The morning sky, tissue-paper fragile, lay overhead, thin, and sun-bleached. Despite the promised heat, Karl McKinnon knew better than to risk a wetsuit in these waters. He'd made that mistake once. Never again. His teeth still chattered at the memory.

Instead, he zipped up his dry suit and shrugged the ten-litre cylinder tanks over his shoulders. He waddled over limpet-strewn ridges, dragging his flippers across the rocks with the ungainliness of an arthritic penguin. 'Yes,' he thought, 'Shore dives are a bugger.' He came alive when he finally slipped into thirteen degrees of inky sea, free from gravity and the weight of clunky equipment.

A pair of greater black-backed gulls, thick-necked and adorned in crisp white and grey plumage, came thumping through the air. They swooped low enough for their wing tips to stir the surface as they flew alongside him for a blissful moment before he arched his body and kicked downwards.

The Janet Clark lay in nine metres of water off the nor-eastern edge of St Mary's Island. She had run aground on Christmas Eve 1894 in a worsening storm. Waves breached the vessel and carried away her wheelhouse, bridge equipment, and compasses leaving her at the mercy of tide and weather.

She broke up around three a.m., her engine room shorn from her on impact with the reef. All that remained of the engine was the boiler, which stood upright, aft of the main wreck, and served as a navigation point for divers.

When Karl McKinnon came across it, he flicked on his torch and immediately the blackness all around him awakened. Through a jungle of kelp, the mass of the Janet Clark loomed at right angles to the reef. Barnacles and anemones had adopted the hulk and they reflected in his torchlight like an underwater rainbow of pinks, greens, and yellows.

Karl circumnavigated the hull and kicked down to deeper waters where the Janet Clark's propellers lay. He withdrew his waterproof camera and snapped away, uncertain whether the beam of his torch offered sufficient light to penetrate the murk at this depth.

He felt something nudge against his legs; once, twice and a third time. He flipped around to catch sight of a grey seal, increasingly common in the waters around Whitley Bay, watching him with her enormous bug eyes. He raised his camera only for her to swim off coquettishly before he had her in focus.

Karl moved on. West of the wreck, in a deep gully between shards of reef, he discovered a series of rib-like girders protruding from the seabed and a scattering of rusted metal plates wedged in crevices. He snapped these, too.

Another nudge on his legs told him his seal was back. Smiling beneath his mask, Karl McKinnon raised his camera, tumbled one-hundred and eighty degrees in the waters, and snapped away on repeat.

The shots were perfect.

But, they weren't shots of a seal with doleful eyes.

The eyes he captured were the empty sockets of something much less palatable.

**

'Bloody hell. It's quiet as a grave in here,' Ryan said as he entered the open-plan squad room universally but inaccurately referred to as the bullpen.

Gavin O'Hara looked up from his computer screen. 'Aye. Another quiet day in the office.'

'Where is everybody?'

'Sue's checking out a counterfeit sportswear importer, Ravi's downstairs with the tech guys, and Hannah's on leave - but you know that already.'

'Todd?'

'He's around somewhere. Treblecock's not due back from Cornwall 'til tomorrow. Lyall Parker's on lates.'

'What about the DCI?'

'Foreskin's in with the Super. Connor wanted an update on the course he'd been on last week. You know what the Super's like. If it's not value for money, nee bugger else will get the chance to go on it.'

Ryan agreed. Not that he had any inclination to go on a course anyway, but Superintendent Connor's penny-pinching and obsession with budgets was having an impact everywhere.

Especially on the coffee supplies. 'Ah man, just tea again?' Ryan complained to the vending machine.

'Yep. 'Fraid so,' Gavin confirmed.

Ryan wandered to the water dispenser instead and filled a plastic cup. 'I remember last summer was quiet as well, but at least we had coffee.'

Gavin spun on his chair like a kid on a merry-go-round. 'Swings and roundabouts, Ryan. Something'll turn up.'

'As long as it's not today. I'm after an early one. I've got plans.'

'Care to share?'

'Suffice to say they involve beer, food, and DC Hannah Graves.'

Gavin smiled. 'Pretty serious, you and Hannah now, isn't it?'

Ryan tapped the side of his nose. 'Keep it out, Gav,' he smirked.

'You started it,' O'Hara chuckled.

Ryan held his hands in front of him, wrists together. 'Fair cop, guv.'

He fished a pile of folders from a drawer while his computer booted up. 'Right, let's see what the Gods of Forth Street have in store for us today.'

The answer was, not a lot. It was looking good for his early finish.

DCI Stephen Danskin emerged from one room and slipped into his own. Ryan followed him in. 'Can I have a word, sir?'

'Aye, take a pew, son.' He pulled a face at a sip of stone-cold tea and popped a mint imperial between his lips instead. 'What's up?'

'Nothing really, sir. I was just going to say if nowt new turns up today, I'd like to shoot off a bit early, if that's okay.'

Danskin rolled the sweet around his mouth. 'You're not in the civil service now, Jarrod. You're big enough and ugly enough to make your own decisions, just so long as you get your report on the racist attacks in Elswick to me before you go. What you got planned, like?'

'It's the last day of Hannah's week off. You've got us on different shifts for a couple of weeks so I thought we'd have a night out. Pop down to Whitley for some scran or summat.'

Danskin shook his head. 'Some scran or summat,' he chided. 'How romantic. You sure know how to treat my stepdaughter.'

Ryan knew the DCI was joking but he still felt the blush heat his throat. He began to explain himself when Danskin's phone rang.

Danskin held up a hand to shush him. A few 'Uh-huhs,' 'I sees,' and 'Yeps' followed. He ended the call and looked at Ryan.

'How do you fancy gannin' to Whitley Bay a bit early? Like, in half an hour? Something nasty's just been washed up.'

**

The Lighthouse Keeper

By the time Ryan arrived at Curry's Point, the uniform boys were busy taking down the cordon tape which held back a gaggle of rubberneckers.

Ryan flashed his ID. 'What are you doing? We can't be done already, man.'

A young cop, younger even than Ryan, shrugged. 'False alarm, apparently.'

'Who's call was that?'

The cop tipped his head. 'His.'

Ryan shielded his eyes from the sun as he followed the man's gaze. A figure stood three parts along the causeway. 'Is that who I think it is?'

'If you mean the pathologist, aye; it's him.'

Ryan was already making his way towards Aaron Elliott.

Dr Elliott was an oddball, but Ryan guessed it came with the line of work. And, he had to admit, he quite liked him.

'If it isn't Young Sherlock. How are you?' Elliott greeted him.

'Canny, man. I didn't recognise you with your clothes on.'

Aaron Elliott laughed. 'I know what you mean. I have to say it's a pleasure to be in my civvies for once.'

'And not like you at all. Why no PPE? You're normally obsessed with it.'

Elliott tossed his head. Long, unkempt hair flew out like a solar flare. 'No need.'

'Why's that?'

Elliott bent and retrieved something from behind a boulder. The sun caught the object and reflected white light into Ryan's eyes.

It was a skull. And, unmistakably, a human one.

'Jesus Christ,' Ryan gasped. 'The lads up top said it was a false alarm. They need to get the cordon back up pronto.'

'I wouldn't bother.'

'Howay, man. It's a crime scene.'

'Nope. You're wrong, Sherlock. Well, if you're not wrong, you're not going to arrest anyone for it.'

'How can you be so sure?'

'Because this little beauty,' he said, cradling the skull, 'Dates back to the sixteenth century. Properly interred it's been, as well.'

'What? You can tell that just by looking at it?'

'I wish. No, he told me.'

Ryan looked the length of the causeway, island-side. A man stood at its tip, legs astride, arms folded, watching them.

'His name's Freddie. He's the island warden. Told me all about our friend here. I dare say you'll want a word?'

'Too right I would.'

'The diver who found it is there somewhere, too. Poor chap. He looks like Richard Dreyfuss did when Ben Gardner's head popped out in Jaws.'

Ryan offered a grim smile. 'I bet he does.'

Elliott tossed the skull into the air and caught it one-handed. 'I'll get Yorick here back to the lab while you chat to old Freddie. You might need a translator, mind.'

Ryan soon understood what Elliott meant. He introduced himself and asked the man to confirm he was Freddie.

'It's Ferdie, man, Ferdie Milburn but divvent worry: they ayll get it wreng.' He spoke with the elongated, flattened vowels of the Northumbrian burr.

'Okay, Mr Milburn. I gather you believe the remains are historic.'

The man removed a sailor's cap from his head and scratched a thatch of grey hair. 'Bound to be.'

'And you would know that, as the warden here, I guess?'

Ferdie nodded.

'How long have you been here, Mr Milburn?'

'Two years next month. Afore that, I worked a Bert from Emble to the Ferns.'

Ryan took a moment to digest the information. *'He ran tourist boat trips from Amble marina to the Farne Islands,'* his brain translated.

'So, not long, then. What makes you so sure the remains Mr McKinnon found are ancient?'

Ferdie Milburn rubbed an anchor tattoo on his forearm. Idly, Ryan thought all Ferdie lacked was a pipe, a can of spinach, and an overly-thin wife.

'Let me show you something,' the warden said.

Ryan followed the man to the rear of an ancient stone cottage. Through the window, he saw a female PC talking to a shell-shocked Karl McKinnon, dry suit hanging loose to his waist, towel around his shoulders, mug of tea in his hands.

At the back of the cottage, Ryan looked down into a six-metre long trench and signs of abandoned groundworks.

'They wanted to build a tearoom here,' Milburn explained. 'I didn't, like, but I didn't have much say. Me cottage used to be a pub. The Square and Compass, it was called. Been here since 1861. Rumour has it, they fund human bones when they durg the foundations.'

Ryan's brow furrowed, but not at the warden's dialect. He was growing accustomed to it by now. 'I don't buy it. 1861 until now, and nowt else has turned up in the meantime? Nah, doesn't ring true to me.'

Ferdie pointed to the abandoned works. 'Aboot nine months ago, this started. They turned up a load of skeletons and such like. When they checked the records, they fund a chapel used to be here. And a graveyard. Seems the burial ground lies under me cottage. Their work came to a turtle stop.'

Ryan stifled a smile as a vision of a stationary amphibian, rather than an absolute halt to the development, sprang to mind.

'The remains were reinterred on the mainland but it looks like some got washed oot to sea,' Milburn concluded.

Ryan glanced back at the cottage. 'And then washed back in on the tide.'

'That's aboot the size of it.'

Ryan rubbed his nose. 'Okay, Mr Milburn. Thanks for your time. I'll leave you to it.'

'Aye, and tek Jacques Cousteau with you. You've got less than fifteen minutes before tide comes in. I cannot be minded to be stuck with him for the next few hours.'

Ryan extended his hand. 'You've been most helpful.'

Ferdie Milburn pirouetted three-hundred and sixty degrees. He saw Ryan's perplexed expression. 'An owld tradition,' Milburn explained. 'Bones belong to Davy Jones's locker, not wi' me.'

He spun again. 'Sends the curse back out to sea. You better try it.'

Ryan declined the invitation.

It was a decision he'd live to regret.

CHAPTER THREE

They set their menus down on crisp white linen. Ryan's hand dipped in and out of his pocket as he waited for service.

'Are you okay, Ry?' Hannah enquired. 'You seem a bit edgy.'

He gave her a thin smile. 'Aye,' was all he said.

'Has the call out to St Mary's bugged you?'

'No, man. I'm aal reet. Maybe I shouldn't have brought the car. If I'd had a pint or two, I'd be fine. Kaliber doesn't exactly hit the spot.'

Hannah's fingertips alighted on his. 'Have a beer with your meal. One can't do any harm.'

'I think I will.' He signalled to a waiter. 'We're ready when you are, mate.'

The waiter wandered over, Ryan assumed to take their order but, with his plastic visor face-covering, he might have come to weld their table.

'Pint and a half of Cobra, please. I'll have a chicken chaat to start and a lamb dopiaza.'

Hannah ordered the veggie samosa and chicken tikka Balti. They'd share a naan.

'Any popadoms?' the waiter asked in an accent more Cullercoats than Kolkata.

They declined and held hands again as their server disappeared into the kitchen.

'You got your stuff back home okay, then?' Ryan asked.

'Yeah. I didn't realise I had so much at yours.'

'You could have stayed, you know.' He avoided her eyes.

She sighed. 'Can I be honest with you?'

He sucked air between his teeth. *'Here we go,'* he thought, nodding.

'It's still your gran's house. You bought it from her to fund her care, but nothing's changed. It's all floral chintz. Old furniture. It's even got net curtains, for God's sake.'

Ryan said nothing, his hand leaving hers and burrowing into his pocket. This wasn't going the way he'd planned.

The waiter delivered their starter at the same time as a second arrived with their drinks.

'I don't want to be unkind, Ryan, but I don't want to live in a shrine to your gran.'

'You talk as if she's dead,' he answered defensively.

'She's not, but she's never coming back to the house, either. It's yours now. Update it, man.' Her brown eyes were gentle but her words strong.

Ryan sipped his lager. With his other hand, he fingered the box in his pocket. Inside it, his grandmother's engagement ring. It had seemed a good idea at the time. Clearly, it wasn't.

He wished he'd spun with Ferdie Milburn.

Ryan shrugged off the disappointment. There'd be other days, other opportunities, other rings.

Shampan's was quiet in its socially-distanced way, but when The Blaydon Races echoed through it, all eyes turned to him as he answered his phone.

'Sir, I'm in the middle of something.'

Hannah rolled her eyes. Interruptions came with the territory, but it didn't make it any easier.

'Are you still in Whitley?' Danskin asked.

'Yes.' A short, clipped response.

'Good. Then get yersel back to St Mary's. Lyall's already there but he could do with a hand until Robson arrives. You're closest.'

'What's happened now?' Ryan asked through gritted teeth.

'Another one's been washed up.'

'Sir, man, I told you: the remains are centuries old. Elliott's confirmed it. It's nowt to do with us.'

'It has this time. Unless they had lycra running gear back in Chaucer's day, this one's fresh.'

**

The tide had run its full cycle and the island was again accessible via the causeway. Having seen his evening in tatters and his erstwhile fiancée despatched home in a cab, Ryan trudged across it like a man to the gallows.

At the rear of the cottage, on the seaward-facing side of the island, he found Aaron Elliott and the forensic team already there. The fact the pathologist was in full garb told him the find was real this time.

Elliott saw him coming and intercepted him. 'That's as far as you get at the moment, Sherlock. We're still busy with her.'

'So, it's not just bones this time? You can tell she's female?'

Elliott inclined his head. 'A pretty one, too. At least, she was until she got battered against that.'

Ryan looked at a concrete pyramid emerging from the North Sea a few yards offshore. 'What is it?'

'It's a rangefinder tower. Built during the first world war. Our friend got wedged in the rocks alongside it and the current decided it was a clever idea to use her head as a wrecking ball.'

Ryan grimaced. 'Where's DI Parker? I was told he was already here.'

'He is. He's in the cottage with Freddie. It was him who found her.'

'Ferdie, but let's not split hairs.'

A breathless Todd Robson arrived on the scene. 'What we got?'

DI Lyall Parker saw him coming and left the cottage to join the group. Between him, Ryan, and Elliott, they filled Robson in on the detail.

'Do we know if this was an accidental drowning?' the quietly-spoken Parker asked Elliott. 'If it is, we can all get away home before the tide turns.'

'Too early to say,' Elliott replied. 'However, I suspect not. There are recent contusions and haematoma at the base of the girl's cranium, either side of her neck, which weren't caused by tidal motion. Don't quote me, but I'd say they're consistent with downward pressure. Someone forced her face under the water.'

'Hang on, if she was held under, does that mean she wasn't killed here? That it happened nearer shore?' Todd Robson asked.

'I suspect it did. Well, not on shore, exactly. Some of the detritus under her fingernails appear consistent with what I'd expect to see on the causeway. Off the record, I'd guess she was killed on or near the causeway, and her body drifted out to sea on the tide, then back in on it, too.'

Elliott dipped his head towards the forensic team huddled over the body. 'We'll know more when they're done.'

The three detectives turned to watch the forensic activity. The evening air remained warm and humid, but the wind and tides were stronger this side of the island. Breakers crashed against the rocks, spraying the attendants with flecks of greyish foam.

Ryan spoke to Lyall. 'What about Ferdie, the warden? What did he have to say for himself?'

'Och, nae much, and what he did say I couldnae understand. You need subtitles.'

Todd snorted a laugh. 'That's rich, coming from a Jock like you.'

Parker snickered. 'Show some respect, ye ugly bastard. I'm your DI remember?'

'So, what Inspectoring have you been doing?' Todd continued, disrespectfully. 'Has this Freddie…'

'Ferdie,' Ryan corrected.

'Aye, him an' aal; what's he been up to?'

'He's the warden. Protects the wildlife. He reckons he spotted the lassie about twenty minutes before he reported in.'

'Why wait twenty minutes?' Ryan asked.

'He reckons he thought it was a seal carcass washed up. Happens quite a lot, he says. He makes a note of things for the Marine Maritime Agency. Maintains an inventory. He says that's what he was doing.'

'What? He makes a note before he knows what it is?'

'Aye,' Parker said, 'That's what I asked. He said *'What else could it be? Not every day a body gets washed ashore ma island.'* Or words to that effect.'

Ryan thought for a moment. 'Can he account for his movements?'

Parker laughed. 'He's been on the island all the time. I took it at face value. After all, he couldnae go anywhere else once the tide's in.'

Aaron Elliott spoke. 'I'll need to establish time of death back at the lab. She hasn't been in the waters long, I'm certain, but probably long enough for this to happen during a different tide cycle.'

Ryan pulled at his hair. 'Are you still sure the earlier find was historic? I mean, two in one day…'

'Quite sure, Sherlock. There's no connection. Look, I've got to get back out to her. Tides changing and I don't want to lose any evidence that might be out there.'

'Aye, and I'll get back wi' auld Popeye,' DI Parker said. 'He's refusing to budge and I've no call to bring him in. I think I'm going to be stuck oot here all night once tide sets in. You two might as well get back to the station. Run some missing persons checks. See if you can find who the lassie is.'

'I already know. Her name's Chelsea Birch.'

They looked at Elliott.

'What? You can tell who she is from your preliminary examination? How come?'

Elliott smiled. 'Because she's got her name stitched on the inside of her running kit.'

He turned his back on them and walked off towards the body. 'And you call yourselves Detectives,' he said, shaking his head. 'Dear oh dear.'

**

Todd Robson called it in. Back at the station, Danskin borrowed one of DCI Kinnear's lads to run some checks on a Chelsea Birch.

'We've got an address for her,' Todd said before they'd even reached the car park. 'She lives just round the corner. It's a lodge in the caravan park up the road.'

They arrived there in moments. That was the easy part. Finding the lodge was more difficult. Every block looked the same; every caravan, every plot, every turn, identical. They hadn't wanted to alert park management but, in the end, they had no choice.

A charmingly grumpy woman wearing her 'Fiona' name tag upside down led them down nooks and crannies and circuitous loops until she came to a halt outside a downbeat property in a less salubrious corner of the site.

'Are you going to let us in, then?' Todd asked.

'Are you going to ask nicely?' Fiona replied.

'No.'

Fiona tisked but set about fumbling with a set of keys, just in case Todd Robson decided to arrest her, or worse. Eventually, she found the right key and unlocked the door to the lodge. She remained in front of it.

'We respect our client's privacy and their property. I can't let you in there alone.'

'I understand that,' Todd smiled. 'I won't go in alone.'

'Good.'

'I won't go in alone cos me marra here will come in with me. Now, sod off oot the way and let us in.'

Fiona sodded off with a face like a squashed pie.

The Lighthouse Keeper

Inside, the lodge smelled stale and stuffy. Ryan also detected the smell of Chelsea Birch; a reminder that, only hours earlier, their victim had been as alive as they. Ryan shivered.

They found the interior surprisingly roomy. There was a breakfast bar in the kitchen area to their right, which overlooked exterior raised decking and a rusted barbeque. Ryan wandered to the sink. A dirty breakfast bowl and stained mug lay in grey dishwater.

The main living space was to the left of the entrance. The curtains, a dowdy brickwork pattern on them, were closed.

'Christ, they make the place look like a bloody dungeon.' He ripped them open. 'That's better.'

Directly beneath the window lay a beige couch which had seen better days, in front of it, a glass-topped coffee table. Todd's attention was drawn to the laptop on it, lid open. The screen was black, battery dead.

Todd tutted.

Ryan slid into one of two chairs either side of a small dining table. He sifted through some items of mail; a couple of bills, a Dominos menu, nothing much. He put them back and wandered into the bedroom. Todd followed.

The room was orderly, save for a baggy t-shirt and worn panties lying on an unmade bed. Chelsea Birch's phone lay on a side table, charger alongside it. Todd plugged it in, just as his own phone rang.

Ryan left him to the call and checked out the bathroom. It was small and compact, but well-equipped. An array of toiletries stood in a shower rack, one or two of them with their lids flipped open as if recently used. He opened an under-sink unit as Todd Robson entered the cramped space.

'That was the station,' Robson said. 'Our girl isn't known to us. Well, not directly, anyway.'

'What do you mean?'

'She hasn't a record, is what I mean. Born in Stockport. Her mother moved here to be with the bloke who became her stepfather when Chelsea was five.'

Ryan shifted a toothbrush and paste and brought out a white oblong cardboard packet. 'Nowt unusual, then.'

'Oh aye, there is. Chelsea didn't stay with her parents long. Social Services got involved. The lads tell me she was shuffled around foster homes for the rest of her childhood.'

Ryan turned to face Todd, who had moved to the doorway to create space. 'Why?'

'Cos her stepfather was a bloke called Clive Oxley. The name means nowt to me, but seems the bastard was a kiddie-fiddling nonce.'

Ryan's eyes slid shut. He groaned. 'I guess that explains these.' He held up the box. 'Citalopram. It's used to treat depressive disorders and panic attacks, according to the leaflet. There's a few boxes of 'em, an' aal.'

'Poor lass,' Todd said. It was the first genuine display of empathy Ryan had ever witnessed from his hard-faced colleague.

They entered the final room. A spare bedroom, sparsely-furnished. It housed a fold-away bed which would afford more living space once it was stored upright.

Todd checked the drawers of a unit while Ryan flipped through a few items of clothing hanging in a wardrobe. They found nothing of interest. Ryan and Todd each grabbed one side of the fold-away bed and hauled it upright. Beneath it, they found two suitcases. Todd carried one into the living room while Ryan fiddled with the zipper of a second.

The case was heavy. When the lid opened, he realised why. It was crammed full. Lying on the top was a one-piece item of clothing. He fingered the material. It had a strange, almost rubbery feel. Beneath it lay a mask. Ryan understood what it was. At least, he thought he did.

'Todd,' he called. 'Look at this.'

A shadow fell over him, telling him Robson was behind him. 'Seems like Chelsea was the athletic sort. We know she was into running. Looks like she was a diver, too.'

He held up his find and was surprised to see Todd crack up with laughter.

'Howay, man. That's not diving gear.'

'Then what the hell is it?'

Robson laughed again. 'It looks like there's more to wor lass than we first thought.'

'Waddya mean?'

'That's a bondage suit. Chelsea Birch was a fetishist.'

CHAPTER FOUR

'She ran towards me, still holding the gun in her hand. She took me in her arms and squeezed me tight. I felt I was suffocating all over again, this time in the folds of her enormous saggy breasts. I think I preferred the mattress. In fact, I know I did.

I felt her tears on my cheek, and she planted horrid wet, sloppy kisses on my forehead. Uncle Jed's brain matter still hung from my hair but it was preferable to her drool. I wanted to wipe it all away but I couldn't. I couldn't because she had my arms pinned to my side, and she was crushing me with her tits.

All I could do was listen to her telling me it would be alright. That the policeman would understand. He wouldn't send her to jail, and she'd be there to protect me.

She didn't realise that's why I was crying. I didn't need her to protect me. I wanted her to go to jail. Even better, I wanted the ground to open up and swallow her.

Just like it has you, my dear.

But, don't worry. You'll soon be covered up. I'm going to do that right now.

I just thought you deserved an explanation, that's all.'

**

On the third floor of the Forth Street police HQ, Ravi Sangar sat with Chelsea Birch's laptop and mobile phone in front of him. Ryan and Todd had recovered the items from the lodge having been unable to access either. They knew Ravi would soon hack in, and he weaved his technical wizardry over them while Stephen Danskin leaned over his shoulder. Todd Robson sat at the desk alongside.

Ryan stood, cursing, at the vending machine's lack of coffee. He retrieved a femmer plastic cup from the tray and sipped a tasteless powdery drink known by the alias 'Vegetable Soup.'

The Lighthouse Keeper

'Wish you'd had the decency to wait until I'd had me main course, sir,' he complained. 'I'm famished but even I'm struggling with this muck.'

'Stop your whinging, Jarrod. It was your choice to stay. I told you to get off home an hour ago. Besides, you could be stuck on St Mary's island for the night, like Lyall.'

Ryan couldn't disagree. Instead, he wandered over to the threesome busy hacking into Chelsea Birch's private affairs. He felt a degree of disquiet, wondering what Chelsea would think of a group of men about to poke their noses into her business.

Todd Robson had no such qualms. 'Howay man, Ravi. Hurry up.'

'I shouldn't be much longer.'

'Odd name, 'Chelsea', isn't it?' Todd mused.

'I quite like it,' Ravi replied. 'And it's more common these days. There's Chelsea Clinton, Chelsea Halfpenny...'

'Who?'

'Chelsea Halfpenny. She was in Emmerdale and Casualty. She's from Leam Lane, you know. I used to live there.'

'Poor bugger.'

'How, there's nowt wrong with the Leam.'

'Nah. I meant, being in Emmerdale. Anyway, it's still an odd name. You don't hear of anybody calling their kid Arsenal, do you? Or, Queens Park Rangers?'

'Robson: stop prattling on, man, will you?' Danskin said. 'It's a murdered lass we're talking about. Show a bit of respect.'

They were saved from Todd's riposte by Ravi. 'Right, lads. We're in.'

'Phone first, Sangar. I want to see if she contacted anyone this morning.'

Her activity log was suspiciously bare. No calls – incoming or outgoing – for three days. There were a couple of calls from unrecognised numbers before that, a call from a

Lennie, three from a Natalie, and one from an Ahmed. The last outgoing call was over two weeks ago.

'Check texts,' Danskin instructed.

Lennie and Ahmed turned out to be guys from Heaton Harriers. There was nothing significant in the exchanges. It seemed like the three of them were sharing progress reports on their running performances.

'What about this one?' Ravi asked. Four days ago, Ahmed had texted, '*Do you wanna hook up?*'

'Hmmm. For a run, or something more personal? I wonder.'

'Whatever it was, Chelsea didn't reply.'

Danskin made a note to check Ahmed out.

There were a series of chats with Natalie. One caught Ryan's eye. The exchange ended with Chelsea saying, *'I've had another one from him. Think I'll change my profile. Can't be too careful lol'*, and a couple of smiley face Emojis.

'Another what? And who's he?'

'Whoever he is, there's nowt here to give us a lead. In fact, for a young lass, she led a pretty humdrum life judging by how few contacts she had. Let's try her laptop.'

Ravi's programme bypassed the password screens. 'Let's start with her e-mails.'

The monitor screen filled with text. Chelsea's in-box overflowed with hundreds of e-mails.

'Whoa, whoa, whoa,' Danskin said. 'Whatever she lacked in phone contacts, she more than makes up for in her e-mail list. There's hundreds of the damn things. Looks like this is where she did most her communicating and correspondence.'

'Look at the addresses. I'd wager most of these are blokes,' Ryan noted.

'Aye, it looks like it, doesn't it? Let's see what they've got to say for themselves.' Ravi opened the first.

Hiya Miss Styx. You were so strict with me last night. I'll have to be naughty again very soon xxx.

'What the fuck?'

Ravi opened the next e-mail in the list.

I look forward to our session in two weeks. Would you be so kind to wear the rubber outfit I sent you? Wearing something of mine would make me so horny. And I know what you do to horny boys.'

'Jesus Christ, what is this?'

Ravi randomly clicked on a third e-mail.

My Dear Miss Styx, my wife says she would LOVE to watch our next session. Do you have anything special to wear just for the ladies? My wife likes VERY high heels and she says she can imagine you trampling all over my balls in them.

Danskin stared at the laptop open-mouthed while Todd Robson guffawed heartily.

'That explains the stuff we found in the lodge. Our Chelsea girl had a nice little earner performing to camera for a load of saddos.'

Stephen Danskin blew out air while tugging an earlobe. 'We've got enough suspects here to fill St James's. Where the hell do we start?'

Ryan made a suggestion. 'What about social media? Check her Facebook account, or Instagram. Cross-match them with the pervs in her e-mail list. It might be a starting point if any crop up on both.'

'Good idea, Jarrod. Ravi – do it.'

Accessing the account was the easy bit. 'Silly, silly girl,' Sangar said. 'Her profile's set to public. Will they never learn?'

Chelsea Birch's friend list extended to no more than forty-eight. Precious few more than her phone contacts. A quick scroll through them rang no alarm bells.

'Check Messenger. Any Tom, Dick, or Harry could message her.'

There were a few chats with Natalie, but none with either Lennie or Ahmed. A couple of meaningless GIFS from someone called Leia, a few harmless photos of an Annie Mee's pet rabbit, an image of a friend snorkelling in the

Caribbean, an innocent exchange over site fees for her lodge; nothing from anyone tagged '*Your murderer.*'

'Okay, guys. Let's shut this down 'til morning,' Danskin suggested. 'I'll hand over what we've found to Kinnear's night shift to follow through, and we'll pick up again first thing.'

Ravi was about to close down Chelsea Birch's laptop when Ryan spotted it.

'Hang on,' he said. 'I might have something. The rabbit pictures. Zoom in on the one of it in its hutch.'

'I don't see owt, Jarrod.'

'A bit closer, Ravi. There's summat on top of the cage.'

There was. It was a copy of a magazine. *Bound and Gagged*, it was called.

And an envelope addressed to Ahmed Nuri.

**

The Range Rover wasn't in the car park. That would have been plain stupid. Instead, he'd parked off-road, beneath overhanging trees on East Park Road, far away from the nearest streetlight.

The killer kicked a foot against the wall, dislodged loose soil from it, and did the same with the other foot. The dirt stuck fast to the sole of his left shoe, so he picked at the earth with his fingers. His mouth curled in distaste at the grime lodged beneath his fingernails.

Once inside the vehicle, he removed a bottle of hand sanitizer from the glove box and worked the gel between his fingers. The dirt remained. Goddamn it; he'd been so content just a moment ago. Now, he was angry.

He started the car and headed onto Saltwell Road South and down past the Gold Medal pub onto the A1 at the Team Valley. Before he knew he it, he was beyond Askew Road, on the flyover leading onto the Redheugh Bridge.

He checked the fuel gauge just as its light flickered red. He thought he'd sufficient to get home. He had to, and quickly, because he needed to wash his hands. It was all that bitch's fault. Just like it had been his mother's all those years ago.

He hadn't intended to strike again. Two in one day was one too many. He preferred the anticipation but, because of her, he'd been denied that pleasure.

She shouldn't have replied. If only she'd ignored it and not asked, *'Who is this? Do I know you?'* he'd have enjoyed the build-up to the act the way he'd planned.

He wished now he hadn't given her an explanation. She didn't deserve one. Not after spoiling his fun.

He'd make sure the next one went to plan.

CHAPTER FIVE

Ryan levered himself off the old mahogany-framed bed an hour before his alarm was due. In the continued absence of DS Sue Nairn, Danskin had partnered Ryan with Todd Robson for the early morning knock on Ahmed Nuri's front door, and he'd spent most the night running over the approach he'd take.

Much as he liked Todd, he'd have preferred to work with Nigel Trebilcock. Known to all as 'Treblecock', Nigel was nearer Ryan's age, and considerably less Gene Hunt in approach. But, he wasn't back from holiday until later that day so Todd Robson it was.

When Ryan went to cancel the alarm on his phone, he saw the message notification blinking. '*Yes, I got home alright, thanks for asking.*' No kisses. Hannah was miffed. Tough. He was, too. He reached into the pockets of the trousers crumpled at the foot of his bed and stuffed his grandmother's engagement ring deep inside a bedside drawer.

Perhaps it was for the best their shifts would keep them apart.

He called Todd Robson who, from the sleepy tones and husky voice, clearly hadn't had similar sleep problems. They agreed to meet outside Benfield School, five minutes' walk from Nuri's address in Walkergate. Robson still looked half asleep when he turned up ten minutes late.

Nuri lived in a terraced flat above a takeaway near the dilapidated Railway pub. He answered the front door with bed hair and stale breath. He was older than either had expected; late thirties, Ryan guessed.

'I'm Detective Constable Ryan Jarrod, and this is my colleague, DC Todd Robson.'

'At this time? Seriously?' Nuri asked.

'Deadly,' Todd said.

Nuri led them up a dark narrow staircase adorned with posters of near-naked cartoon characters, women with exaggerated breasts, tight shorts, and huge eyes like something from Area 51. The men sported angular haircuts and even sharper features.

Ryan and Todd followed Nuri into a living space cluttered with an array of artist's easels, free-standing lamps, and a simple desk strewn with charcoal sketches.

One wall was plastered with a giant mural, its vivid colours glistening under a spotlight. The style and vivid colours reminded Ryan of something from CBeebies, the content not so.

The mural portrayed a line of naked women kneeling at the feet of muscle-bound men. All bore the stylised features of the posters on the staircase. The wall bore the signature of its artist, Keifer, in large black paint in the lower right quadrant.

The room contained no furniture, as such.

'You're an artist?' Todd asked.

'Kind of. I produce graphic novels.'

'Comics,' Todd replied, disparagingly.

'Not exactly. Hentai.'

Todd raised an eyebrow.

'It's a Japanese art form. I guess you would call it cartoon porn.' Nuri watched for their reaction. When he got none, he continued. 'What can I do for you?'

'We want to ask you some questions.'

'Should I call a lawyer?'

'I don't know. Should you?'

Ryan took up the questioning. 'Chelsea Birch. You know her?'

Nuri tipped his hand like a set of scales. 'Sort of. We're in the same running club.'

'Anything else?'

'No. Like I say, I know her vaguely through the Harriers.'

'Mr Nuri, you asked if you could hook up with her. What did you mean by that?'

He rubbed his nose. 'Go for a run. That's what Harriers do.'

Todd's turn. 'Do you have a rabbit?'

'What?'

'A rabbit. Do you have one?'

'Look, this is ridiculous. Yes, I keep rabbits. I confess. Lock me up and throw away the key. I keep rabbits in my bedroom. Guilty as charged.'

'Is that where you keep your chains, and your whips, and your dick clamps? Anything else I've missed off the list?'

Ahmed Nuri looked at Todd, then at Ryan. He cleared his throat.

'Okay, officers. Is this where I throw myself to the floor begging you not to tell anyone my dirty little secret? Yes, I like a bit of S and M. You'd be surprised how many people do.'

Ryan and Todd let a silence settle. Quietly, Ryan asked, 'Do you like a bit of S and M with Chelsea Birch? Or, Miss Styx, whichever you prefer to call her.'

Nuri blinked several times. 'We share an interest. That's all. Harmless fun.'

'Did you kill her?'

'What?'

'I'm asking if you killed Chelsea Birch. She was murdered. Yesterday morning.'

Ryan and Todd watched his reaction. The man blanched. Swallowed hard. Rested against the desk. He shook his head.

'Chelsea? Never. I don't believe you.'

'Where were you, Mr Nuri?'

'Where was I when?'

'Yesterday morning. All of it.'

Nuri thought. It took time for the process to kick into gear. 'I was on-line. A zoom workshop with Kendo Ito. He's a world-famous anime artist. You can browse my history if you like. That'll confirm the times. Listen, Chelsea and I never hurt each other. We never even got together. Not in that way.'

Ryan inclined his head; a sign for Todd to follow outside for a con-flab.

'What do you reckon?' Ryan asked.

'I divvent knaa. He could be kosher. It'd be too easy for us to disprove his alibi. But, if he had nowt to hide, why send Chelsea Birch a photo of his rabbit from a fake account? What was it he called himself? Annie Mee, wasn't it?'

Ryan snapped his fingers. 'I think it was an in-joke. For Annie Mee, read anime.'

'Ah, shit, man. Of course.'

They re-entered the room. Ahmed Nuri sat cross-legged on the floor.

'This isn't a wind-up, is it? Chelsea's really dead.'

'I'm afraid she is, Mr Nuri. We'll be off now. Thank you for your help. You need to understand we will be in touch again, though, so don't go anywhere.'

Ahmed Nuri twiddled with his hair. He understood well enough.

**

When Todd and Ryan returned to the station, they found Superintendent Connor next to one of the whiteboards with the DCI alongside him. Treblecock, looking bronzed and healthy after a week in his home county, had been invited to join them for an update.

'How's the case going?' Connor asked.

'The victim's name is Chelsea Birch,' Stephen Danskin said. 'She's twenty-four years old. She was found on the eastern rim of St Mary's Island. Her residence is listed as a lodge in Whitley Bay caravan park, within walking distance of where she was found. She moved there six months ago. Robson and Jarrod have already checked it out.'

Connor looked at a map pinned on the whiteboard, alongside a photo of Chelsea's battered and bruised face.

'Did she rent?'

'No, sir. Owned it outright.'

'I see. She wasn't penniless, then.'

'On the contrary, sir. She had a nice little earner displaying herself on-line in, let's just say, various costumes.'

'Really?' he shook his head, 'You see all sorts in this job.'

'Aye, sir. I'm thinking of taking it up mesel, as it happens. Looking at her PayPal account she was earning more than me.'

Connor inspected the photograph. 'Family been informed?'

'As far as we can tell, she hasn't any. Her stepfather was the last to go, around eight years ago. Found hanging in his cell in Frankland.'

The Super raised his eyebrows. 'Suicide?'

'He was a convicted paedophile. It looked like suicide, but nobody really cared whether he'd topped himself or somebody had made it look like it.'

'Any suspects?'

'For the stepdad or Chelsea?'

'The girl, man.'

'Well, there's her two hundred or so clients for starters.'

'Any local?'

'There's at least one, sir.' Heads turned towards Ryan. 'And we've just interviewed him.'

'And?'

'His name's Ahmed Nuri. He not only shared her interest, as it were, but he also knew her from Heaton Harriers.'

Danskin spoke next. 'Have we enough to bring him in?'

'Nah. He'll remain a person of interest but he seems to have a watertight alibi. Dozens of people aal ower the world were on a zoom conference with him at the time Dr Elliott reckons Chelsea Birch was killed.'

'Bollocks,' Danskin and Connor said together.

'Any other leads?' Connor asked.

Danskin picked up a dry-marker and wrote the name '*Ferdie Milburn*' on the crime board. 'He's the guy who found her. He's the warden on St Mary's. Milburn didn't report it straight away, which is suspicious, but he's given a plausible reason for the delay, sort of.'

'We've not much else to go on,' Robson jumped in, earning a scowl off Danskin who wanted Connor to believe they had a handle on the case.

'We have a few more of her contacts to check,' the DCI added in a damage-limitation exercise. 'Starting with a mate of hers called Natalie Hoffman.'

'Keep at it, Stephen. Oh, and use that whiteboard properly. That's not how you set 'em up these days. Don't tell me I wasted my money sending you on that course.'

Connor marched into his office, where the smell of percolating coffee reached out to them like a banquet to a starving man.

**

Todd Robson was consigned to desk duties where Danskin could keep an eye on him. He and Gavin O'Hara trawled through Chelsea Birch's client list.

The DCI despatched Ryan to speak to Natalie Hoffman. Although perfectly capable of doing it on his own, Jarrod didn't object when Danskin suggested he took Treblecock with him in order to bring the Cornishman up to speed.

They traced Natalie to a restaurant on Clifford Street, off North Shields fish quay. It was a low-key establishment squashed between a warehouse and a fishmongers but it seemed popular enough despite the contrived name 'Mr Mussels.'

The interior consisted of eight square tables each covered by a black-and-white check tablecloth. Six were occupied, meaning the place didn't come close to adhering to social distancing etiquette. The menu was displayed on a crab-shaped chalkboard and consisted of nothing but shellfish.

A tall, slender woman with piercing blue eyes which smiled even when the rest of her face didn't, stood behind a counter. Her badge told them her name was Natalie.

'Natalie?' Ryan asked, nonetheless.

She looked from Ryan to Treblecock, trying to decide if she knew them. After a moment, she smiled.

'What can I get you?'

Ryan flashed her his ID. 'Is there somewhere we could talk?'

She looked through a hatch into a kitchen area resembling a bombsite. 'I'll need to get someone to cover for me.'

A waitress pushed open a swing door with her hip. In one hand she carried a plate of shrimps, in the other a bowl of moules mariniere swimming in a greasy liquid which could have been discharged from BP's Deepwater Horizon.

'Rosalind, when you're done with that order can you cover for me? I'm just popping outside for a moment to help these gentlemen.' Natalie looked at Ryan. 'Ten minutes. That's all I can give you.'

Beneath the overhang of the neighbouring warehouse, Ryan introduced Natalie Hoffman to Trebilcock, remembering to pronounce his surname correctly, as in Sergeant Bilko.

She dragged a forearm over her brow, wiping beads of sweat from it. As she raised her arm, Ryan realised she'd carried the aroma of fish outside with her. He tried not to let distaste show on his face while making a mental note never to bring Hannah to Mr Mussels.

'Reet,' Natalie said. 'I've no idea what you want, so fire away.'

'How do you know Chelsea Birch?' Ryan asked.

The smile disappeared from her eyes, replaced by suspicion and wariness. 'I want to see your badge again.'

'Where did you meet?' he asked as he held his ID in front of her face.

'Here. She came here for a trial. It didn't work out. Look, what is this?'

'Why didn't it work?'

'Not for me to say. You'll have to ask her.'

Ryan's eyes roamed her face, assessing her. 'I can't ask her. Miss Hoffman, Chelsea Birch was found dead yesterday morning.'

Like someone from an am-dram production, her hand shot to her mouth. She leant against the wall and slid all the way down. From her position on the floor, she asked, 'Was it one of her clients?'

'We didn't say she was murdered,' Nigel Trebilcock said.

'Well, no, but...' Natalie stuttered, 'You wouldn't be here if it were natural causes, would you?'

Ryan helped her up. 'Why did she leave Mr Mussels?' he asked again.

'Because she had to deal with people. Natalie doesn't...didn't do people.' She paused for a moment. 'You know about her upbringing, yeah?'

Ryan nodded.

'It affected her. It would anyone,' Natalie concluded.

'You mentioned her clients. Did she ever talk about them?'

She shook her head. 'No, never. Not in any detail.'

'Do you know if she ever dated any of them?'

Natalie barked a laugh. 'You are joking me, aren't you? She hated them but doing what she did give her a sense of control. That was important to her, after her start in life. To the best of my knowledge, I don't think she ever dated anyone.'

'You received a text from her four days before she died. She told you she'd *Received another one from him.*' Do you know what 'it' and who 'he' was?'

She shook her head. Sniffed back tears.

'And why didn't you reply?'

'She sometimes let off steam to me. It was just a release. She must have come across some pretty sad bastards doing what she did. I just let her get things off her chest. She wasn't looking for a reply from me, Mr Jarrod.'

Treblecock spoke next. 'Chelsea ran. Did she always follow the same route?'

'I think so. It made her feel comfortable. She had to have routine. It was the way she was.'

'Why so early?'

Natalie shrugged. 'Who knows? Because of the tides? So she didn't come across people? You'll have to ask h…' She realised what she'd almost said and broke down again.

'Okay, Miss Hoffman. I'm sorry I had to break the news to you this way,' Ryan said, meaning it. 'Would you like me to have a word with your employer? Get you excused for the day?'

'No,' she offered a wan smile. 'I'll be okay. If I think of anything else, I'll let you know.'

'That was my next ask, Natalie. You beat me too it. Thank you again.'

The woman sniffed, rubbed her eyes, and stepped back into the odorous Mr Mussels.

Ryan stared after her. 'You know,' he said to Treblecock, 'I sometimes wonder why I ever wanted to do this job. It bloody stinks.'

CHAPTER SIX

Ryan dropped Treblecock back at Forth Street. He checked in with Danskin. He was knackered, he claimed. Asked if he could take yesterday's excess hours as time in lieu. Much to Todd Robson's chagrin, the DCI had agreed on the proviso he worked the case from home and develop a theory to throw into the mix.

The house in The Drive was empty and hollow after a week of Hannah's presence. Ryan sat in his Gran's favourite straight-backed armchair and tried to focus on the case. It was impossible. His mind drifted, lost to Hannah and a head full of might-have-been.

Ryan slipped outside. Above him, the cornflour blue afternoon sky, streaked with delicate ribbons of cirrus clouds, lay still as a placid lake. Doris Jarrod's old house – his house – stood little more than a mile from her care home. Ryan could have walked it but, instead, he found himself in the womb of his trusty old Fiat.

Ryan's world was inhabited by empty thoughts to such an extent he drove straight on by his Gran's home and pulled into a small forecourt further downhill, more Swalwell than Whickham. When he clambered out the Fiat, he had no idea why it had brought him here.

Pedalling Squares was a quirky establishment. Once home to a garage unit, it was now part bicycle repair shop, part café/tearoom/restaurant. The latter had built up a reputation for excellence. He'd brought Hannah once. She'd loved it. Perhaps that's why his autopilot had directed him here. That, and the fact he'd get some proper coffee.

The tables outside were occupied by guys in cycling gear. He took a single table just inside the French doors, beneath a

Jimi Hendrix portrait which provided an odd juxtaposition to the cycling memorabilia adorning the walls.

Although only two other interior tables were occupied, he felt guilty taking up one in these challenging times for the sake of an Americano, so he also ordered a Froome Dawg from the cycling-themed menu.

Ryan lay back against gaudy pink brickwork and propped his feet against a floor-to-ceiling girder. He closed his eyes and, quite literally, smelt the coffee. He tried to visualise Chelsea Birch's last moments; the coffee aroma replaced by salty sea air.

He pictured the girl running downhill towards the causeway in the silence she loved. It had been a warm morning so, in his mind, he had her sprinting to generate a cool air. But it had been towards the end of her run. Perhaps she was tired. He slowed her pace.

In front of her, at the end of the causeway, the lighthouse stood proud. He visualised her straightening her back, becoming upright so she mimicked its stance.

She was on the causeway now. It would be slippery, seaweed strewn across the uneven concrete surface. She'd plant each foot with care. So, he thought, why wasn't she equally wary of her attacker? Especially if she had trust issues? She should have turned tail and fled. She was young, fit, and healthy. Chances are, she'd have escaped him.

He tried to picture the scene. It was daybreak. The sun would hang low in the sky. What was its angle? Had her attacker been waiting in plain sight, safe in the knowledge its glare would mask his presence the way a cheetah preys on a gazelle?

He considered other possibilities. Did she know her assailant? If so, she'd have no need to evade him. Or, perhaps, she'd been approached from behind. Ryan pondered on the thought. She was running, he realised. So, if the killer had come from her rear, he'd have to run faster.

Could he be an athlete, too? Or, what if he was both someone she knew AND an athlete?

Someone like Ahmed Nuri.

Nuri had an alibi. Ryan made a note to double and triple check it.

He took a sip from his cup, waited for it hit to the spot, then forced his thoughts back to Chelsea Birch's last moments.

He sought inspiration from his surroundings. His gaze settled on a David Baird portrait of Bradley Wiggins which Hannah had much admired on her visit to Pedalling Squares. What if her killer had been a cyclist? If he'd ridden up to her from behind, would she have heard him approach?

Ryan blew out his cheeks, sighing noisily.

Questions, questions, questions. That's all he had.

If only Ryan had chosen a different coffee shop less than a five-minute drive away, he could have put his questions to the killer directly.

**

Towards the rear of Caffe Nero, the man gazed out at the automatons stalking the MetroCentre malls. Faceless wonders, all of them, even without the masks which turned them into clones of one another.

He returned his focus to the tablet in front of him. He scrolled upwards, images and profiles gliding by at an ever-increasing speed. Still, he took in the detail of each one. Nothing escaped his attention.

When he looked up, his eyes locked with those of another. She stood at the window, gazing in. At first, he thought she was just another nobody queuing for a table. She wasn't.

The girl looked directly at him, her eyes bright and alert. The eyes reached into his soul. Beckoned him towards her. His mouth dropped open. She was there for a purpose. She was the one. The next one.

The girl continued to stare at him. Her long, carroty hair tumbled beyond her shoulders. She was perfect.

An older woman came up behind her. She slid her mask down to her chin, mouthed the girl's name, and walked off.

The girl – his girl - continued to gaze into Caffe Nero. She was looking at him, for sure. Slowly, she turned and set off towards the House of Fraser department store. He raised himself from his seat. Like the rats of Hamlyn, he prepared to follow his Pied Piper.

He forced himself back down. Fool. What was he doing? He knew nothing about her. How could he play the game if he didn't know her? Where would the fun lie? The last one had spoilt his fun. He wouldn't make the same mistake.

He shook his head. It had been a lucky escape. For him, not her.

He returned his focus to the i-pad in front of him. She'd be on there, somewhere. He'd find her; he'd recognise those eyes. Besides, she had a name, now. He'd lip-read her friend.

The killer scrolled through countless Facebook profiles of those named Jasmine.

Oh, yes: he'd find her, for sure. Then, the fun would begin.

**

The cycling party outside had left their tables. Ryan slipped outside and pulled his phone from his pocket. He called the station. DI Lyall Parker picked up.

'The Birch case,' he began. 'None of it makes sense.'

'We're struggling with it back here, too, sonny.'

'Help me out here. I'm trying to work out how she didn't see her killer. All I can come up with is, he lay in wait for her.'

'He didnae need lie in wait, is what we're thinking.'

'How's that?'

'He knew where she'd be, and when.'

'Stalking her, you mean?'

'Aye. Our theory is he knew her routine to the second.'

It made sense. It linked with his own thoughts that she knew her murderer.

'Still doesn't explain where he hid. Unless he didn't need to. If she knew him, she had no reason to be afraid…'

'Careful, laddie. You know what Danskin would say.'

He did. *'Don't see what you expect to see,'* was his mantra.

'Lyall, can you remember what the causeway looked like? Could he have hidden behind a rock or summat?'

'Possibly.'

Another thought struck Ryan. He visualised Karl McKinnon rising from the water, terror-struck at the sight of an ancient skeleton. No, that was the wrong case. Or was it?

'What if someone came at her from out of the water? I'm thinking of Karl McKinnon, yeah?'

Lyall seemed to give the possibility some thought before answering. 'Not at low tide, they couldn't.'

He was right. 'I guess, but we're missing something here. There's something nagging away. It's a bit like when you start to speak then forget what you were about to say, y'knaa? Or walk into the kitchen and wonder what you came in for.'

Lyall snickered. 'You're a bit young for that, Ryan.'

The comment took him by surprise. He suddenly realised this was what life was like for Doris Jarrod; forever grasping at fragments, never seeing the complete picture.

Thoughts of his Gran didn't help the case. He returned the conversation to Chelsea Birch and her killer. 'There's something else, as well: why do it the way he did? Why didn't he just come up to her, stab her, and keep on walking? Drowning her took time. Why'd he take the risk?'

'Because, Ryan, it meant something to him. He didn't just drown her, remember; she suffocated in the detritus on the seabed.'

'What are you getting at?'

'What I'm getting at is, he did it because it was meant to happen that way. It was how he planned it. She needed to suffocate. Your mission, should you choose to accept it, is work out why? That's what we're all struggling wi' here.'

On that note, Lyall ended the call. Ryan's brain swam. He drained his cup just as a waiter delivered the food he didn't really want.

The waiter wore a black T-shirt. It bore the image of a white racing bike. Above it, the slogan *'Cycopath.'*

A psychopath.

Ryan hadn't encountered one in his time with the force, but he knew they were renowned for their meticulous planning; a trait which made them highly able to evade capture.

They were also the brand of killer most likely to strike again.

A chill ran through him. Ryan abandoned his food, sunk his hands in his pockets, and trudged out the café with the ominous cloud of foreboding above his head.

CHAPTER SEVEN

Ryan Jarrod was seventeen years and eight months old when he passed his driving test at the first time of asking. It was the only good thing to come out of an annus horribilus.

He'd lost his mother to cancer four months earlier. His father stumbled through the intervening period like a man under hypnosis while his younger brother, James, struggled to comprehend what had happened.

Ryan bought his first car, a Micra, from a dealer in Burnopfield who went by the contrary name of 'Honest Roy' Porter. It was a clapped-out heap of junk. Nevertheless, Ryan squeezed father, brother and grandmother into the rust-bucket and treated what remained of his family to a day out in Bamburgh.

It turned into a disaster.

For starters, Doris Jarrod insisted on calling Ryan 'James', and James 'Ryan'. It was the first hint of things to come.

They stopped off at Seahouses for fish and chips. James took a hissy fit at the length of the queue. Norman Jarrod couldn't be arsed with the fuss meaning they went hungry.

During a walk on Bamburgh beach, it rained. Pissed down, to be precise. They trudged back to the Micra. Ryan felt in his pocket for the car keys and his fingers brushed bare thigh. The keys had slipped through the same hole as his fingers and were buried somewhere on the beach.

Norman Jarrod had a meltdown, James laughed, and Doris disappeared into the Lord Crewe for a brandy while Ryan slunk back to the beach in the vague hope of locating his car keys.

He recounted the tale to DCI Danskin and the rest of the squad as they stood around a depressingly sparse crime board, their moods as mixed as the Jarrod clan in Bamburgh.

'Get to the fucking point, man,' Todd Robson complained.

'My point is, this case is the same. Everything that could go wrong has gone wrong. We've spent five days trawling through Chelsea Birch's entire client list. Most have alibis, those who don't live hundreds of miles away and we've no evidence that any of them have been anywhere near Whitley Bay in the recent past. The obvious suspect is Ahmed Nuri and we've checked his alibi over and over again.'

'There's others it could've been – McKinnon the diver, or the warden.'

'Todd, man. There's no forensics to link them. No means or motive.'

'Nuri had a motive. If she'd threatened to reveal his fetish…'

'Who to? He's a single bloke. No wife to worry about. He's self-employed, ergo: no job to lose.'

Todd thumped the desk. 'There's got to be something, man.'

'There is,' Ryan said. 'That's what I'm saying. It's like me car keys. I knew they were on the beach. I retraced my steps and, eventually, I found them.'

He looked at the board. 'The answers out there, somewhere. It's a bloody big beach, that's all.'

**

Danskin's crew searched the beach for a week but the car keys didn't show.

They had no DNA, no fingerprints. Aaron Elliott's report was categorical: no evidence of sexual activity. Rape wasn't a motive, nor was it a sex game gone wrong.

Ryan's theory of a psychopath at large was given due consideration. A psychopath would repeat the act. There were no other murders, no cold cases, no sign of recidivist behaviours. Psychopaths also tended to be trophy hunters.

As far as anyone could tell, nothing had been taken from Chelsea Birch.

Ravi Sangar enlisted help from DCI Rick Kinnear's lads and, together, they trawled through the criminal record PNC database. They drew another blank.

Danskin even contacted Scotland Yard. Scotland Yard were as Scotland Yard are: no help to anyone beyond the metropolis.

Ryan and Todd Robson revisited Ahmed Nuri so many times, his solicitor threatened to file a harassment suite.

Lyall Parker spent another high tide marooned on St Mary's Island with his Man Friday, Ferdie Milburn. He even began to understand him. When the warden invited Parker *'Ti hayve a dek arund'*, he knew he was being invited to inspect the island.

Lyall counted ever one of the one hundred and thirty-seven steps up the lighthouse tower and counted them all back down again. In between, he was rewarded with impressive views from a guano-encrusted platform but learnt nothing which helped the case.

Hannah Graves, Nigel Trebilcock and Gavin O'Hara focussed once again on the weirdos amongst Chelsea Birch's client list and were dismayed to discover most of them weren't weird at all. Embarrassed at being traced, yes; but most turned out to be perfectly normal apart from their liking for a bit of humiliation. None of them leapt out as obvious suspects.

Put bluntly, the car keys were all at sea.

And Superintendent Connor knew it, which is why he summoned Danskin to his office with an ominous crooked finger.

'You've been at this the best part of three weeks, Stephen. Cards on the table: are we any further forward?'

'Honestly?'

Connor nodded.

Danskin's lids slid downwards. 'No, sir. We're not. We've ruled out most of the lass's clients. We've still a couple to run checks on. I've got DS Nairn heading up a team of uniforms chasing them up as we speak. Nuri remains our most likely suspect but his alibi holds up; so far, at least.'

He waited for Connor to speak. When he didn't, Danskin continued.

'Ravi's doing something incomprehensible with the victim's e-mail lists. Something to do with IPT protocols, or summat. You know what he's like…'

'You're telling me we've diddley-squat, aren't you?'

Danskin sucked in air. 'I wouldn't put it that way.'

'What way would you put it?'

'The enquiry's ongoing, sir. In a case like this, we need to cover all the bases. As well as completing the checks on the victim's clients, Sue's command are doing door-to-door on the caravan site. It's proving tricky 'cos the majority are holiday lets. It'll take time to track them all down.'

'And, in the meantime, you've got a backlog of cases stacked so high you'll need ropes and crampons to get over it.'

'Sir, with respect…'

'Don't give me that 'respect' crap, Stephen. Seems to me, you haven't a strategy here. You're grasping at straws. Client lists and holiday-makers: there's hundreds of them and it's all a shot in the dark anyway. You know what it sounds like? It's as if you're in a nightclub half an hour before kicking out time and you're desperately tashing around trying to score.'

Danskin stared at the Super, muscles twitching above his jawline.

'It doesn't look good, Stephen,' Connor continued. 'You need to divert some of your resources away from the Birch case. The brass are on my back. They want results. We're not giving them any. Our arrest figures are way down. It's time to scale down the Birch operation. Move on.'

Danskin met Connor's eyes. 'So, we let the bugger go Scot-free? Is that what you're telling me?'

Connor flipped open a file. 'I've been looking at Dr Elliott's report. He can't categorically state Birch was murdered. It may have been an accident.'

'The imprints on the girl's neck…'

'…Could have been caused by some of the gear she wore. You know well enough what cuffs can do to the wrist. Imagine a collar around your neck. It'd do the same.'

Danskin shook his head vigorously. 'Na. Not having it. Elliott said they were caused by fingers.'

'PROBABLY, is what Elliott said. They were caused by external pressure, PROBABLY fingers; not conclusively.'

'You're telling me it's a cold case, aren't you?'

Connor turned to gaze out the window, hands clasped behind his back.

'I'd describe it as lukewarm,' he said. 'Let Jarrod keep a watching brief for a while before we declare it cold. I'm open to the idea of resurrecting the case if we get something concrete to work on, but I can't afford to have my budget tied up on one enquiry. Especially when our own pathologist couldn't win a court argument with a 'probably', even if we do pin down a suspect.'

Connor turned from the window. 'Forget about it, Stephen. Leave it with Jarrod while you get out there and climb your case mountain.'

Danskin's arms clung to his side, fists clenched. He knew he'd lost the battle.

Until the polite knock on the door.

'Sorry, sir,' Hannah Graves interrupted, 'We might have something.'

**

Sue Nairn stood while the rest of the squad remained seated around her. She'd adopted her usual straight-backed stance, her features as stoic as a marble bust, but Danskin noticed the glint in her eyes.

'What you got for us, Sue?'

'We're still tracing some of those who stayed at the caravan park at the time of Chelsea Birch's murder.'

Danskin gave Connor a sideways glance and tried to conceal his smug satisfaction at her use of the word 'murder'.

'It'll be a long haul to get through everyone and it's still work in progress. However, we've found a connection with a possible suspect. The static van two along from our victim's is registered to an address in New Hartley.'

'That's just a few miles from the site, isn't it? I presume the owner rents it out. There'd be no point owning a van so close to home.'

Sue agreed. 'That's what we thought, too. Thing is, according to the park's records, no-one's ever stayed there. Far as they can tell, if it's ever been occupied at all, it's been by the owner.'

'Interesting,' Superintendent Connor conceded.

'It is. More so when we checked the electoral register for the New Hartley address. The property is owned by one Karl McKinnon.'

'Yess!' Todd Robson exclaimed. 'Nailed the bastard.'

'Sir,' Ryan explained to Connor, 'McKinnon is a scuba diver who we know was at St Mary's on the morning Chelsea Birch died.'

'Good work, Nairn,' Connor commended.

Danskin wasn't so complementary. 'It is, but McKinnon's name was one of the first in the frame. It shouldn't have taken us three weeks to discover he was living on top of our victim.'

Rather than appear admonished, Sue Nairn smiled. 'It was only when we checked the electoral roll we were able to make the connection. You see, the owner used a pseudonym when he registered the van with the site.'

'Fair enough,' the DCI conceded.

'It's even more interesting when you learn the name he was using.'

'Go on. You know you want to.'

DS Nairn paused for dramatic effect.

'Peter Sutcliffe.'

The stunned silence was broken by Danskin. 'The Yorkshire Ripper.'

'The very same.'

Connor clapped his hands. 'What are we waiting for? Bring him in.'

'That's just the thing, sir. We can't. Like I said, he's not at the van, nor is he at the New Hartley address. We've talked to the neighbours…'

'And?'

'McKinnon's gone AWOL. He's not been seen for a week or more.'

CHAPTER EIGHT

Last time he'd sat in this spot, it had been the dead of night. The park looked vastly different in the warmth of a summer's afternoon.

Today, he could see the splendour of the Gothic Saltwell Towers mansion directly in front of him, its spikes and turrets and linear slopes reminiscent of Gaudi's La Sagrada Familia.

Sagrada, Spanish for Sacred. He glanced to his left, northwards, towards the sacred spot where she'd lain undisturbed for two weeks. He wished he could resurrect her for the day. He was sure she'd appreciate the beauty of the location he'd chosen for her.

The man closed his eyes and tried to imagine what it would be like if she were with him. The weather was perfect; one of those days where there was almost no weather; just a pleasant ambience which drifted by like a lazy butterfly. The man breathed in the fragrance of flower beds, freshly mown grass – and cat's piss.

Behind him, a group of schoolchildren lost within the depths of the park's maze traced their hands along the angular series of privet and yew trees, which released their pungent feline spray aroma.

The man's lips curled as he swore his distaste. He levered himself from the park bench and strolled towards Saltwell Park Dene, a densely wooded area which separated the Towers from the boating lake.

He'd be close to her by the dene.

The bench he chose to sit on was occupied by an elderly woman who nibbled on a crustless triangular sandwich. 'Another lovely day isn't it?' she smiled.

He didn't reply; just shuffled nearer until his thigh brushed her leg. She hurriedly dropped the remains of her picnic into her bag and scuttled away.

He chuckled. 'Works every time,' he said aloud.

The place was so perfect, he knew the next one would have to be extra special to better it. Excitement mounted within him. A rose-bloom flushed his cheeks and his breathing picked up pace.

He fingered her profile picture displayed on his phone. The profile was public, just as her eyes had told him it would be when they settled on him through the window of Caffe Nero.

Jasmine Peters was young. Seventeen at the time of the photograph. He'd checked often enough to know she was now nineteen. He had everything prepared for her. All that remained was for him to clip the image he'd selected and send her the message.

He copied the image. Pasted it into the message bar. Readied his finger above the 'send' arrow.

Behind him, leaves rustled. Branches snapped as if a wild boar rampaged towards him. A figure emerged from the undergrowth, twigs and foliage clinging to his hair. The man's eyes were wide, face deathly white.

'Help! For God's sake, someone call the police,' he managed to yell before his lunch slid from his throat and pooled at his feet.

The killer smiled benignly. 'How fortunate,' he thought. 'He's found her. She'll get to see the day, after all.'

He clicked 'Send' and sauntered away, hands in pockets, confident in the knowledge Jasmine Peters would be looking at her phone right now.

**

Ryan Jarrod collected Spud from his father's house and, back at The Drive, fed the dog a bowl of evil-smelling raw food. The old pug devoured it and looked to Ryan for more.

'No chance. That's yer lot, Spuddy-boy. Howay, let's go for a walk.' The dog pranced an excited circular jig, leaving Ryan to spin on the spot as he battled to attach the lead.

Once outside, Spud led Ryan beyond Washingwell Primary school, down towards Bucks Hill plantation, and into the green fields beyond.

Ryan didn't object. The route reminded him of childhood walks when he'd clutch his father's hand while his mum pushed James in his buggy. He was sure his memory played tricks on him, but the sun always seemed to shine back then.

He smiled wistfully until the view shimmered like a mirage through his teary eyes. He pulled at his lip until it hurt; until the pain released him from his melancholia.

He unleashed Spud and watched the dog trot away, snuffling at each bush along the track of rutted, parched earth. Ryan felt himself relax, thoughts of Chelsea Birch exiled to the back of his mind as he listened to birdsong filter through the trees, magical as a flute, as improvised as a jazz saxophonist.

He couldn't imagine living anywhere else but here. He wondered if Hannah felt the same about her home, and whether that was the real reason she'd chosen to remain in Jesmond.

Ryan knew Hannah led a nomadic life as a child. When she was two, her mother took her off to live in Majorca on a whim which lasted until the Spanish waiter she'd shacked up with moved on to his next conquest.

On their return, and before Debra Graves wooed and settled down with Stephen Danskin, she'd rented accommodation in Throckley, Wideopen, and Kenton Bank Foot. Worse, after her mum split from the DCI, she dragged Hannah to the dark side when Debra set up home with a bus driver from Hylton Castle.

After all that, perhaps it wasn't surprising Hannah's apartment was, for the first time in her life, somewhere she, too, could call home.

The Lighthouse Keeper

The late afternoon warmth proved too much for the short-nosed Spud. The little dog knew when to call it quits and was already scuttling home, his master in his wake, when Ryan felt the phone vibrate against his thigh.

'Sir?'

'Are you home?' Danskin asked.

'Almost. Why?'

'Can you get yersel' to Saltwell Park in less than fifteen minutes?'

Subliminally, Ryan checked his watch. 'I dare say. What's up?'

'A body's turned up.'

'Jeez. Look, I'm oot with the dog. Can no-one else get there quicker?'

'Negative. We've a jumper on the Tyne Bridge so traffic's at a standstill, which means the Redheugh's clogged, too. Lyall's on his way but he's stuck in tailbacks. You're the only one we've got that side of the water.'

Ryan vibrated his lips. Not because he was off duty. He wasn't keen on dead bodies, that's all. 'Aye. I'll see what I can do.'

'Good lad. There's a uniform presence from Gateshead on the scene but I need one of my crew there to take charge. Lyall will take over once he gets there. Just do the initial checks, yeah?'

Ryan agreed. He didn't mind the extra duties. Not on this occasion. It wasn't as if he had any plans to propose to the DCI's stepdaughter this time.

**

Danskin hadn't been wrong about the uniform support. A flotilla of patrol cars penned in the rubberneckers, while other cops checked the grounds to ensure the park was empty.

Ryan marched towards the dene; the entrance marked by a couple of hastily-erected incident tents. A PC accompanied Ryan into the trees and directed him to a shaded patch of land where a couple of forensic investigators crouched over a shallow hole. One took photographs while the other worked a small trowel as if he were unearthing ancient fossils. Opposite them, a woman stood hands on hips, ice-blue eyes showing above her PPE gear.

She stepped towards Ryan. 'You are?'

'Detective Constable Ryan Jarrod, City and County Police.' He flashed her his ID. 'Dr Elliott not here?'

Ryan sensed the woman scowl.

'No. He doesn't need be, either. I'm perfectly capable,' she said. 'I'm Dr Josie Gustard, duty FME. I'm Home Office registered.'

Ryan held up his hands. 'I'm sure you are.' He wondered why the Forensic Medical Examiner was on the defensive, but he let it ride. 'What we got here?'

'Come closer and have a look.'

Wow. That was a change from Elliott. Aaron Elliott wouldn't allow anyone near a corpse unless they'd offered him their first-born.

The grave was only partially uncovered. All but the body's head and legs remained concealed, yet the smell of rot permeated the burial place. The body was far from fresh.

Ryan took short breaths through his mouth as he stared into the open grave.

As far as he could tell, the corpse was that of a young woman. Her hair was largely detached from her scalp; her eyes and tongue protruded from her face like some grotesque Hallowe'en mask. At the other end of the grave, the flesh around the victim's legs glistened black and pulsed with insect activity.

'Shit.'

Ryan pulled his T-shirt up to cover mouth and nose. 'Found anything significant yet?'

The fossil-hunting Scene of Crime Officer laid down his trowel and moved aside to reveal a pile of evidence bags. Most contained soil samples. 'It's a busy park. Folk walk their dogs every day and,' the SOCO said. 'It's not as if this happened yesterday. I think there's a limit to what we'll get.'

Ryan spoke to Josie Gustard again. 'Any idea how long she's been here?'

'I won't know until I get her back to the lab. I dare say Elliott will want to get his paws on her so you might want to ask him.'

There it was again: the defensive tone. 'If you had to guess?'

'DC Jarrod, I don't do guesses. Not in my line of work.'

Ryan took a step back. Tried to visualise the murder scene. 'Like your colleague just said; this is a busy place. Must've happened at night, I reckon, for it to happen unseen.'

'That's your question to answer, Detective,' Gustard said.

'Aye, but I'm sure I'm right. And, if I am, the park's locked up at night, which means this can't have been a chance meeting.'

The fossil hunter held up an evidence bag. 'You didn't let me finish what I was saying. I said, there'll be a limit to what we'll find. I didn't say we'd find nowt.' He shook the bag. 'This mightn't be relevant to the case because it could've been left by any number of passers-by, but you'll want it checked out.'

Ryan squinted at the transparent bag. Tried to decipher the grubby item it contained. 'What's in there?'

'I'm sure DNA evidence might just be a game changer.'

'Howay, man. What is it?'

'A used condom, that's what it is.'

CHAPTER NINE

When Lyall Parker finally arrived at the scene, he spoke to the guy who'd unearthed the corpse, happy to leave Ryan at the shitty end until their initial on-scene enquiries were done.

Back at the station, DI Parker took ownership of the briefing. It was an informal affair. Most of the squad had signed off for the day. At this stage of an investigation, the majority of leg work was down to the uniform lads, with Forensics adding brain power. Danskin hadn't deemed it necessary to recall those who'd left.

Stephen Danskin perched on the end of a desk, Todd Robson leant against a wall, while Hannah remained seated behind her computer screen. Ryan rested a hand on her shoulder. She offered him a sad smile and raised her own hand, fingers momentarily locking with Ryan's.

'The duty FME at the scene was Josie Gustard. She refuses to put a time, or even a date, to the death, but one of her SOCO laddies let it be known it was probably two, possibly three, weeks ago,' Parker explained. 'They've removed the body to the lab. We'll ha'e a better idea once Dr Elliott's had a wee look at her.'

'Cause of death?' Danskin asked.

'The FME's not committing herself on that, either.'

Danskin tutted and rubbed chin stubble so dense he could strike a match on it. 'I take it she had no ID on her?'

'If only it were that simple. Nae, she didn't.'

The DCI turned his attention to Ryan. 'What do we know about her?'

'Dr Gustard reckons she was five foot three tall. Probably in her twenties. Can't tell weight because of the

The Lighthouse Keeper

decomposition, but Gustard reckons she was slim build. She had auburn hair and a taste in expensive jewellery.'

'Hang on. We know that, how?'

'The hair because it was still attached to her. Well, some of it, anyway. The jewellery because she still wore it.'

From a folder, Ryan pulled out three polaroids the SOC photographer had taken. He blu-tacked them to the crime board.

'There'll be more digi prints to follow. They won't be pretty.'

Hannah shivered as she looked at the decaying corpse. 'Has the jewellery been bagged?' she asked.

'Aye,' Ryan confirmed.

'Good. It's the only way we'll get an identification, I reckon. Wouldn't want the next of kin to see her in that state.'

They fell silent as their thoughts turned to the victim's mother and father, boyfriend, or husband – although the lack of a wedding ring made the latter unlikely.

Stephen Danskin stared out the bullpen's floor-to-ceiling window while he gathered his thoughts.

Like a toddler battling sleep, the long summer's day had finally conceded defeat. The lights of the quayside reflected in the thick mass of the Tyne while, downriver, the Gateshead Millennium Bridge glimmered glow-stick green.

Danskin brought the silence to a close. 'Saltwell Park's always heaving this time of year. Why did it take so long to find her?' He knew the greater the delay between event and discovery, the more difficult their job became.

Ryan answered. 'She was buried in Saltwell Dene, sir. It's woodland. Loads of people will have walked right by her but they'd be making for the Towers in one direction, or the boating lake in the other. Neebody's that fussed about the Dene.'

'In that case,' Todd Robson asked, 'How did she turn up at all? Lyall, you've been talking to the gadgy who found her, right? Does he seem kosher to you, or is he in the frame?'

'Och, I'd bet my life on him being in the clear.' His reply came without hesitation. 'There's no earthly reason why he'd dig her up now, not after this length of time. Besides, you didnae see the state he was in.'

'Surely worth checking him out, though,' Todd persisted.

Lyall Parker gave him the stare. 'D'ya think I'm an idiot? I already have. His name's Ronnie Dougall. He's a detectorist.'

Robson's eyes widened. 'Really? Never heard of 'im. From the Prince Bishop force, is he?'

'What?'

'Detective Dougall. Is he one of the Durham lads?'

Robson scowled when the others laughed.

'Are ye for real, Todd?' DI Parker asked. 'A detectorist; not a detective. Detectorist as in metal detector. He was in the Dene searching for stuff. That's how he discovered her. His wand, or whatever it's called, picked up her bling.'

'So,' Hannah surmised, 'Not only does it put Dougall out the frame, we can also strike mugging or robbery off the motive list.'

Danskin scribbled Hannah's observation down on a notepad. 'What else do we have as a motive?'

'Sir, there was a used condom found nearby. Forensics have it now. Could be a sex crime,' Ryan said.

'When will they know?'

'Doubt Forensics ever will. Only Elliott will be able to confirm it one way-or-another but, once he does, there'll be DNA ready.'

'Let's hope it was rape, then.'

Hannah cringed. 'Sir,' she admonished.

'Sorry, Graves. Bad choice of words, but you know what I mean.'

She stared into space. 'Aye. I do. It's the best chance we have of catching him.' She paused. 'How sad a world do we live in?'

They had no answer.

Danskin sighed. 'Okay. That's us done for the day. Let's see what tomorrow brings. Thanks for putting in the extra hours, Jarrod.'

'Again.'

'Aye, 'again'. What do you want; a medal, or summat?' He said it light-heartedly.

The squad began to disperse. Hannah hung back.

'Sir, if it's okay with you, I'd like to work a double-shift. Keep me mind working, if you know what I mean.'

Danskin did. 'You sure you're up for it?'

'Yes, sir. I'll check out missing persons. See if I can find who our Jane Doe is. If I do, the next of kin might appreciate the news coming from me rather than the likes of Todd.'

The DCI snickered. 'Aye, you've got a point there, like. Don't overdo it, mind.' His eyes searched her stepdaughter's face. 'You okay?'

She smiled, her dimple puckering her cheek. 'Yes. I'll take Tuesday in lieu, if you're worried I'm working too hard.'

'Should be okay unless Saltwell Park turns out to be like the back garden of 23 Cromwell Street.'

'Cheers,' she said. She saw Ryan's back disappearing out the door. 'I've got plans.'

**

In the silence of a near deserted bullpen, Hannah pulled up the missing persons database. She began by searching for young females reported missing in the last two months.

Only one name appeared, but it showed promise. The girl was a student at Gateshead College, less than a mile from Saltwell Park.

Hannah's fingers drummed against the desktop whilst she waited for the information to load. When it did, Hannah swore in disappointment.

The girl's name immediately ruled her out. Her name was Ling Liu. The image on the screen confirmed she had long, sleek, black hair. Not auburn. Besides, one of the few things they knew for sure was that their Jane Doe was white.

Hannah added another month to the search parameters. She gained two hits. She pulled up the photograph of the first. The girl was pretty but slightly overweight. And blonde. She also had lip and nose piercings. Not her.

The second case gave Hannah more encouragement. The young woman was slim and only an inch taller than their victim. Close enough. Hannah knew those who reported missing loved ones often over or under-estimated their height.

She studied the girl's picture. She had sandy hair. Was it sufficiently similar to the auburn colour Ryan had described? Could the girl have dyed her hair? Could death alter its shade?

Hannah tugged at her curls as she read through the report. The girl's name was Vivien Stratton. She was twenty-five and had learning difficulties sufficient for her to be classed as a vulnerable adult.

She was reported missing by her boyfriend on 10th May. His statement said they'd had a row over an unpaid mobile phone bill. Viv Stratton stormed out. He'd called her parents the next day. She wasn't there. The boyfriend called it in a day later.

At the bottom of the report, Hannah noticed the file was cross-referenced with another crime ID. She pulled up the second report. Vivien Stratton had been arrested on Westgate Road for soliciting on the 19th May, nine days after supposedly going missing. It looked like another blind alley.

The charge sheet gave Stratton's address as that of her parents. Hannah called them. Mr Stratton picked up.

Did Hannah know what time it was, her father asked. Yes, Vivien was there, he confirmed. No, they hadn't let the police know she'd turned up. Yes, they'd assumed her boyfriend would have. He was sorry.

'Not half as sorry as I am,' Hannah said to herself as she clicked and dragged the Missing Person file into the Closed Archive folder.

She yawned. Pulled down the hem of her top as it rose with her stretch, exposing the tail of a dragon tattoo on her abdomen.

Hannah ripped open a Yorkie bar and took a man-size bite before resuming the search.

This time, her filters took her back to the beginning of March. Again, two new names appeared. Or, at least, one did. The other file was marked 'CLASSIFIED: Authorisation Required.'

Hannah stared at the screen for a minute or more, intrigued. She'd never encountered a 'Restricted' file in her years with the force. Intrigued, and frustrated. There was no-one present to grant her access.

Instead, she moved onto the second case.

Terri Grainger was twenty-one. The photograph showed a sullen-looking, thin-faced, and Scouse eyebrowed young woman. She was the right age, build, and had reddish-brown hair which needed the attention of a good hairdresser. More importantly, it met the victim's profile.

From the file, Hannah learnt that Grainger had set off from her widower father's home for a Friday night 'on the toon.' There'd been no arguments; she simply went out and never came back.

Hannah gulped air, reached for the phone, and prepared herself for the conversation she most hated.

She re-read the file. Noticed Mr Grainger lived in Fenham, a few miles from the station. She could be there in minutes. Face-to-face was a more empathetic, humane way to break what must be the worst news a parent could receive. Hannah set down the phone.

She knew procedures advised female officers to be accompanied by a male colleague in such circumstances, but it was listed under 'advice', not as a 'mandatory instruction.' Besides, there was no-one suitable around.

Hannah grabbed her jacket in one hand and her car keys in the other.

CHAPTER TEN

Jasmine Peters struggled to pay the rent, let alone her baby daughter's childcare, despite holding down four part-time jobs.

She often wondered why she bothered. The answer always came down to the same thing: they got her out of the tiny bedsit and, she hated to admit, away from dirty nappies and baby's sick.

Or, at least, they had until Covid hit.

Three of Jasmine's jobs were zero-hour contracts, which meant she neither worked nor got paid. It also meant she didn't benefit from the furlough scheme. The only job which gave her regular hours was the one she disliked most: bar work at the Marlborough Social Club, on the western fringe of Newcastle city centre.

Tonight, the club had been even quieter than usual, yet the gaffer still insisted she stayed until last knockings. So, at the same time as the final customer's shadow left the premises, Jasmine slipped out the club's rear exit.

Coat and bag in one hand, motorcycle helmet in the other, she dodged traffic on Blandford Street and headed along Lord Street.

The narrow road was deserted, its darkness punctuated by tiny full-stops of light from ineffective streetlamps. In near silence, Jasmine walked towards the patch of derelict scrubland where she'd chained her scooter to a fence.

She hooked the helmet over her wrist while she buried her head in her handbag. She fished out her mobile phone, opened her contacts, located 'Lucy (Babysitter),' and began typing a text message.

'Back in about half an ho…' was as far as she got.

Her first thought was, 'Why is my phone flying through the air?' before she realised it wasn't just her phone.

She, too, was somersaulting like a seal pup tossed by a predatory Orca.

**

'I don't know what changed her mind, but something did.

Perhaps it was the mess Uncle Jed made of the bed. Perhaps it was the stain his brains left on the wallpaper. Perhaps it was something else entirely but, whatever it was, it seemed she no longer thought the police would understand.

She looked at Uncle Jed, the parts of him that were left, and started to bubble again. Christ, she was a mess. She spoke nonsense words. More a jumble of sounds than words. Like a witch around her cauldron.

Yes, that's what she was. A witch.

She grabbed my hand. I felt her dirty, jagged fingernails dig into my wrist. I told her she was hurting me, but she didn't listen. She dragged me downstairs like I was a piece of luggage. I stumbled. Twisted my ankle. Fell again. But it didn't stop her. She kept pulling and pulling.

We're outside now. It's dark and it's cold, a gale howling like a Banshee. Next thing I know, she's throwing me into the back of the car.

She slammed the car door before I was in properly. My elbow banged against it. It hurt like Hell. She still didn't care. She just jumped in the front seat and started the engine.

I told her to wait. That I didn't have my seatbelt on. Did she wait? Not likely. She drove off so fast I was thrown off my seat.

I banged my face on the back of the driver's seat. I heard my nose break. Tasted blood. But she didn't give a toss. She just drove faster and faster into the night.

And that's all there is to tell, really. I thought if I explained it to you, it'd help you understand.'

**

It didn't help. Jasmine Peters didn't understand at all.

She lay on her back, hair fanned around her head as if she'd posed for a Vogue cover. Except, she lay on a darkened roadway, not velvet cushions.

She felt no pain; not at first. Just a stunned confusion at the turn of events. It wasn't until she tried to stand, and realised she could move only her eyes, she began to panic.

Something was wrong. Very wrong.

A man looked down on her. She saw his lips open and close but didn't hear his words.

Jasmine attempted to speak. Ask him for help. Tell him it was little Nina's first birthday next week. She'd want her mummy.

But the man turned his back on her. He was walking away. Surely, he could see this wasn't right?

With every ounce of effort left within her, she managed to open her mouth. She waited for the words to pour from her.

Instead, a dark crimson sliver dripped from the corner of her mouth and trickled down her jaw.

**

He ran gloved hands over the front of the car. Flakes of paint and rust showered the tarmac as his fingers traced the bumps and indentations where the girl's torso had left its mark. He shrugged. The vehicle was a wreck, anyway, and it cost less than three-hundred quid. He'd more than got his money's worth.

The man swung himself into the driver's seat and reversed just far enough so he could see Jasmine lying in the road.

The contours of her broken and misshapen limbs fascinated him but, once again, it was her eyes which captured his attention. They stared at him, just as they had at Caffe Nero. They were huge now, round and pleading. He watched as their lids slowly blinked, then opened just as sluggishly.

He thought of his Great Aunt Emily. She'd had a giant porcelain doll. It sat on a wicker chair in her bedroom. Once in a while, when someone walked by, its eyelids would slant downwards over coal-black eyes.

It scared the shit out of him.

When Jasmine's eyes did the same thing, he'd seen enough. He floored the accelerator and sped over the young woman's fractured body.

The car squealed to a halt. Slowly, he reversed until the rear wheels rose over the stricken girl as if the vehicle had mounted a speed hump. Just as slowly, he nudged the car forwards until the rear wheels fell once more.

It was so much fun, he did it again.

And again.

With a heavy heart, the man decided it was time he left. He reversed thirty yards, sped forward, and bounced over Jasmine so hard the impact levered him off his seat.

The car barrelled its way onto George Street amidst a squeal of tyres, leaving Jasmine Peter's remains flattened like roadkill hedgehog.

**

Hannah had steered her Renault onto St James's Boulevard on route to the Fenham address of Malcolm Grainger when the call came through. By rights, the report of a hit and run wasn't hers to respond to; her traffic cop colleagues were the intended recipients, but she was too close to ignore it.

She veered into the warren of avenues behind the Discovery Museum and swung onto Lord Street. Despite her close proximity to the incident, Hannah heard the sirens of a squad car approach, and found another already at the scene as she pulled her vehicle onto the wasteland car park.

She left her headlights on as she jumped from the Renault. They bathed the dim street and illuminated the stricken figure prostrate on the tarmac. They also revealed a traffic cop already throwing up in the gutter.

When Hannah saw the extent of the girl's injuries, she, too, reeled back. She stepped away, felt her groin pull as her foot slipped on something visceral, and almost fainted when she realised the girl's entrails were wrapped around her heel.

Hannah marked herself with the sign of the Cross, something she hadn't done for a dozen years or more, as the occupants of the second car stood around horror-struck.

'Howay, man,' she said. 'Jump to it.'

'Ambulance already on its way,' an ashen-faced cop stuttered.

'Get back onto 'em. Let them know it's not a blue light job.'

'Why?'

'It's fucking obvious, man. She's gone. Let them attend to those with a chance.'

The cops remained static, glassy-eyed.

'Look,' she instructed, 'Get Forensics here PDQ. Search the scene. See what evidence there's around.'

They looked at her, blankly.

'This is no hit and run. It's more than that. Some sicko knew exactly what they were doing. This is a murder scene. So, get off your fat arses and onto your hands and knees. Mark and number anything you find. You know the score.'

Hannah knelt alongside the victim. She felt blood soak through her trousers, tried not to think of it, but failed. The fact the victim's head and face remained unscathed above a squashed and flattened torso made the scene ever-more ghoulish.

She stood. Walked away from the body. She told herself she wasn't going to cry. No way was Detective Constable Hannah Graves going to let any uniformed cop see her cry.

She cried.

Behind her, she was vaguely aware of the muffled sounds of activity as more vehicles attended the scene. Seven or eight cops were on all fours, inching over the road, fingers delving into every crack and crevice in the tarmac.

She heard someone shout for a DC Graves. She kept on walking.

'DC Graves,' she heard again. 'Ower here.'

'That's me,' she realised. She sniffed. Rubbed her eyes. 'Yeah, on my way.'

One of the cops signalled towards her. He was a tall, rangy youth; probably a Special Constable, just as her Ryan had been when she'd first met him.

'What you found?'

'It's a mobile phone. Boond to be hers, isn't it?'

'Probably, yes. Good work.'

The young lad flushed with pride.

'Just like my Ryan,' she thought again as she fumbled in her pocket for an evidence bag.

DC Graves turned the bag inside out and used it like a glove, picking up the phone as if it were dog-poo. A spider's web pattern radiated across the shattered screen, but the phone still worked. She knew, because the screen glowed with its owner's wallpaper photograph when Hannah's fingers touched it through the bag.

The screen displayed an image of blotchy-faced teenage mother in a hospital bed, new-born baby suckling at her breast.

Hannah felt her heart freeze and melt in the same instant.

She cried like an infant herself as she frantically shook the young mother's innards off her footwear.

CHAPTER ELEVEN

Sleep hadn't come easily to Ryan but, when it did, it was the sloth of hibernation. The extra shifts, coupled with the stress of his aborted marriage proposal, had done for him.

He awoke slowly and reluctantly, daylight penetrating eyelids which refused to open. He tried to kid himself he was still asleep. It almost worked.

He was in a twilight zone, somewhere between wakefulness and slumber; a dream-like state in which he felt in some way restrained, yet sufficiently conscious to sense Spud's drool on his bare back and hear the dog's snuffles behind him.

Ryan screwed his eyes tight and buried his face in the pillow.

Until he realised Spud was at his dad's house.

'What the hell...?'

Ryan sat up. Or, tried to sit up. He couldn't because he really was under restraint. His eyes shot open.

He lay entwined in Hannah's arms, his back drenched in her tears.

'Hannah?'

'Don't speak,' she sniffled. 'Just hold me. Please.'

'I don't understand. What're you doing here? What's wrong?'

'I need a hug, Ry. That's what's wrong.'

Ryan rolled over. Traced a finger down her tear-stained cheek. His mouth opened, but Hannah's finger hushed him.

'No words Ryan. Just a hug. That's all I want.'

He obliged, holding her so tight she could barely breath, but it was just what she required. Tears flowed. They soaked his chest, his biceps, his pillow.

They lay in silence, woven together, for endless minutes. Finally, Hannah released her grip.

'Thank you,' was all she said.

'What's up, love?'

She shook her head. 'A bad day, that's all. No, the worst.'

Ryan thought back to the time Hannah had been abducted in the line of duty; a time when he was sure he'd lost her.

'You don't mean that,' he said.

She didn't miss a beat. 'Yes. I do.'

Ryan propped himself on an elbow. Beneath him, Hannah appeared as vulnerable as a robin in a sparrowhawk's shadow.

'How long you been here? I mean, why didn't you wake me?'

He felt her shoulders shrug beneath the thin sheet.

'I got in about two. I don't know; maybe three. I just wanted to be with someone.'

'Someone', or him, specifically? Ryan bit his tongue.

The buzz of his alarm clock jolted him back to reality. 'Listen, I've got to get ready. I promised I'd be in sharpish. Will you be aal reet here by yersel'?'

Hannah flipped back the sheet. Got to her feet. 'No. I won't. That's why I'm going in, too.'

'Hannah, man. You can't. You're working too hard. You need a break. Look at the state of you.'

'No, I don't need a break. A break is the last thing I need. I needed a hug, and I got one. Thank you. What I need right now, is to work. And, if you want to find out why I spent last night here, get yersel' dressed and doon to Forth Street.'

Ryan watched her naked backside beat him to the shower.

**

A sombre atmosphere descended over the bullpen. A new set of photographs pinned to a crime board explained the mood. They also helped Ryan understand Hannah's surprise visit.

The Lighthouse Keeper

'Jasmine Peters. Nineteen years old,' DCI Danskin began. 'A single mum of one. Lives in a bedsit in Station Road, Wallsend. Last night, she was the victim of a hit and run. There's no doubt it was a deliberate act. DC Graves was amongst the first on the scene and she did a commendable job organising the traffic and uniform boys.'

Ryan glanced towards Hannah. She was staring at the photograph of Jasmine Peters. He saw her swallow, but her eyes never left the girl's picture.

'Now, our resources are stretched. I want O'Hara and Treblecock to work with Sue on the Saltwell Park find. Graves, you were doing some background checks last night. Bring the guys up to speed, yeah?'

Hannah remained fixated on Jasmine Peters' face.

'DC Graves?' No response. Danskin tried again. 'Hannah? D'you hear me?'

She blinked. Nodded.

'Good. Robson and Jarrod – you report to Lyall on the Peters' case. Sangar, I want you to provide geek support to both investigations.'

A robotic voice asked, 'What about me?'

'You're going home, Graves. The minute this briefing's finished and you've handed over what you know, you're oot of here.'

Hannah's tongue moistened her dry and cracked lips. She shook her head. 'I'm not.'

Danskin's tone was stern. 'I can't afford anyone going sick. You're at breaking point, Graves. Do as I say.'

'I told you I'd be off on Tuesday. I'm sticking it out 'til then. I'll be fine.'

Danskin and Ryan exchanged glances. Ryan gave an almost imperceptible nod.

Sweat glistened on the crown of DCI Danskin's head. He wiped it with the flat of his hand. He took a swig of water from a sports bottle and released a long sigh. 'Okay. You win. You're with us until Tuesday. No longer; understand?'

'I've a question, sir,' Ryan asked.

'Gan on, then.'

'Who's taking the Chelsea Birch case?'

Stephen Danskin hesitated. 'No-one. Super wants us to prioritise and says the Birch investigation stays on hold. There's insufficient evidence to warrant deploying resources to it.'

The DCI addressed Lyall Parker. 'I want you to take your guys back to the Lord Street scene...'

'What if they're linked?' Ryan asked.

'Come again?'

'What if there's something linking all three cases?'

'There isn't, Jarrod. Chelsea Birch's death may be accidental, we don't know enough about the Saltwell Park case yet, and last night's an entirely different MO. There's nowt linking them at all.'

'Apart from the fact all three are female.'

'Well, yes...'

'Young females.'

'That's nowhere near enough to draw a conclusion, man.'

'Young, unmarried females.' Ryan fixed DCI Danskin with a glare. 'Young, unmarried females with red hair.'

Danskin looked between the three crime boards. Studied the girls' photographs. Scanned their faces. 'Bugger me backwards. I see what you mean.'

'What are ye getting at, laddie?' Parker asked.

'He's back to his serial killer psychopath theory again. Aren't you, Jarrod?'

'Yes sir, I am.'

The squad fell silent, then spoke all at once. Danskin and Parker fought to regain control of the briefing. Finally, order restored, they reached a consensus: they needed hard evidence or, at least, something more robust than what they already had, before narrowing the enquiry down to a single path.

Ryan argued he was right. In fact, he was certain of it. But his was a lone voice. After ten minutes to-ing and fro-ing, he accepted he'd lost the battle.

Ryan agreed he'd go along with the others.

For now.

**

During a brief recess, Hannah brought Sue Nairn up to speed on the Saltwell Park case.

DS Nairn despatched Nigel Trebilcock to Fenham to confirm the victim as Terri Grainger, while she and Gavin O'Hara took themselves off to pore over witness statements and chase up forensic reports.

Danskin ushered Ryan, Hannah and Lyall Parker into his office. The aroma of stale sweat invaded their nostrils. Danskin slid open another window, only for the city's oppressive heat to push fetid air back into the room.

'Hell's teeth,' Danskin cursed, 'You can stick this global warming lark right up your arse. Whatever happened to a good old-fashioned miserable Geordie summer?'

He ripped the plastic cap from another water bottle, took a swig, and tossed it from hand-to-hand as he spoke.

'Robson and Sangar will join us in a mo. Once we're done, I want DI Parker and Graves back up to Lord Street. The scene's still cordoned off and I want the pair of you to have a gander in daylight. See if you can spot something that wasn't visible last night. The trail of evidence will be laid out for you, an' aal, so it'll give you a clearer picture.'

Hannah shuddered. The picture remained all too clear to her.

Ryan noticed her wince. 'I think I should accompany them, sir.'

'No need to go overboard, Jarrod. There's plenty for you and Robson to work on back here.'

'No, sir. I disagree.' He gestured towards Hannah with his head.

Understanding showed in the DCI's face. 'On reflection, Jarrod, that's a sound proposal.' Danskin mouthed '*Thank you*' to the young detective.

The office door opened. Todd Robson strode in, his bent nose wrinkling like a rabbit. 'Christ. Smells like a Sumo's jockstrap in here.'

He began whistling Springsteen's *Wreck on the Highway*. Fortunately, before Hannah picked up on the crude case reference, Sangar entered, SD card flat in the palm of his hand.

'I've recovered data from Jasmine Peters' phone,' he announced. 'I've got the squaddies trawling through it as we speak but I thought you'd want the edited highlights so far. I'm not sure there's owt game changing on it, but there'll be summat useful once we've sorted the wheat from the chaff.'

'Excellent. Load it up.'

Everyone in the squad knew Ravi Sangar was the 'go to' guy if you wanted to dig into someone's digital life. He had a knack for cross-referencing social media accounts across all platforms in a way which extracted endless titbits about an individual's habits, behaviours and, most importantly, their secrets.

On the surface, Jasmine Peters appeared the polar opposite to Chelsea Birch. Her Facebook account totted up four-hundred and sixty friends. Yet, if truth be told, most ended up being little more than acquaintances. Close friends were at a premium.

Sangar revealed Peters had been something of a child protégé. Musician, singer, and actress, she'd enrolled in drama school at an early age. Many of her contacts – her so-called 'friends' - stemmed from that period in her life. Most were now slung far and wide throughout the British Isles. Jasmine Peters hardly ever met up with any of them.

Ravi switched to her photo gallery. It, too, was luvvie-centric. There were several shots of a young Peters alongside Ant and Dec, an older Peters engulfed in a Brian Blessed bear-hug outside the Theatre Royal, an unshaven Sir Ian McKellen under the London Palladium portico, and countless selfies taken at random music gigs.

Mostly, her recent photo gallery comprised of hundreds of shots of a baby girl. 'Nina,' Ravi divulged.

Hannah averted her eyes from the display and gulped back tears.

Sangar had mapped Jasmine's Facebook friends with her contact list, and here the truth emerged. Like Chelsea Birch, she was in regular contact with fewer than a dozen people.

'Where's the boyfriend in all this?' Danskin asked.

'He isn't. The father remains anonymous. Around nine months to a year prior to the child's birth, she engaged in some sexting with a lad called Ethan Hodge. Seems they met at drama school. Most of the messages were idle chit-chat between them but some of them were suggestive. Nothing too overt, but enough to suggest there was something between them even if it didn't appear too serious.'

'Serious enough to put her up the duff,' Todd Robson observed.

'His last message to her was about seven months before the child's birth. He said his folks were emigrating, and he'd be going to Oz with them. There was no hint of it before that message. Peters didn't reply, and there's been no further contact between them since. As far as I can tell, the lad doesn't even know he's a dad.'

'Aye, that's assuming he is the father,' Parker said.

'He's the only one in the frame for it. There's nothing in her messages to indicate she's been close to anyone, before or since. Of course, you can't rule out a one-night stand, but she doesn't seem the sort.'

'Child Maintenance records?'

'None, sir. She's supported the child by herself.'

Danskin rubbed his brow. 'What else we got?'

Ravi moved onto her messages. He began with text messages starting four weeks ago. It didn't take him long to run through them. It was clear she used text almost exclusively for childcare arrangements.

When the unfinished message to the babysitter appeared, Ryan watched Hannah anxiously. Her reaction wasn't what he expected.

'Brilliant! This gives us an exact time of death, to the very second. When we get our suspect, he'd better have a cast-iron alibi for where he was at precisely eleven twenty-seven last night.'

'Great point, Graves. That's the best lead we've got to date.'

Ravi selected a few of her social media posts, explaining they were typical of the messages across all her accounts. They were the usual mix of unfunny memes, sponsored product ads, and pictures of people's pets.

There were a few messages shared from other accounts. A couple from single-parent groups like Gingerbread and NetMums, a few fake Covid news articles, pictures of rock stars and their cars, a promo from a random on-line store; nothing out the ordinary.

'Basically, nowt alarming,' Ravi summed up, 'Especially seeing as her Facebook profile was public. That's usually an open door for all sorts of shite.'

Ryan couldn't resist interjecting. 'That's another similarity to Chelsea Birch. A public profile.'

'Similarity? Or coincidence?' the DCI countered. 'Jarrod, don't…'

'…see what I expect to see. I know, sir, but; howay man, it's all adding up.'

'Aye. Like two and two make five. Owt else for us at this stage, Sangar?'

Ravi could see the sweat stains under Danskin's armpits. Sensed the DCI was keen to get on the streets and do some 'proper coppering,' as he would call it.

'I think we could leave it there, sir. Take my word there's nothing of substance in her e-mails as far as we can tell.

There has to come a time when you stop rooting through someone's digital life. We're not quite at that stage yet - like I say, the lads are still working on it - but I'll report back if we get anywhere.'

'Excellent, Sangar. You've worked hard on this. Get yersel off for a break. In fact, I think we could all do with one, yeah?'

The group muttered their agreement. 'Okay, then. Get a cuppa and, when you're ready, you might as well all head up to the Lord Street scene and see what you find there. The SOCOs are all done but we don't need open the street up again until rush hour. Gives you more than enough time.'

They began shuffling out Danskin's office. Made their way towards the break-out area with their plastic cups of lukewarm dishwater in hand.

All except Ryan. He remained seated in Danskin's office. Something nagged in his subconscious like toothache. Something Ravi had said.

Ryan was back in his Gran's world; a world where everything meant something, but nothing meant anything.

What the hell had Ravi said?

CHAPTER TWELVE

A belligerent parliament of grey clouds gathered on the horizon as Hannah emerged from the car. She gulped down a lungful of air thick with humidity and looked around.

The contrast with last night couldn't have been greater. The site was calm; serene, even. The only reminder of the horror she'd witnessed came in the form of a series of yellow numbered markers strewn across the road like chunks of Toblerone. The numbers matched those allocated to evidence bags already indexed and secured in the bowels of Forth Street, cross referenced with images captured by the scene of crime photographer.

DI Parker despatched Ryan to obtain an update from the duty sergeant manning the barricades at one end of the road, while he marched to the far end and took ownership of a handful of witness statements from the PCs in the incident van.

Hannah and Todd checked the road for anything the SOCO search may have missed. Although temporary floodlights had been wheeled in to help officers comb the road surface, there was always a possibility crucial evidence had remained hidden in the shadows of night.

Todd stood back and observed from a distance while Hannah prowled the markers like a hungry wolf. She viewed them as if they were a join-the-dot puzzle. Soon, the picture was as clear as it had been the night before.

A nebular cluster of markers indicated where the vehicle had hit Jasmine Peters. They indicated the point of impact and where her body landed. They outlined blood spray, showed the spot where fragments of glass from a broken headlamp were found, indicated rubber laid down by wheelspin, and highlighted the location of the girl's handbag.

Hannah pictured it all. As she walked backwards from the centre, her heel bumped against a yellow indicator numbered 'Seven.' She turned her head and saw numbers 'Eight' and 'Nine' nearby.

With a sense of dread, she realised they signified the spread of Jasmine Peters' organs, and the point where her own feet had smeared them over the tarmac. She felt herself gag.

'You aal reet?' Todd shouted.

Hannah raised a hand in reply. She moved towards the kerb. Kicked over another marker. Number thirteen. This was where Hannah had found the girl's phone. The phone containing the pictures of orphaned baby Nina.

Hannah sank to the ground. She sat on her haunches, head down.

Todd shook his head. Looked around. There was no-one else nearby to offer Hannah comfort. He supposed he'd better do it.

'Shit.'

It wasn't his thing.

As he approached, he witnessed Hannah trail her fingers through the gutter. She brought her hand to her eyes. 'The pathetic cretins,' Todd heard her say. 'Utter useless tossers.'

'Cool yer jets, man, woman, will you?'

'Piss off, Todd.'

'What the matter, lass? Wrong time of the month, or summat?'

She stood. Slapped him across the face, hard.

He rubbed his cheek. 'I'll take that as a 'yes', then, should I?'

Lyall Parker emerged from the Incident van. 'What the bloody hell's going on, you two?'

'My fault, Sir. I said summat out of turn,' Robson confessed. 'Divvent knaa what, mind,' he added, quietly.

'No, Lyall. I'm more to blame,' Hannah said. 'I let myself get frustrated 'cos the search missed something. Look.' She held her palm out flat in front of her.

'Och, I cannae make oot what it is.'

'It's rust and, I reckon, flecks of paint. I bet it's off the perp's car.'

Parker peered closer. 'You could be right. Bag it up and let's get back to the station. They want the road open 'soon as', and the DCI's after an update.'

'Not yet, Lyall. Look, the tyre treads show the car disappeared onto George Street, and uphill from there.' She glanced at the dried paint on her palm. 'We're after a sky-blue vehicle which drove towards Rye Hill at or around eleven twenty-seven. It's bound to be on CCTV.'

'Aye, except for one thing. We dinnae have any cameras until we get to Westmorland Road.'

'We don't, Sir, I agree.' She turned towards an austere building at the junction with George Street. 'But the Sixth Form College does.'

Parker pulled out his phone. 'I'm on it already. Noo, back to the station and brief the DCI.'

**

They arrived in Forth Street as rain began falling and Sue Nairn rose to her feet in the bullpen.

'Sir, we got a lead,' Lyall Parker said.

Danskin held up a hand. 'In a minute, Lyall. Let DS Nairn say her piece on the Saltwell Park case first.' He addressed Nairn. 'Go on, Sue.'

'Aaron Elliott's given us more information about the circumstances of Terri Grainger's death. It's not pleasant.'

'Howay, man. Spit it out.'

'Dr. Elliott is certain the girl was alive and alert when she went into the grave.'

They fell silent, other than for a 'Holy shit' from Todd Robson.

'Elliott can't say for sure whether she'd been subjected to a sexual assault, but we can rule out the condom we found at the scene. The semen inside was fresh.'

'Are we sure?' Todd asked.

'Elliott says so, yes.'

'Aye, but our detectorist bloke – have we checked his DNA?'

Danskin scowled. 'What's your point, Robson?'

'What if he came back to dig her up for a bit of fun?'

They looked at him, open-mouthed.

Robson held up his hands. 'I'm only saying.'

'Well, don't say,' Danskin retorted. 'Christ, you're one sick bastard, do you know that?' Despite himself, he did wonder if Robson had a point.

Superintendent Connor stood, arms folded, propped against a wall. 'You called the victim Terri Grainger, Sue. Does that mean we have a positive ID?'

'I've spoken to Malcolm Grainger. He says it's his daughter,' Trebilcock confirmed.

'He identified the jewellery?' DCI Danskin asked.

'That's the thing, sir. He couldn't explain the bling.'

'Hang on. If that's what you showed him, and he doesn't recognise it, how's he so sure?'

Trebilcock rubbed an eyebrow. 'Everything else fits. Timescale, height, build, hair colour. He says it's his daughter.'

Danskin studied Trebilcock. 'But, I sense you're not convinced.'

The Cornishman shrugged.

'Why aren't you sure, Treblecock?' Danskin persisted.

'I think Grainger just wants closure, so's I do. Wants to put an end to the endless wondering. Put it all behind him and move on, is what I'm thinking. I mean, it might be her, but… I don't know.'

'How do we prove it, though?'

'Mr. Grainger mentioned his daughter had vision problems as a child. Turns out it was caused by something called ethmoid sinus disease.'

'What's that when it's at home?'

'He said it was because she had a highly pneumatized posterior ethmoid sinus.' Nigel Trebilcock saw their blank looks. 'I know; it means nothing to me, either.'

'So, why tell us?'

'Because I'm sure it'll mean something to Dr. Elliott, I do.'

'Then what are you waiting for? Get onto Elliott and have him check it oot.'

Superintendent Connor tisked. 'Of course, it's Terri Grainger. A man wouldn't say his daughter was dead if he wasn't sure. Right, Lyall – what you got for us on the Peters case?'

Ryan pulled a face at Connor's haste to move things along, but let it lie as Lyall Parker began his team's update.

'We have a positive ID, a time of death, and the means. We also know the vehicle used in the assault was light blue in colour and sustained damage to at least one of its headlamps in the collision. What we dinnae have at this stage is a motive or a suspect.'

Parker's phone vibrated in his pocket. 'Excuse me, sir. I need to take this.'

He moved to a far corner of the bullpen as Stephen Danskin slid open a window streaked with rain which fell in solid vertical lines. The DCI stared out over the River Tyne, its earthy-brown surface rippled by the downpour's onslaught, while he gathered his thoughts.

Superintendent Connor was less patient. 'DC Graves, Jarrod – do we have a witness?'

Chagrined at his omission from the Super's rollcall, Todd Robson replied with a, 'No, sir; we don't.'

'So, who called it in?'

Ryan interrupted. 'It's not strictly correct to say there isn't any witnesses.'

Robson glowered at him as Ryan continued.

'We don't have any eye-witnesses, true; but there is an ear-witness, if there is such a thing. The duty sergeant told me a guy having a late-night smoke in his garden heard a thud. *'Like someone dropping two bags of builder's sand one after another,'* was how he described it. A couple of minutes later, he heard a vehicle screech from the scene. He says he went to see what was gannin' on, and that's when he noticed Jasmine Peters in the road. He called it in immediately. DI Parker has his statement.'

Lyall Parker hurried back to join them. He struggled to gather his breath. 'Sir, I said earlier we might have a breakthrough. We have.'

'Tremendous. What is it?'

'Hannah suggested the Sixth Form College might have something on CCTV. They've just called. Only four vehicles passed the College between eleven twenty-five and eleven forty-five.'

'Great stuff. That narrows it down.'

'Och, it gets even better, sir. One of the vehicles was a Citroen Xsara. It just happens that one's turned up abandoned in Belgrave Parade, a cul-de-sac nae more than a wee spit from the College. What's more, it's blue, got a broken headlight, and blood stains on the hood.'

Amid the squad's shouts of triumph, Todd Robson asked, 'Do you think it could be wor car?'

Danskin stared at him. 'Of course, it's ours. Fucking hell, Robson. You get more like Trigger every day.'

The squad dissolved into hoots of laughter as the DCI said, 'Howay, I'll treat you all to a celebratory cup of piss from the machine.'

**

Ravi Sangar charged into the bullpen just as the squad were tipping the drinks machine's filth down its drip-tray.

'DVLA have identified the vehicle. As we know, it's a Citroen Xsara. DVLA confirm it was first registered in 2001 but, as of now, it's neither taxed nor insured.'

'Well, what a surprise,' Danskin commented.

'Its previous MOT certificate expired four months ago and was renewed only last week. It passed with flying colours.'

'At least summat about it was legal,' Hannah commented.

'Aye,' Ryan said, 'But it's a bit odd, isn't it? I mean, I'm no Edd China but a 2001 registered car that's been off-road for months passing first time? Howay, man.'

Stephen Danskin considered it for a moment. 'True, but we can't argue with the facts. On the bright side, the fact it's not taxed or insured gives us enough to bring the owner in, never mind all the other evidence stacked up against him. So, let's go get him. Who's it registered to, Sangar?'

When Ravi said the name, Ryan's jaw fell open.

'Honest?'

Ravi blinked at him. 'Yes. Why would I make it up?'

'No, I mean that's his name.'

'I know it is. I've just told you, man.'

'You don't understand, Ravi. I know him, sort of. I bought my first car from him.'

Ryan thought back to a disastrous family outing to Bamburgh.

'He's known to everybody as Honest Roy Porter.'

CHAPTER THIRTEEN

The deluge emptied the streets of Whitley Bay faster than a colon cleanse.

Ferdie Milburn couldn't have been more pleased. He didn't like crowds. In fact, the warden of St Mary's Island didn't much like people so, when he came across a near-deserted circle of uncomfortable metal seats outside The Victoria, he was delighted. He could hijack the pub's Wi-Fi.

He had considered nipping into the nearby Fat Ox. He preferred the beer there but there'd be people in, even with the current restrictions. People and crowds; they were all the same to him.

No, he'd settle for the metal seats.

He gave a surreptitious glance at the bloke opposite. The other man acknowledged him a tacit nod of the head. Ferdie looked away immediately.

Ferdie pulled his phone from his pocket and, when he saw the other man do exactly the same, he set about his work.

Ferdie quit ten minutes later when his screen became unreadable beneath a kaleidoscopic splatter of raindrops. His companion came to a similar conclusion at the same moment. Both men rose, brushed themselves down, and walked off in opposite directions.

One turned right, the other left onto Marden Road and then into a leafy avenue behind the Deep Blue Dive Centre.

There, in the shelter of a branch bowed by saturated foliage, the man set the next phase in motion.

**

Lyall Parker took the wheel of the unmarked vehicle, Ryan giving directions with Todd sat in the rear. A squad car trailed in their wake.

After weeks of inactivity, the wiper blades screeched on the windscreen like an unoiled hinge. 'Switch the radio on, Lyall. The blades are doing me heed in,' Todd complained from the back seat.

Lyall obliged. A Wagnerian opus filled the confined space.

Todd tutted. 'Lyall, man. Turn the wipers back up, will you? It's better than that racket.'

Ryan filled the void with a running commentary. 'Me Gran's care home's just to the right, there. The one that looks like a hotel.' Once on Fellside Road, he pointed out his old school on the right, the Fellsider pub to the left and, back on the right, Whickham golf club.

When the car crested a rise and Ryan indicated the Woodman's Arms, Todd Robson told him to cut the tourist guide act. Or, more accurately, he told him to 'Shut the fuck up.'

The road became a narrow switchback, twists and turns left and right. Ryan warned Lyall of a Stop sign coming up beyond the Pack Horse Inn. The two vehicles crawled to a halt and, when a gap finally arose, they crossed the busy A692 in convoy before swinging into the village of Burnopfield.

'It's on the left just up here.'

Lyall opened comms lines and spoke to the squad car. 'Hang back, laddies. Let's not spook him.'

The car containing the three detectives trundled to a halt outside an unremarkable car dealership. A few decent enough vehicles stood out front, many more wrecks hid out of view to the rear.

'I suppose we should see if he's in,' Ryan said.

'You know the number?' Robson asked.

'I've got a fairly good idea, aye.' He dialled the number etched across the showroom's windows in four-foot high, red figures.

'Could I speak to Mr Porter, please?'

Parker and Robson heard him say, 'When are you expecting him back?'

They listened as Ryan said, 'No, it's okay, thanks. I'll call later. No; no message.'

'Well?'

'They're expecting him back any minute. We'll pull across the road there. If he's not looking for us, we should be out of his field of vision and we'll still be able to watch the forecourt. Advantage us.'

Parker gave instructions to their uniformed escort and the cars pulled into the residential tranquillity of Grove Terrace.

Five minutes later, a short man with wispy, greying hair emerged from a silver Audi. He flapped torrents of water off a cream raincoat and bustled into his own showroom.

'Methinks it's time for a chat,' DI Parker said.

**

Lyall Parker waved his ID in the general direction of Porter's receptionist as he led the entourage towards a cramped office at the rear of the showroom.

Lyall remained in the doorway, uniform support behind him, as Ryan and Todd approached a polished mahogany desk out of character with the rest of the office.

Honest Roy Porter sat behind it, a pile of stamped MOT certificates awaiting his signature. Without raising his head, Porter pointed a pen towards a Government poster on the office wall.

'You need masks on inside here, gentlemen. *Hands Face Space*, and all that.'

Todd let out an exaggerated sigh. He laid his hands on the desk. Put his face in Porter's. Invaded the man's personal space.

'I don't give a monkey's chuff whether it's Hands Face Space, or Shoulders, Knees and Toes. If I had me mask on, you wouldn't be able to identify me, would you, pal?'

Ryan couldn't disguise a laugh. Despite Todd's faults, he had his uses. Ryan thrust his ID under Porter's nose.

'I'm Detective Constable Ryan Jarrod, City and County Police. This is my colleague, DC Todd Robson. We're accompanied by Detective Inspector Lyall Parker.'

Parker gave Honest Roy a mock salute.

The car salesman pushed back his chair, swallowed hard, and cleared his throat. 'All the same,' he said, 'You do need to wear face coverings. If you'd care to oblige, I'll be happy to help you gentlemen. I've a nice 1982 Ford Capri Fastback outside which I'm sure would suit your friend from the Sweeney, here.'

Lyall moved into the office and placed himself between Todd and Honest Roy. 'Seeing you brought up the subject, we're here about you and your car.'

Porter looked at the three detectives and the uniform presence lurking in the showroom. 'You've come a bit heavy-handed, haven't you?'

They remained silent.

'Look, since that Rogue Traders expose – which was a set-up, by the way – I've replaced all my mechanics. There's no scams going on here, I assure you. Feel free to look around. I've nothing to hide.'

DI Parker's next words hit Honest Roy below the belt. 'You were seen running over a young girl. Four times, to be precise.'

Honest Roy paused. Frowned. 'Are you mental? I wouldn't run over four people if I were pissed out my head. And, before you suggest otherwise, I don't drink so I wasn't.'

Lyall leant in. 'Och, you misunderstand me. It wasn't four different lassies. It was the same girl, four times. There's nae need for me to spell oot the fact she's dead, is there?'

Porter shook his head so fast it became a blur. 'Nope. Not me. Wrong guy. Wrong car.'

'What car do you drive, Mr Porter?' Ryan asked.

'I've three. Which one are you talking about?'

'Tell me what they are, and I'll tell you which one it is.'

'I've got a Merc and an Audi. Would you like to inspect them for damage?'

'That's two. You said you drove three.'

'That's incorrect, Detective Constable. I said I owned three; not drove three. The other's my wife's. She slums it.'

Ryan felt his pulse quicken. 'Slums it, you say? As in, slums it in a Citroen Xsara?'

Porter spat out a laugh. Spittle hit Ryan's face. He wished he'd donned a face covering.

'A Xsara? Are you taking the piss? No, she slums it in a MG sort of way, not a frigging Citroen sort of way. What sort of a schmuk do you take me for?'

Ryan held out a hand. Todd placed a photograph of a damaged, sky blue Citroen Xsara in his outstretched palm.

'This Citroen Xsara is registered in your name.'

Honest Roy stared at the photograph. Blinked several times. Quietly, he said, 'I sold it.'

'How convenient. When did you sell it?'

Porter shrugged. 'Couple of days ago. Four, at most.'

'Mr Porter, it's registered in your name. Do you have any paperwork for the transaction?'

Porter shook his head.

'Like I say, how convenient.'

'Listen,' the salesman said, 'It's registered in my name because I do everything by the book, now. All the cars out there are registered to me before they're sold on.'

When he saw the detectives weren't impressed, Porter continued.

'Look, a guy walks in. Tells me he's seen a car he fancies out back. He offers me three hundred quid in cash. I take it. I didn't put it through the accounts, okay? Three hundred quid isn't going to break the tax man, is it?'

'And they call you Honest Roy. Tut-tut, Mr Porter,' Ryan chastised, 'You've just told us you do everything by the book. You don't, do you? If you lied to us about that, I think you could lie to us about owt. You're in a spot of bother, my friend.'

'You're taking everything I say out of context. Trying to twist things.'

Ryan held a silence. He watched Porter's face twitch like he had St Vitus's dance before he spoke again.

'Can you describe the man you say bought the car from you?'

'I don't *say* he bought it. He did buy it.'

'What did he look like?'

'I don't know what he looks like, okay? He wore a mask. Like we're all supposed to. Everybody looks the fucking same, don't they?'

Todd Robson spoke next. 'Do you ever go to Saltwell Park?'

'Not often. What's that got to do with anything?'

'How about bondage? Like a bit of kink now and again?'

'What???'

'I'm curious, that's all.'

'I want my solicitor. Now.'

Lyall Parker summoned the uniform officers into the cramped room.

'You'd better tell him to meet you at Forth Street because that's where you're going. Right now.'

CHAPTER FOURTEEN

Roy Porter's lawyer was unavailable. He refused the services of a duty solicitor and stayed good to his word – there'd be no co-operation without a legal presence.

Parker ran what they had past Danskin. They both knew it wasn't enough to charge him with Jasmine Peters' murder, but they sure as hell weren't prepared to release him. Instead, Ryan and Todd did a bit of digging and soon came up with a basket-load of charges relating to Porter's dodgy dealership; charges sufficient to afford him an uncomfortable night in the custody suite.

At nine the next morning, Porter's lawyer turned up, bustlingly angry, with the demand his client be released immediately. By nine-thirty, the solicitor sat glum-faced alongside Honest Roy in an interview room.

Fifteen minutes later, Lyall Parker and Todd Robson joined them.

The interrogation rooms in Forth Street were all identical. They were modern yet sparsely furnished and decorated a depressing battleship grey. The lighting was harsh and blinding. The wall to the left of the entrance consisted of a two-way mirror which reflected both interviewers and interviewee.

Behind the mirror, Stephen Danskin observed proceedings alongside Ryan Jarrod, Hannah once again consigned to office work upstairs.

Parker and Robson stared through a sheet of plexi-glass at Honest Roy. Porter stared back. He was unshaven and rheumy eyed after a sleepless night on a hard bunk in a cold cell.

Lyall started proceedings with a tap on the plexi-glass. Honest Roy jumped.

'Did I startle you? Och, what a shame. We're in a secure environment. Please remove your face coverings. We want to make sure the tape picks everything up.' He didn't add: *'We want to see every tic, every nervous twitch of your guilty little mug,'* but that's what he meant.

Honest Roy removed his mask with the resignation of a surgeon who'd just lost a patient in theatre.

The detectives introduced themselves, and Porter's solicitor, an angsty man with a bushy black beard he kept touching as if to assure himself it was still there, identified himself as Jake Gellner.

Straight to the point, Parker asked, 'Tell me about the man you say bought a blue Citroen Xsara from you.'

'I've nothing to add to what I told you yesterday.'

'You say you cannae describe him.'

'I have nothing to add to what I said last night.'

'Okay then, let's try an easier question. How did he pay for it?'

'Cash. I told you yesterday.'

'You didnae complete any paperwork. The car is still registered in your name.'

'It's only a few days ago. I never got round to it. Besides, the bloke who bought it also has a responsibility to notify DVLA, as well you know.'

'If he exists.'

Lyall left his words hanging.

'I told you everything I know yesterday,' Porter repeated.

Jake Gellner interjected. 'My client has already told you he does not own the vehicle in question, nor did he own it at the time of the incident.' He tugged at his beard and shivered violently. 'Could we have some heating on in here?'

'Nee chance,' Todd said.

'Where were you at eleven twenty-seven on the night in question?'

'At home. With my wife. Asleep.'

'That's not the strongest alibi I've ever heard, I have to say.'

Porter made a dismissive noise.

'Detective Inspector,' Gellner objected, stroking the beard as if it were Blofeld's cat, 'My client has told you what he knows. Now, unless you have a witness able to positively identify him as being behind the wheel of the car, I suggest we're all done here.'

Porter ignored his solicitor. 'Listen, I didn't drive the car. I sold it. I was at home with my wife. What more do you want me to say?'

Todd placed the flat of his hand against the plexi-glass. Pressed it until the shield bevelled. 'If I drag your wife here, put her in a different room, and she tells me something different – you are in the shittiest shit you've ever been in.'

'This is outrageous,' Gellner objected.

'Shut yer gob,' Todd replied.

'Mr Porter, you don't need answer any more questions,' the brief spluttered.

Honest Roy didn't take the advice. 'My wife won't know. She has sleep apnoea. Snores like a water buffalo. We sleep in separate rooms. It's possible she mightn't be able to vouch for me.'

Lyall and Todd shared a knowing look.

'But, if you check my landline phone records, they'll prove I was home.'

**

Babestation is a non-subscription soft porn channel where semi-naked women of various shapes and ages parade themselves in front of a camera while encouraging viewers to call them on a premium line number for a 'personal chat.'

Back upstairs in the third-floor bullpen, it didn't take Hannah long to determine Roy Porter was indeed engaged in a sparkling bout of wit and repartee with an Asian Babe called Prita from eleven-four until ten minutes after midnight.

For once in his life, Honest Roy had lived up to his pseudonym.

'Shit.' Hannah put her head between her hands and writhed at her curls. She sighed, rubbed her eyes with the heels of her hands. 'I thought we had him, Ry. I thought it was over.'

Ryan's brow wrinkled with concern at his girlfriend's torment. 'Love, get yourself home. You're off tomorrow anyway. There's not much else you can do here for now. Danskin won't mind. Leave me to explain it.'

He waffled on, anticipating her objections.

Instead, what he got was, 'I think I will.' She was in the elevator even before Ryan had time to ask if she'd be okay alone.

A thought struck him. 'Do me a favour, man, Ravi. Call up the Chelsea Birch file for us, will you?'

'Super says it's all but a cold case. Not to waste time on it.'

'Hadaway, man. It'll only take a couple of minutes. Five, max.'

Ravi subconsciously glanced towards Connor's office. 'What're you after?'

'I want you to run through her contacts. See if we've missed summat.'

'Any contact in particular, or just all of 'em?'

'Her client list.'

Ravi loaded a browser and brought up the Birch file. 'I'll get shot with shit if Connor finds out.'

'Relax, man. Reet, I want to check for a name.'

'Which is?'

'Roy Porter. If he's into iffy TV channels, he might have other predilections, an' aal.'

It took Ravi less than a minute.

Roy Porter wasn't on the list.

The Lighthouse Keeper

**

He couldn't find his car. All his planning, all his preparation, and it came down to the fact he couldn't remember where he'd parked his fucking car.

On his second circuit of the Park View car park, he discovered his vehicle tucked away on the upper floor, in the shade of a utilities building. He relaxed and began breathing again.

His mind had been focussed on the pleasures to come. He couldn't let that happen again. He had to be ready for her, at the right time and the right place. If she followed her usual routine again today, he'd know it was safe to strike.

But, if he wanted to be sure, he'd have to get a move on.

He reversed out of the bay. Almost ran over an old dear who thumped the roof of his car with her stick. Once out on Park Avenue, there was traffic. Of course, there'd be traffic. Lots of it.

Just. Fucking. Great.

'Relax. It'll be alright,' he told himself.

And, of course, it was.

Once he reached the Nord Bottle Shop, he knew he'd make it. A left and a right, and his car was on Marine Avenue headed towards Monkseaton Metro Station.

He pulled up across the road and watched.

'*Florabundance*' was an unprepossessing establishment. Little more than a glorified kiosk, it lived up to its name. Inside, there was barely room to manoeuvre between a forest of orchids and wreaths and garlands of all sizes and colours.

From across the road, the man saw the proprietor load up a van. He counted him in-and-out of the shop three times. Once the florist loaded the van with his fourth armful, he hopped into the driver's seat and set off with his deliveries.

Four-eighteen. Three minutes later than usual, but the man knew four armfuls of flowers meant he'd be out the florists for at least thirty-five minutes.

The man settled down in his car. Seven minutes later, as he knew she would, the proprietor's daughter began restocking the window display.

He watched her struggle to manoeuvre a step-stool into position. Saw her climb atop it, hidden beneath an array of roses and carnations and delphiniums.

As she restocked the display, the girl slowly materialised from behind a decreasing shrub of flora. She had a roundish face etched with a perma-smile which seemed to inflate her cheeks like a Puffer fish. The girl wore a plain, mid-calf length dress and sensible shoes. Her hair was scraped back behind her ears and held in place by clips, apart from a single strand which worked its way loose and hung in front of her eyes.

Across the road, the man placed an object on his lap. He withdrew his phone from his pocket, took a picture of it, and copied and pasted the image. He clicked 'send'.

On the counter behind her, the girl's phone pinged with a message alert.

She glanced down at it. Decided she'd check it later.

She refocused on her stock and tucked the errant strand of blush red hair behind an ear.

CHAPTER FIFTEEN

Ryan reported for duty the next day to find his colleagues in the same downbeat mood as himself. The atmosphere in the bullpen resembled the aftermath of a party when only dirty plates, empty bottles, and stained carpets remain.

Roy Porter wasn't their man, just as it hadn't been Ahmed Nuri or any other potential suspect they'd investigated. The enquiry landed on a snake and slithered all the way down to square one without a ladder in sight.

No-one spoke. They sat with heads down, engrossed in paperwork, trawling through statements, and reviewing evidence. Some even drank tea.

Outside, the weather sulked with them; dull skies and a strengthening wind consigned the heatwave to history. Only Stephen Danskin welcomed the change in climate. He stood by an open window dressed in short-sleeved shirt and open necked collar. Ryan sidled across to him.

'Things are a bit bleak, sir, aren't they?'

'I think better when it's like this,' he replied.

The scent of the DCI's antiseptic mouthwash rinsed Ryan. When Danskin overdid the Corsodyl, it was a sign he, too, felt the pressure.

'Better than the vodka, though,' Ryan thought. 'I didn't mean the weather. I was talking about the investigation.'

Without taking his eyes from the river, Danskin replied, 'So was I. Nowt like a bit of pressure to focus the mind.'

'Where do we go from here?'

'We keep at it, that's where we go. You work with Lyall and co on Jasmine Peters, DS Nairn and her troops on Terri Grainger.'

'And when we find out it's the same person, what do we do then?'

'IF it's the same perpetrator, Jarrod. It's a big if. Divvent get ahead of yersel' again.'

Superintendent Connor's head emerged from his office door. 'A word, Stephen.'

'Be right with you, sir.'

He lowered his voice. 'When I'm with the Super, you get on with proving me wrong. But remember - don't see what you expect to see.'

Ryan returned to a desk weighed down with paperwork. He popped in a set of AirPods and lost himself in an Arctic Monkeys download and the detail of Jasmine Peters' life.

He was still at it two hours later. He ferreted through everything they knew about the case. He trawled the internet for all references to Jasmine Peters, trying to determine whether another Jasmine Peters may have been the intended victim. Finally, he accessed the file Ravi Sangar created from the victim's social media feed and scrolled through it, back and forth.

Something, somewhere, struck a chord.

What was it?

Bingo!

'Lyall, come here, will you? I think I've got something. In fact, I know I have.'

Parker was at his shoulder in seconds. 'What is it?'

'I'm in her social media account.'

'No' again. We've been through it a dozen times, man.'

'Aye, we have. And we've missed it a dozen times.'

'What am I looking at?'

'This is her Facebook photo gallery. Things she's photographed, or pictures she's been sent.'

'And?'

'Look.'

Ryan enlarged a series of images. Freddie Mercury on the bonnet of a Studebaker Champion. Springsteen alongside a Chevrolet Corvette. Tony Iommi and a Jag E-Type.

'Aye, Ryan. We already knew she had a thing about rock stars and their cars. We've looked at these already.'

'Exactly. And, like I say, we missed it.'

Sandwiched between Iommi and Brian Johnson's Mustang GT sat another image, an image out of place amongst its stablemates.

It was a picture of a clapped-out Citroen Xsara. A sky-blue one.

Parker rarely swore. 'Fuck me,' he whispered.

'Look at the time, an' aal, Lyall. It was sent at 11.20 pm the day before Jasmine Peters was killed by the very same vehicle. Almost exactly twenty-four hours before, to be precise.'

All hell broke loose. Lyall shouted for Stephen Danskin. Ryan shouted for Todd Robson. Sue Nairn and Gavin O'Hara broke into a gallop.

'Fuck me,' they all said.

'Get Sangar here, quick,' Danskin ordered. 'I want a digital footprint of the sender.'

'The message is from someone calling himself Jim Smith. Name mean anything to anyone?' Parker asked.

No-one responded.

'Pretty common name,' Ryan said.

'Aye. A bit too common for my liking. Made up?'

'Possibly. Sue – cross-check the name Jim Smith with the stuff you got for the Grainger case, yeah?' Ryan urged.

This was it. He felt it in his bones. Jim Smith would be on the file. It would prove his theory was correct; the same person was responsible for both murders.

'Negative,' DS Nairn said.

'What?'

'It's a negative. There's no-one of that name linked to my case.'

While the rest of the squad celebrated the breakthrough on the Peters investigation like they'd scored the winner in the Cup Final, Ryan slumped back in his chair, crestfallen.

He'd so wanted to be right.

**

On the journey home, Ryan's head buzzed with information overload.

Ravi had established the message to Jasmine Peters came from an unregistered Android device. The SIM used was an over the counter, ten-quid-a-pop job; untraceable even by Ravi Sangar's standards.

In the Grainger case, and despite Nigel Trebilcock's initial reservations, DS Nairn and Gavin O'Hara were sure the victim was indeed Terri Grainger. In the absence of a denial from Aaron Elliott, there was no reason to doubt them.

Nairn set Trebilcock and O'Hara the task of combing Terri Grainger's profile for the umpteenth time. They confirmed and double-confirmed Jim Smith definitely didn't feature anywhere. Nor were there any images of Saltwell Park, or any stills taken from the set of Shallow Grave.

The flames of Ryan's theory were doused once more. Superintendent Connor instructed Stephen Danskin to maintain separate lines of enquiry.

To put the old tin lid on it, when Ryan arrived home, he couldn't find a parking spot outside his own house. He squeezed in nine doors up, on the curve of The Drive, and cursed the blue van which had snaffled the space outside his home.

The van was outside his house for a reason. His front door was ajar, and his possessions were being loaded into the back of the truck.

He broke into a trot, balled his fists, and burst through the opening. 'Stop right there. Police. You're under arrest.'

'Oh, hello, Ryan. What do you think?'

Hannah Graves stood in the centre of a living room which wasn't his. She had a scarf wrapped around her head and wore paint-splattered dungarees.

'What the…?'

'I knew you'd never get round to doing anything yourself, so I thought I'd grab it by the whatnots for you.'

He gazed around the alien room. Gone was the large floral-patterned wallpaper, the chintz sofa, uncomfortable upright chair.

The walls were painted a fashionable light green. 'Fern green, it's called,' Hannah explained.

'I don't like green.'

The ceiling glistened glossy white.

'It hurts me eyes,' he complained.

Two men lugged in a cream-coloured leather recliner sofa and set it against a wall.

'It'll get filthy once Spud gets on it, man.'

The wooden-framed print of The Hay Wain had been replaced by an oversized close-up of a bee on a bright yellow sunflower.

'I'll get hay fever just looking at it,' he moaned.

Hannah signed for the deliveries and bid the delivery men goodbye.

'Who needs Nick Knowles?' she beamed, her dimple puckering her cheek for the first time in an age. 'What do you think?'

Ryan looked around. 'It's not me Gran's anymore,' he sighed.

'So?'

'Hannah, man. You can't just wipe her oot like that.'

She blinked. 'I'm not…'

'You are. Yes, you are.' He espoused the new sofa for a seat on the floor. 'That's exactly what you've done.'

'I thought you'd be pleased.'

'I'm bloody not, okay? In fact, I hate it.'

Tears welled in her eyes. Spilled over. Clung to her eyelashes then dripped onto her cheek like a melting icicle.

'I thought you wanted us to be together, Ry.'

'I do. Did. Still do.'

'I told you I couldn't live in a shrine.'

'It wasn't your decision to make, Hannah. It's my house; my decision.'

Hannah sat against the far wall, knees drawn up, chin resting on them. 'I needed it, Ryan. You know I've found this case hard. I wanted something to take my mind off it. Needed summat to look forward to, y'know?'

They sat in sullen silence.

Ryan moved over to her. Lowered himself beside her. 'Actually, I don't.'

'What?'

'I don't know. I don't understand, at all.'

She shrugged.

Ryan took her hand. Spoke softly. 'I suppose something good's come out of it. It'll make the neighbours jealous.'

She half-laughed. 'What? In snooty Whickham?'

'Says she from snooty Jesmond.'

This time, she gave a proper laugh.

'Besides,' Ryan continued, 'It's not snooty roond here. A lot of these were council houses once. In fact, this street used to be called Lenin Drive. The Crescent, Marx Crescent.'

'So, why'd they change it?'

His turn to shrug. 'Cos they're snooty, I guess.'

'I love you, Ryan.'

His eyes widened. 'Anyway, moving on...'

She kissed him. 'I said, 'I love you.''

He returned her kiss.

A thought struck him. The ring. Upstairs, in his drawer. Why not now?

'Just a minute, Hannah. I'll be back in a tick.'

She kept hold of his hand. 'Just a few more minutes, yeah?'

A few more minutes. He could manage that.

'How was work?'

He snickered. 'You know how to break a spell, don't you?'

'That bad, eh?'

'Aye. That bad.'

He told her about the breakthrough, about his theory, and how it all came to nothing.

'That's always assuming the Saltwell Park body was that of Terri Grainger,' Hannah said.

'We're quite sure it is. Neebody's heard from Dr Elliott yet but it can't be anyone else, can it?'

'Shit. It could be.'

'You what?'

'The other file. I was so tied up with Jasmine Peters, I forgot to tell DS Nairn about the other file.'

He shook his head. 'I'm not with you.'

'There was another possible Miss Per.'

'Who?'

'That's it. I don't know. The file was marked 'Restricted Access.' I was going to query it after I'd spoken to Malcolm Grainger. But I never got. I never got because of Jasmine Peters.'

Hannah began weeping again.

Ryan took her in his arms. 'Hey, howay man. Everybody makes mistakes.'

She sniffed. Shook her head. 'No, it's not that. It's every time I think of Jasmine…' she couldn't finish the sentence through her sobs.

'Sssh, sssh.' He pressed his lips against her headscarf. 'I know. It must have been a shock seeing her like that. I think we'd all have reacted the same.'

She wiped away a tear. 'It's not that. I just can't help thinking about her baby. Nina. The poor child. No mother, no father. What sort of life's she going to have? Thing is, I'm not even sure it's Nina I'm grieving for.'

Ryan understood. Hannah's background had come back to haunt her. He held her tightly. 'You survived it, Hannah. Nina will, too.'

'It's not me I'm thinking of, either.'

'Then, who?'

'I just can't stop thinking about the baby.'

He still didn't get it, but he held her just the same.

'I can't get the baby out of my head, Ryan.'

She turned to face him.

'My baby. The one I lost.'

'Oh God, Hannah. I didn't know. We've been together two-and-a-half years, and I didn't know that about you. I'm so sorry.' His heart ached for her loss. 'How long ago?'

She cast her head downwards.

'Six weeks and three days.'

CHAPTER SIXTEEN

Ryan struggled to remove his head from the cement mixture in which it was trapped.

'What did you say?'

'Six weeks and three days ago.'

'You mean six years, yeah?'

She shook her head.

'You never thought to tell me? Why?' A thought hit him like a runaway truck. 'It wasn't mine, was it?'

Hannah hunched her shoulders. 'I don't know.'

Ryan's stomach lurched. He feared he was about to vomit.

'Jesus. You don't KNOW if it was mine? How many could it be, for Christ's sake?'

'Get lost, Ryan. I meant I don't know why I didn't tell you. Of course, it was yours.'

He began breathing again. 'Right. Let's get me heed around this. You were pregnant with my baby and you didn't think to tell me. What does that say about us?'

'I didn't tell you because I didn't know.'

'Hadawayandshite. You must have, man. How couldn't you know something like that?'

Hannah edged away from him. 'Ever since…well, you know – last year, I haven't been regular. The stress of being taken hostage and all that, it's affected me. Not just mentally, but physically, too.' She pinched the bridge of her nose. 'I might have come out of it with nowt more than a broken nose but, up here,' she tapped her temple, 'It nearly broke me. I guess it had to come out somehow, and it disrupted my cycle.'

Ryan got what she was saying. Self-consciously, he glanced at his scarred hands. From personal experience, he knew the psychological scars could run deeper than the physical ones.

'The fact I missed a couple of periods,' she continued, 'Didn't bother me. It's happened a few times before, so I thought nowt of it.'

'Then, how did you find out?'

'When I did come on, it felt different. Painful. Heavy. I don't expect you to understand, but I knew something wasn't right. Doc checked me out and that's when she told me. *I'm sorry to tell you, I think you've had a miscarriage,* she said.'

Hannah fell silent. Ryan hated himself for it, but he spoke coldly; selfishly.

'You could have told me once you'd lost it.'

'Didn't think there was any point. Nowt either of us could do about it by then.'

'You didn't think there was any point? Howay, man. I could have comforted you. Been there for you.'

'Ryan, be honest with yourself. You couldn't. You'd have been, well, like you are now. Besides, I had work. I just threw mesel into it. And it worked. Until Jasmine-sodding-Peters. She had to bring it all back, didn't she? Her and baby Nina.'

Hannah sobbed. Craved for Ryan to put his arm around her, to take the pain away.

'I thought you were on the pill,' he said, oblivious to her need.

'I am. I was. But, you know, with the hours and the shifts, I guess I forgot. I. Just. Bloody. Forgot. Okay?'

'So, it was a mistake?'

'Of course, it was a mistake, man. The last thing I want is to have your baby.'

She realised how that sounded. Saw his crestfallen face.

'I didn't mean it like that,' she said. 'I meant it wasn't the right time, that's all.'

He didn't respond. He just sat there, in sullen silence.

'Say something, Ry.'

He did. 'I think you should go home.'

'What?'

'I need to get me heed round this. Go home, Hannah.'

She sniffled. 'How? I came with the decorators. I haven't got me car. I came with the decorators because I thought you'd want me to stay the night. To thank me for doing up the house. Sod you, Ryan Jarrod. Just, sod you.'

Ryan ran his hand through his hair. He was being a twat, he knew it; he just needed time. He put his arm around her, but it was a perfunctory act.

'I'm sorry, love. It's been a shock. You can stay. Of course, you can. But I need space, yeah? So, sleep on the sofa. Please. Just for tonight.'

Hannah didn't look at him, but she nodded her understanding. 'I'm sorry, Ryan. For everything. I should have told you.'

He kissed the top of her head. 'No, I'm sorry. Now, get yersel' some kip. We've work tomorrow, then we've the rest of our lives to get over this.'

'Thanks, Ry. I love you.'

'Give ower, man. Make yourself comfy and gan to sleep. As someone once said, *'Tomorrow is another day'*. Let's both remember that.'

As he headed upstairs, he shouted back down to Hannah. 'And take your shoes off. Can't have you scuffing me lovely contemporary furniture, can I?'

**

Shortly before three a.m., Ryan snuck downstairs and lay under the sheet with Hannah. They didn't say a word; just lay there, holding each other. It made for a less tense journey into Forth Street.

'Aye, aye. We know what you two have been up to,' Todd leered when they arrived together. 'Cosy little support bubble you two got going on there, isn't it?'

Ryan gave Todd a hand gesture before joining Hannah at Sue Nairn's desk.

'Sue, there's something I overlooked in my handover,' Hannah apologised. 'If Dr Elliot can't confirm the Saltwell Park victim as Terri Grainger, I have another possible for you.'

'It's Terri Grainger, right enough.'

'Elliot's got back to you?'

'Not yet, no.'

'Okay. So, what if it's not?'

'We'll cross that bridge when we come to it, shall we? Now, I've leads to chase up and I'm sure Lyall would appreciate you doing his work, not mine,' Sue Nairn concluded.

Nigel Trebilcock raised his eyebrows towards Hannah and Ryan, but the conversation was at an end.

'She was a bit off, wasn't she,' Hannah said as they returned to Lyall Parker's quadrant.

'There's a few things a bit off if you ask me. For example...' Hannah's phone rang, preventing Ryan from finishing his statement. But it didn't interrupt his thoughts. For a moment, he was sure he had it, then the revelation drifted away on a breeze.

He wandered to the breakout area, revelled in the silence which allowed him to gather his thoughts.

Ravi Sangar sat two tables away, scrolling through his phone.

Ryan remembered.

He knocked over his chair in his haste to get to the evidence storeroom. In the cool, climate-controlled basement, Ryan signed for the item he wanted and, in the corridor, set about confirming his fears.

Like the last few pieces of a jigsaw puzzle, everything snapped into place.

The elevator took an age to arrive, longer to ascend. It stopped at Ground, First, and Second floors. When it

The Lighthouse Keeper

reached the third floor, Ryan's impatience was at breaking point.

'...We haven't a connection,' Sue Nairn was saying to the assembled squad in the bullpen.

'Okay. Lyall, what you got for us?' the DCI asked.

'Never mind what Lyall's got. Look what I've got,' Ryan shouted, bursting into the bullpen.

'Jarrod, what do you think you're doing?'

'I'm solving the cases, that's what I'm doing. Or, at least, proving we've a serial killer on our hands.'

'For fuck's sake, man. Change the record, will you?'

'Shut up.'

Danskin's face darkened.

'Aal reet, then; 'shut up, with respect, sir.' Is that better?'

The look on Danskin's face told Ryan it wasn't. He didn't care.

'Listen up. We've ruled out a connection between Jasmine Peters murder and that of Terri Grainger. Two things: first, what if it isn't Terri Grainger?' he held up a hand to stem the objections, 'Second, what if there's a connection with Chelsea Birch?'

'You're obsessed, man.'

Ryan fixed Danskin with a glacial stare. 'No, sir. I'm not obsessed. I'm right, that's what I am.'

The DCI saw the fervour and utter conviction in his young protégé. Danskin lay down a challenge. 'Prove it.'

Ryan held aloft the evidence bag. 'In here is Chelsea Birch's phone. There's something we missed. We thought she'd been sent a holiday picture from a friend. She hadn't.'

'Slow down, man. Talk us through it.'

Ryan took a gulp of air. Decelerated his brain. 'Jasmine Peters was sent an image of the car which killed her in the hours before her death. We know that.'

The squad stared at Ryan.

'What we thought was an innocent holiday snap on Chelsea Birch's Facebook account, wasn't.'

Ryan passed the phone and its image around the squad. It was a picture of a snorkeler emerging from the ocean with an island in the background. An island with a lighthouse.

The image came from a 'friend' with a name they all recognised.

A friend calling himself Jim Smith.

'Sir, we have a serial killer out there. Worse, he's taunting his victims.'

Ryan looked at each of them in turn.

'He's letting them know how they'll die.'

**

Dorothy Jackson helped her father load up the delivery van. Lockdown and social restrictions may have affected many businesses, but one thing remained true: you can always say it with flowers.

Dorothy returned to the shop and, just as she always did, lay her phone on the counter-top while she fine-tuned the window display of Florabundance. She hummed a tune from Beauty and the Beast as she went about her task, climbing and descending the step-stool.

Dorothy was putting the last display on show when the bell jangled at the door. 'I'll be with you in a moment,' she said from behind a pale blue facemask.

'I've all the time in the world,' the man replied.

She leant back from the top of her stool. Took in the display. 'There. That's good. Now, what can I do for you?'

Dorothy turned her neck to look at the man as she spoke. Veins and arteries and tendons bulged at just the right angle.

Just the right angle for the man wielding the secateurs.

Blood sprayed from Dorothy Jackson's carotid artery. The window was covered by a thick red curtain. Every bloom in the shop turned crimson. A maroon pool spread across the wooden floor.

The man knew he had to tell her quickly, before it was too late.

**

'Mum knew what she'd done, alright. And without a shadow of doubt, she knew what the consequences were.

I think she had some sort of epiphany or, at the very least, a realisation. She may even have regretted what she did to Uncle Jed. Whatever it was, the stupid bitch decided she had to unburden herself. She had to go to church. Of course, she made sure I went with her. I didn't have a choice.

I remember three things about our visit to church. First, I remember the cold. Bone-chilling, it was. Like death itself. Second, I remember people looking at my black eyes and bust nose where I'd hit my face on the car seat. What I remember most, though, is the way they looked at her.

She'd done herself up to the nines. She probably thought she looked smart. In reality, the bitch looked like a cross between a pantomime dame and Elton John dressed for a party.

Everyone stared. Everyone. Some even laughed. Me? I wanted to hide. Hide beneath the pews, or the altar, or in the alcoves in the cold, stone wall.

Except, I couldn't hide there. I couldn't because the alcoves were full of flowers. Putrid, wilting, flowers.

There. You know now.''

Dorothy Jackson's trembling body gave one final shudder before her eyes glazed over.

CHAPTER SEVENTEEN

With the investigation into Dorothy Jackson's murder fresh as a butchered calf, Stephen Danskin's team worked through dusk and late into the summer's night until the lights on the Tyne Bridge cast elongated reflections across the great river like the flares of flickering candles.

They were exhausted to a man, but not one of them considered calling it a day. Even Superintendent Connor remained behind in a show of solidarity to his troops. Only when petty squabbles broke out and mistakes began appearing in their work did Danskin bring the day's toil to a close.

'Listen up. It's been a long day, and you've all shown the qualities and dedication I've come to expect from you. I know I don't say it often enough but, thank you. Give us another half an hour and we'll call it quits.'

They murmured their reluctant consent as Danskin wheeled in an item of office furniture. It resembled a dining room table on its side, a vertical rather than horizontal plane.

'Before we go, I want to outline where we're going to pick up tomorrow.' He flipped open the leaves. The 'table' revealed itself as an outward-folding whiteboard, one hidden on the back of each leaf, another concealed by the closed doors; three in total. 'Say hello to our new recruit.'

Todd screwed up his face. 'Christ, is that where our coffee money went? On a bleedin' fancy crime board on wheels?'

Connor stood in the doorway of his office. 'It's the way things will be done from now on, Robson. Carry on, Stephen. I'm glad to see you put what you learnt into practice. Money well-spent, I'd say.'

The DCI pointed to the left whiteboard. 'On here, we'll have the crime scenes. Diagrams, maps, photos – the works. O'Hara, you'll be in charge of that.'

Gavin O'Hara yawned and stretched but nodded his agreement.

'The right side, I want to see timelines, as detailed and thorough as we can. This is all yours, Treblecock. Dates of death, when the bodies were discovered and when they received their messages, yeah? Stick the images on as well. Birch's snorkeler, Peters' car, and the image of the shears Sangar retrieved from Jackson's phone.'

'They were secateurs, sir, not shears,' DS Nairn corrected.

He waved a hand dismissively. 'Whatever.'

Ryan spoke. 'Sir, what about the Saltwell Park case?'

'Terri Grainger. Aye, what aboot it?'

'Are we sure it fits?'

'Why aye, man.'

'Her social media profiles weren't public, unlike the others. She didn't receive a message. The others did. It looks and feels different to me.'

'Listen, Jarrod. She fits the age profile. The hair colour's right. The bizarre mode of death. It fits.'

Ryan didn't let it lie. 'Sure, all that fits. But only if the victim's not Terri Grainger. We need to chase up Elliot and check the other file…'

'Her father's identified her, Jarrod,' Connor interrupted. 'Let's move on, Stephen. We're getting bogged down in minutiae. It's late. I'm sure we all want to get home. Carry on and make it quick.'

Hannah moved to object. Before she could do so, Ryan rested a hand on her forearm. Put a finger to his lips. She raised an eyebrow and shrugged as Danskin continued.

'Will do, sir. Okay. In the centre whiteboard, we'll record the victims' basic details. Photos, occupation, close friends, and relatives; that sort of thing. I'll take care of that.'

'What about suspects? Where do they go?' Trebilcock asked.

'Does it matter? We haven't any, have we?' Todd scoffed.'

The DCI spun the centre whiteboard. 'Ta-da. The piece de resistance. This has two sides. Suspects go on here. As the investigation progresses, our focus moves from the victims to the suspects. We'll flip the board at that point.'

'Howay, man. It doesn't matter how fancy yer whiteboard is, if we've nee suspects, it's no good.'

'For now, we'll stick Ahmed Nuri, Ferdie Milburn, and Roy Porter on here. They seem in the clear but summat might turn up. Besides, they're aal we've got.'

Danskin picked up a blue marker pen. Tapped it against the board. 'They're all we've got 'til we work out who this bugger is.'

In large letters, he wrote 'JIM SMITH', followed by three question marks.

**

Gavin O'Hara's first task the following day was to stand back and watch the faces of dead young women unfurl from the printer at a funereal pace.

He meandered to the whiteboard and pinned the photographs to the board. He wasn't more than mid-thirties himself, but the girls were all so young. He released a heavy sigh.

Lyall Parker and Sue Nairn followed up on information Ravi Sangar gleaned about the devices used to send the messages. They each called a dozen places which sold non-contract mobile phones. They both came up with pretty much the same answer. Parker updated the DCI.

'The numbers on the phones aren't issued in advance so we cannae link them to the purchaser. In fact, even if they were, it wouldn't get us far. Anybody can buy their own SIM and replace the original with it. It wouldn't prove anything.'

Danskin rubbed his hand across his shaven head. 'What about the stores? I don't suppose they remember anyone walking in wearing a Hannibal Lecter mask and asking for a device they could use to send pictures of murder weapons?'

The Scotsman laughed. 'You suppose right. Och, Sue and I probably wasted oor time phoning them, anyway. You can order a phone on-line and ha'e it delivered to your hoose. No way would we ever find out. No, Stephen, I don't think there's anything we can do with those phone numbers.'

Todd's task was to have further conversations with the bereaved. At least, it was until Hannah heard him ask a contact of Chelsea Birch whether they knew she was a dominatrix. She took over and sent Todd off to see if Ravi needed a hand.

Hannah spent the entire morning on the telephone, offering her condolences to those who were closest to the victims. They'd already been through most of Chelsea Birch's acquaintances and her colleagues at the running club, so those conversations were the easiest.

Chelsea hadn't complained about anyone stalking her, on-line or in real life. No-one had seen any strangers approach her, nor were they aware of any changes to her daily routine; always a red flag to a detective.

She moved onto Jasmine Peters. These calls were more difficult. Her associates were in various states of grief, and disbelief. Her boss at the Marlborough club displayed anger; anger at himself for preventing her from leaving earlier.

Hannah could handle anger. It was inconsolable grief she struggled with, which was why she was delighted Family Support officers were on hand to deal with those close to the latest victim, Dorothy Jackson.

Which left her with Terri Grainger.

She read the statement given to Trebilcock by Terri's father. The more she read, the more questions reared in her mind. The calls to her friends proved nothing one-way-or-another.

There was only one common denominator. They all expressed genuine astonishment when asked if she had expensive tastes in jewellery. None of them had seen Terri Grainger adorned in anything more luxurious than a silver St Christopher pendant.

With growing certainty, Hannah knew the victim wasn't Terri Grainger.

She needed permission to access the Restricted case. She spun her chair in the direction of Stephen Danskin. He had his head buried in paperwork.

'Sir, I need your permission for something.'

'In a minute, Graves.'

A man had breezed into the bullpen. Tall, upright. His expensive brown shoes clashed with his royal blue suit.

Danskin hurried to the crime boards and flipped the leaves closed. 'Sir, you can't come in here. It's off-limits.'

There was something vaguely familiar about the man; something the DCI couldn't place. His hair was fashionably styled, but too young for his age. He was equally unsuited to its glossy black, 'Just For Men' colour. He had a long, angular face with flattened features, almost as if he'd modelled for an Easter Island statue.

The intruder looked at Danskin with disdain. 'And you are?'

'I'm Detective Chief Inspector Stephen Danskin. Now, if you'd kindly leave the floor…'

'I'm here as a guest,' the man said dismissively.

'I don't think so…'

Superintendent Connor's door opened. 'Sir Guy. Thank you for coming. Let me get you a coffee.'

The door closed behind them and their conversation became inaudible.

'Aye, some fuckers can get their mitts on coffee. Not like us plebs doing aal the work out here,' Todd Robson commented. 'Who does he think he is, anyway?'

The Lighthouse Keeper

Danskin knew who the man was, now. 'That,' he said, 'Is Sir Guy Haswell.'

'THE Guy Haswell?' Ryan asked.

'The very same.' the DCI replied.

'Means fuck all to me,' Todd said.

'You really need brush up on your current affairs, mate,' Ryan chided. 'He's the MP for North Tyne Coastal. He also happens to be junior minister in the Ministry of Justice.'

'What's he doing here, like?'

Ryan shrugged. 'Maybe Connor's after an increase in his budget. We might get our coffee yet.'

Todd snickered. 'Doubt it. Connor's more likely after a bum-prod.'

Whatever Sir Guy Haswell was after, it was enough to distract Danskin from Hannah's initial question. She turned, instead, to Lyall Parker.

'Listen, Lyall. I hear what the Super and the DCI say about Terri Grainger, but I want to keep all doors open.'

'Aye, I've nae bother with that.'

'Good. In that case, I need your authority.'

Puzzled, he asked, 'What for?'

'Access to another Miss Per file. A girl went missing the same time as Terri Grainger. I want to rule out the possibility of it being the Saltwell Park victim.'

'You don't need my permission, lass. Get on wi' it.'

'I'm sorry, sir; I do. The files Restricted.'

'Are you sure?'

'Yes. I am.'

'Then, I cannae help you. There's nae many Restricted files but those that are need the Super's authority.'

Hannah let out air. 'Okay. Guess I'll follow up with Elliot, then. See if he can confirm it's Grainger. If it is, there's no need to bother anybody.'

'Aye. Well, what are you waiting for, DC Graves?'

Lyall Parker disappeared in the direction of Sue Nairn who was engrossed in animated conversation with O'Hara.

Ryan had eavesdropped on the discussion between Hannah and Lyall. He signalled for her to join him. 'Don't call Elliot just yet.'

'Why?'

He considered his words carefully. 'My gut tells me this isn't right. There's something off. Bring the file up. Let us see what it says.'

'I told you what it says. It says 'Restricted.''

'Divvent get arsey, man. Let's try it.'

Hannah wheeled a seat alongside him. She rustled through her notebook. Typed in the same search parameters she'd used last time she'd accessed Miss Per.

The monitor fed back the results.

Cases Found: One

Hannah frowned. 'Eh?'

She hit 'Display.'

A name appeared. *Terri Grainger*.

She looked at Ryan. 'I swear, Ry. There was another case. I swear to God.'

'I believe you, Hannah. Let's keep this to ourselves for now, though; yeah?'

His head turned towards the barricade provided by Superintendent Connor's office door.

'Something stinks, and I'm going to follow my nose 'til I find it.'

CHAPTER EIGHTEEN

On the second loop of the car park, the Fiat squeezed itself on the white hash markings separating the parent and child parking bays from the yellow disabled spots.

'See, having a small car has its advantages,' Ryan smiled.

'Hmm. I'm not sure this is strictly legal, though.'

'Hadaway, man. We're CID. We can do whatever we want.'

Hannah held the edge of the car door away from a neighbouring Mazda as she eased out. 'I still say we should have just rung Elliot, you know.'

'Too many ears in the bullpen. I don't know what's going on but I want to find out before raising anyone's suspicions.'

They pulled on their standard issue face coverings as a pair of automatic doors slid open. 'Maybe so, but the least we could have done was make an appointment. Folk aren't supposed to turn up unannounced these days.'

'I think you'll find we're a bit different, Hannah.'

Their voices echoed around the tiled, tunnel-like corridor, rank with an antiseptic smell.

'This reminds of a tube station's toilets,' she said.

'I was thinking more a Victorian lunatic asylum. Speaking of which...' he pointed to a sign on a door which proclaimed itself to be a portal to *Dr. Aaron Elliot.*

Ryan knocked and entered.

A woman looked up from behind a Perspex screen. 'Yes?'

'We're Detective Constables Ryan Jarrod and Hannah Graves, City and County Police. We'd like a word with Dr. Elliot if we may.'

The woman ran her finger down a list. 'You have an appointment?'

'He's aware of our interest.'
'Do you have an appointment?'
'We don't, no.'
'You need an appointment. You can't show up unannounced; not in the current climate. In your position, you should know that.'

Behind her mask, Hannah smirked.

'We're CID.'

'Doesn't make a blind bit of difference. You can't just do what you want.'

Hannah giggled out loud.

'Look, we're investigating a murder and we need Dr. Elliot to confirm the ID of the victim.'

'Then, either call him, or make an appointment.'

Ryan brought out his phone. 'I'll call him from here. I'm sure he'll see us.'

'I'm sorry, Dr Elliot is in the lab. He won't take your…'

Aaron Elliot marched into the room. He pulled off his scrub cap and tossed his hair like a grunge guitarist. 'Sherlock, what are you doing here? You're not in my diary, are you?'

'That's just what I was telling him, Dr. Elliot…'

The medic waved an arm as expressively as his hair. 'Never mind about that. Come through and bring your fetching Watson with you.'

In the back office, Elliot flung himself into a chair, crossed his hands behind his head and plonked his feet on his desk. 'What can I do for you?'

Hannah spoke first. 'The girl buried alive in Saltwell Park. We need to confirm her identity.'

Elliot frowned. 'I thought you already had it.'

'Look,' Ryan said. 'This is a bit tricky. A Malcolm Grainger identified the victim as his daughter, Terri. But we have some doubts about the authenticity. We know Terri Grainger had a medical condition. We'd like you to confirm that the girl who was dug up had the same condition. I believe Sue

Nairn has been in touch about it already and we'd really like an answer PDQ.'

Elliot swung his feet off his desk in a wide arc. 'I'm intrigued. I like a good mystery, me. Tell me more.'

Hannah took up the story. 'Malcolm Grainger said his daughter had vision problems. Can a condition called ethmoid sinus disease affect eyesight?'

'Oddly enough, yes it can. It's not common but optic neuritis, or even neuropathy, can arise as a result.'

'How easy is it to diagnose?'

Elliot chuckled. 'In the living, relatively easily. In a cadaver, not so. There's no mucus to examine, you see, no…'

Ryan was familiar with Aaron Elliot's soliloquys. 'But it's not impossible?' he interrupted. 'You could determine whether the Saltwell Park victim had whatever-it's-called?'

'Ethmoid sinus disease. No, I'm sorry. I can't.'

'Shit.'

Elliot's face brightened. 'But I do know someone who can. Josie Gustard.'

'I'm confused. How can the field FME tell us something you can't?'

'Josie's excellent at her job.'

'Aye, but so are you, Aaron.'

'I take it you haven't met her.'

'I have, as it happens. I don't think she likes you.'

Elliot spat out a laugh. 'She doesn't. She thought she was a shoo-in for this job when it came up. Didn't take it very well when I waltzed in from outside and got it.'

'Still,' Ryan said, 'I don't get why Josie Gustard can tell us something you can't.'

Aaron Elliot steepled his fingers. 'For one perfectly simple reason. Josie Gustard has custody of the body, not me.'

Ryan blinked. After a momentary pause he asked, 'When did that happen?'

'A couple of days after I determined cause of death. The new roster came out and Grainger had been handed over to

Josie. I've more than enough on my plate so Josie was welcome to her.'

Hannah shook her head. 'Why didn't you tell DS Nairn?'

'I knew nothing about it. I assume my secretary deferred the enquiry straight to Josie.'

He pressed an intercom. 'Trisha, can you come through, please?'

The secretary bustled in, hands fluffing her hair.

'Holmes and Watson here are enquiring what happened to a question from their colleague, DS Nairn. It's regarding Terri Grainger. You know, the girl found in the Gateshead park. The girl Jose Gustard's looking after.'

Ryan was used to Aaron Elliot referring to the dead as if they were still alive, but he could see it unnerved Hannah. She cleared her throat.

'DS Nairn asked Dr Elliot to confirm some details to help us identify the girl. It seems the questions never reached him. I presume you forwarded them to Dr. Gustard?'

Trisha fluffed her hair again. Her head twitched as she spoke. 'I don't believe I did, no.'

'You don't believe you did, or you definitely didn't?' Ryan asked.

'I definitely didn't.'

'Why not?'

'Well, I imagined you would know Dr Gustard had assumed possession. I thought you'd ping your enquiry to her.'

'Thank you, Trisha,' Elliot said. 'That'll be all. A misunderstanding, it seems.'

After the secretary left, he ensured the intercom was still on as he spoke. 'You can't get the staff these days.' He winked at Hannah and switched off the intercom. 'I've got Josie's number, if you'd like to ring her from here. Of course, that's on condition I can listen in.'

'We've got her number already,' Hannah informed him.

'Aye, but there's nowt stopping us calling her right now, is there?' Ryan said.

Hannah glanced at Dr. Elliot. 'Anything you hear is confidential, right?'

The medic clenched a fist against the left side of his chest. 'I will abstain from harming or wronging any man by it,' he quoted from the Hippocratic Oath. 'Scout's honour, as well.'

Ryan dialled Josie Gustard's number and was left in an auditory hell of discordant jazz music while someone went to seek the FME. Mercifully, in the midst of an improvised piano solo which replicated a poodle prancing over the keys, Josie Gustard rode to his rescue.

'Dr. Josephine Gustard speaking.' Her voice was tinny, a sure sign they were on speaker phone at her end, too.

'Dr. Gustard, it's DC Ryan Jarrod here. We met at the crime scene in Saltwell Park.'

'Ah yes. I remember. What can I do for you?'

'We need some further information. I'd like you to re-examine the victim for any signs of ethmoid sinus disease.'

A long pause followed. 'And the significance of this?'

'It proves, one way or another, whether our victim is Terri Grainger.'

Josie Gustard's voice came across crisp and clear. She was no longer on speaker phone. 'I'm afraid that's not possible.'

Ryan clicked his tongue against the roof of his mouth. 'Dr. Elliot said it would be difficult.'

'DC Jarrod, I assure you I'm perfectly capable of determining whether the victim had a condition. IF I still had possession of her body.'

Ryan looked at Hannah who looked at Aaron Elliot.

'What do you mean by 'IF' you still had the body?'

'I thought you'd know. Terri Grainger's body was released this morning.'

'Nee way. Released where?'

'To her father. For cremation.'

Ryan scrunched his hair. 'That's impossible. It's an ongoing investigation. Who the hell authorised that?'

'Who do you think? The same person who always authorises the release of the deceased.'

Together, Ryan and Hannah said, 'Superintendent Connor.'

**

Conspiracy theories, cover-ups, and serial killers do not constitute good subjects for pillow talk, but it's what passed for it that night in the
bedroom of a house in Whickham.

'Do we tell Stephen what we know?' Hannah asked through a final mouthful of pizza from Deano's Trattoria.

Ryan flipped the lid of the carton and let the box slide to the floor. 'I've been mulling over the same thing. I know we can trust the DCI, but do we want to put him in such a compromising situation? I mean, we don't have clear proof of anything right now.'

'We know enough. We know Connor's put obstacles in the way of the enquiry at every step. We know he gave authority to dispose of the body despite the ongoing investigation. We know he's tried his damndest to pursue separate lines of enquiry even though you continually told him the cases were linked.'

'Aye, that's true. But, divvent forget Stephen wasn't on board with me serial killer theory, either.'

Hannah let out a roar of frustration. 'So, where do we go from here? We can't do everything ourselves.'

The blinds at the window were open. Ryan looked up at the moon, bright and full in a cloudless sky.

'When Neil Armstrong first stepped onto the moon, he had full faith in his crew. Not only Aldrin and Collins, but those back in Mission Control, too. How many of our colleagues do we really know, Hannah? How many would you trust with your life?'

'All of them, Ry. Every last one.'

'Connor?'

'Well, up until a couple of days ago, aye.'

'Exactly. Until a couple of days ago. Which means any of the others could go rogue, too.'

She tisked. 'I wouldn't go so far as to say Connor's gone rogue.'

'Perhaps not, but we don't know what's gannin' on, do we?'

Hannah let out air until her cheeks vibrated. 'Okay. Right, we're sure we can trust Stephen.'

'Agreed. But not Sue Nairn. She had every opportunity to chase Elliot for the information we needed but she didn't. And now it's too late.'

'Treblecock and Gavin O'Hara are on Sue's team. What about them?'

In the moonlight, she saw Ryan shake his head. 'Gav mentored me for a year and I never really got to know him. I'm not sure about him. I'd say Treblecock's fine, but we can't take the risk. He's on their team so if – and it's a big if – there's something off-cock, we can't chance it.'

'Todd?'

'He's straight as a die. The question with him is, can he keep his gob shut?'

'Fair comment. How about Ravi?'

'Jury's out. Leave him for now. We might need his expertise but he's got a foot in both camps so let's keep him on the back burner.'

Hannah sighed. 'God, this is wor friends we're talking about.'

'I know. Chances are, they're all fine and we're worried about nowt, but that leaves us with Lyall and Danskin. I say we speak to the DCI first thing. Like you said, we can't do this all by ourselves.'

They remained silent in the narrow bed with its lumpy mattress and old springs, lost in their own thoughts.

Hannah laid her head on his chest. Ran her fingers through the fine downy blond hair on it. 'We're good together, you and me.'

On a whim, Ryan propped himself up. He extended an arm and opened the top drawer of his bedside cabinet. His fingers rummaged for the old ring buried somewhere within it.

'I mean it, Ryan. We make a good team. That's why I don't want anything to change between us. It mightn't be strictly against the Code of Ethics right now but, one day soon, one of us will move up the ranks. If I moved in here, there'd be a conflict of interest. We couldn't work together anymore.'

She raised her eyes to meet his. 'I don't think I could bear that,' she said. 'I really don't.'

Quietly, reluctantly, Ryan withdrew his empty hand and let the drawer slide shut.

CHAPTER NINETEEN

They'd agreed in advance there'd be no eye contact with their colleagues. Which was a mistake. If either Ryan or Hannah had glanced towards Trebilcock or Robson as they marched through the bullpen towards Stephen Danskin's office, they'd have picked up the warning signals.

As it was, they entered the DCI's office to find it already occupied. Danskin and Parker sat one side of the desk, Superintendent Connor and Sir Guy Haswell the other.

It didn't need the desk between them for Ryan to know they were on opposite sides. The body language made it obvious.

'Sorry,' Ryan said. 'We'll come back.'

'No, no. Come in. We could use your input here,' the DCI said.

Ryan translated the last sentence as meaning, *For God's sake, agree with everything I say.*

'Do we really need mere Detective Constables in on this discussion?'

Even Connor looked embarrassed as Danskin said, 'We're one team here, Sir Guy.'

'Very well.' The politician sounded less than convinced.

'Where were we?' Danskin asked. He knew fine well where they were but asked as a means of updating Ryan and Hannah.

'A press conference,' Superintendent Connor said. 'A virtual one, obviously. Sir Guy was saying the case has reached the PMs ears. With a by-election due in the marginal Hadrian and Tynedale constituency, it's important we get the killer off the streets. If that means going public, so be it.'

'Wi' respect, sir,' Lyall Parker said, 'We want the killer off the streets period; no' because there's a by-election looming.'

'Well, yes, of course,' Connor spluttered. 'Anyway, we…'

The door banged open. A woman in a beige suit walked into the office. Seeing no-one else wore face coverings, she removed hers.

'Jesus Christ,' Danskin muttered.

'And this is?' Sir Guy asked.

'Imogen Markham,' the woman said. 'I'm the criminal psychologist.'

'Imogen will be working with us,' Connor announced.

Danskin knew the woman. Connor had brought her in to assist on the Tyneside Tyrant case a few years previously. She'd proved as useful as a one-legged man in an arse kicking tournament.

'May I have a private word, sir?' Danskin pleaded.

'No, Stephen; you can't. DC Jarrod, get the lady a seat.'

Ryan leant out the door and trundled in a couple of stand-by chairs. Markham took one, Hannah the other. He remained standing.

'Imogen, can you update the Minister and the DCI with your thoughts on the killer?'

Markham gave a brisk nod. 'There are clear trends present, but I'm sure you've already noticed them. The traceless crime scenes, scrupulous planning, the ritual of the messages; they all indicate obsessiveness.'

'But isn't that typical of any serial killer?' Danskin commented.

She ignored him. 'The murder victims are all young women, all red-heads. Clearly, that means something to him. Also, I suspect he enjoys control.'

'What makes you think that?' Danskin asked, keen to spot a flaw in Markham's work.

'The messages. I believe he enjoys the fact he kills his victims despite them knowing how they'll die. That's why he sends them.'

'There's the first fault in your logic. They don't know he's a killer. They don't know what the messages mean. They don't even know who sent them.'

The psychologist smiled and met his eyes. In them, Danskin saw a different Imogen Markham to the one he'd encountered several years ago. This one was cool and confident, almost to the point of cockiness. She'd changed.

'Detective Chief Inspector, it doesn't matter to him. The victims have the information. That's all that matters. He likes the superiority he has over them. They have all the information, yet they still walk right into his trap.'

Danskin had no answer and was relieved when Connor spoke. 'What can we expect next from him?'

'He'll kill again. Quite possibly, the timescale between killings will decrease as his confidence increases.'

Danskin swore.

'Never fear, DCI Danskin,' Markham continued. 'That's when he'll become careless. He'll think he'll never be caught. Nine times out of ten, that's precisely when he will get caught. Sadly, there's likely to be several more victims before we get to that point.'

She spoke matter-of-factly, as if forecasting sunshine and showers for the next few days.

Sir Guy Haswell intervened. 'That can't happen, Connor. This man must be caught. If there's any more deaths, and if the Government lose a seat as a result, news of your incompetence will reach the highest of authorities.'

Ryan felt Hannah glance towards him, but he stared straight ahead. 'Are we dealing with a psychopath?' Jarrod asked Markham.

'I'd say it's highly probable, yes. Stalking his victims, seeking control, some sort of issue with women, and a distinct lack of empathy are all characteristics of what you laymen would term psychopathy.'

'It's not much consolation,' Danskin said, 'But it looks like you were right all along, Jarrod. Well done.'

Ryan took no pleasure in the compliment. Instead, he asked, 'So, who are we looking for?'

'Jim Smith,' Markham replied, smiling again. 'A common name for a common man. He'll be someone who blends into the crowd. Someone who manages life and society by impersonating the behaviours of others. When you find him, it's almost certain he'll have a history of abuse; either forced on him, or abuse he's forced onto others. Quite possibly, both. He's intelligent. He can plan, and act out a plan, to the letter.'

She locked eyes with them all, one-by-one. 'He's a psychopath, but he's no nut-case.'

Sir Guy Haswell cleared his throat. 'In that case, we must move now. We were discussing a press conference; when and how it should be done. Superintendent Connor – I'm looking to you for a lead here.'

Ryan looked at Stephen and Lyall. It was clear they were not in agreement with the press conference suggestion. Ryan knew Danskin, in particular, had an aversion to them. For some reason, the DCI didn't object so Ryan did it for them.

'Why a press conference? The killer doesn't know we've joined the dots yet. Shouldn't we gather more information first? See what the next few days throw up?'

'Didn't you listen to a word…' Sir Guy floundered for Markham's name, 'This woman said? He'll kill again. I'm not having that.'

'I agree,' Connor said. 'People need to be alerted. If a woman gets a message from a stranger, we want her to tell the police.'

'Surely, though, a press conference will delay him. Make him more careful. Hide his tracks better. He won't want to rush into owt.'

Connor bristled. 'He doesn't need hide his tracks any better because he doesn't leave any.'

Unsurprisingly, Markham didn't support Ryan's plan, either. 'A press conference may push him to act sooner. This is a man who likes control. He'd want to prove he's calling the shots, not the police. It may make him careless.'

'In that case,' Sir Guy said, 'Perhaps we should force his hand – but on the understanding it's your head on the line; not mine.'

The temperature in the room dropped. Danskin sagged. 'It's clear you've made your mind up. But I'm telling you now – this is gannin to be costly. Folk will get hysterical. We'll be inundated with calls. We'll need an army on this, and that's just to man the lines.'

'You'll get everything you need. You have my word,' Haswell promised.

'What,' Danskin mocked, 'Even coffee?'

**

Ryan sat in the confines of his old Fiat Uno outside the care home which housed his grandmother. He spoke to her but talked to himself.

'I don't know when this virus will let me see you again. You mightn't even recognise me when I do. I want you to know you're still with me, though. You always will be.'

He peered up at Doris Jarrod's window, three floors up. 'Hannah's done some work on your house. I hope you divvent mind. Upstairs is still the same, but you wouldn't recognise the rest of the place.'

He wiped away a tear. 'She's done a bit of work in the garden, an' aal. Bless her, she's planted a rose bush especially for you. She says it's called Doris. A Doris Tysterman, or summat.'

His voice broke and he cleared his throat.

'You'd like Hannah,' he said. 'She lives in Jesmond but, one day, I'd like her to be here, close to you. We had a bit of a falling out, Hannah and me, but we're okay now. In fact, when I pluck up the courage, I'm going to give her your engagement ring. I'm sure you won't mind.'

Ryan sighed. 'If things had been different, you might've been on your way towards being a Great Grandma. What do you make of that?'

He felt foolish when he realised he was waiting for her reply. He gave an embarrassed laugh.

'Things are a bit rubbish at work at the minute. I can't show it, but it's a struggle sometimes, keeping it all in. Not letting it show. Being strong.' He laughed. 'Strong. Me. I might've been able to hoy mesel around a high bar in me day, but I've never really been strong.'

He looked up towards the window again. 'These are strange times, gran, and I'm pleased you don't really understand, if I'm honest. Anyhow, I'm going to stop at me dad's tonight. Don't fancy being by myself. I'll give him and wor kid your love.'

Ryan flicked the ignition key. 'See you, gran. I hope.'

As he three-point turned in the car park and waited for a break in traffic on Whickham Bank, the frail figure of Doris Jarrod appeared at the window.

She didn't know who was in the white car but she waved goodbye, all the same.

CHAPTER TWENTY

The kitchen in Norman Jarrod's house always had been illogically designed. Ryan just noticed it more now he didn't live there.

He opened a shoulder-high unit and retrieved a mug. He carried it to the sink, took out a spoon from the drawer beneath, and brought both items to a work surface against the opposite wall. Ryan spooned his morning coffee into the mug, flicked on the kettle, and traversed the kitchen again to collect the milk from the fridge.

Spud followed his master's every move, craning his stunted neck to look up at Ryan's activity. When Jarrod sniffed the open bottle, the dog was rewarded with a splattering of sour milk in his bowl.

'How, Ry. Your gaffer's on the telly,' James Jarrod shouted from the living room.

'Already? What time's it, like?' He tipped his wrist and freshly poured coffee slopped from the mug. 'Bugger.' He flicked the hot liquid from his over-sensitive hands and hurried into the lounge.

James sat one side of a sofa, long carroty hair flopping over his eyes in the absence of its usual litre of gel. Norman Jarrod slouched alongside his youngest son, finger so far up his nose it endangered his brain.

'Thought Foreskin didn't do press conferences these days,' Norman Jarrod said.

'He does whatever he's told to do,' Ryan replied bluntly. 'Besides, I don't think he minds virtual ones. Neebody can catch him off guard or waylay him afterwards.'

His dad removed his finger. 'Just divvent tell us he's going to say, *Next slide, please*. I've had enough of aal that bollocks.'

'Shut up, man. Let's listen to him.' He turned up the volume.

'...two young women from the Whitley Bay area, another found in Gateshead, and one more in the West End of the city. Four in total,' Danskin was saying, the vagaries of Zoom causing the sound to be out of synch with his lips.

'These abominable crimes were perpetrated by the same individual.'

'A serial killer?' James said. 'Wow. How cool.'

'No, knacker-heed. It's not cool. Now, shut up a minute.'

Danskin's mouth had caught up with his words. 'The killer is targeting young women. We have established he contacts his victims via social media platforms. We strongly urge all young women to ensure their profile settings are private. I can't emphasise this strongly enough. For your own safety, do not have a public profile.'

'Are you on the case?' James asked.

'Aye. We all are.'

'Cool.'

'Piss off.'

DCI Danskin was urging members of the public to call the number he was about to read out if they had any information or had seen anything on the dates he'd mentioned.

Meanwhile, if anyone received an image from an unknown source, they should call 999 without delay. He informed the public that all lines would be manned round the clock.

Danskin repeated the importance of remaining vigilant and disclosed the number a second time before ending the conference without inviting questions.

'What's aal that about? The image thing?' James asked.

Without thinking, Ryan answered, 'We think he's sending them pictures of how they're going to die.' He realised he shouldn't have let that slip. 'You didn't hear that. Okay?'

'Cool,' James Jarrod replied.

**

He was watching the press conference.

'*Clever,*' he thought. '*He hasn't mentioned the red hair. Or Jim Smith. Or the significance of the images.*'

The killer knew the shaven-headed cop, who the TV anchor had identified as DCI Danskin, was keeping the information back so they could sort the wheat from the chaff when the calls flooded in.

Then, without warning, the anger hit him.

The detective had called him 'abominable;' the acts, 'vicious'. There'd been no mention of the care he'd taken, the intelligence he'd used in identifying his victims, the intricate planning which meant he'd left no trace for the police to follow.

The story this Danskin bloke presented was the police version of events. The story they wanted the public to hear. Well, there were two sides to every tale and now it was time for everyone to know his side of it.

Only a select few were privy to the fine detail, and that's how it would remain. But there was still a story to be heard. And he'd be the one to tell it.

He opened the internet browser. Found the site of *The Mercury*. Trawled down the list of reporters and their e-mail addresses. The killer closed his eyes and lay a finger on the screen. He made a note of the name his finger rested against. Alongside it, he wrote '*Heads.*'

The man repeated the action, this time noting '*Tails*' next to the reporter's name.

He flipped a coin.

Tails, it was.

**

Those living on the Gateshead side of the river, the ones forced to funnel through traffic onto the narrow bridges, were the last to arrive.

Fortunately, only Lyall Parker and Ryan Jarrod fell into this category and they still managed to join the rest of

Stephen Danskin's watch before the DCI finished his lengthy debrief with Superintendent Connor.

When he eventually emerged from Connor's office, he did so taught-jawed. 'Let the fun begin,' he said.

'If you divvent mind us saying, guv, it's an odd time to hold a press briefing,' Todd Robson commented.

'The Super didn't want us to say anything yesterday evening because he feared we'd be flooded with calls before we'd had a chance to ramp up the number of public lines available.'

'Aye, I get that, like, but why so early today? Normally we'd catch the lunchtime or evening news, not Piers-twatting-Morgan and co.'

A nerve twitched in Danskin's cheek. 'He wanted to get the warning out asap. Just in case Markham was right and the killer decided to act again.'

Ryan spoke up. 'When you say 'he', do you mean the Super or Guy Haswell?'

Danskin raised an eyebrow. 'Connor, of course.' He narrowed the other eye. 'I assume.'

Hannah glanced at Ryan. She flicked her head towards Lyall Parker. Ryan nodded.

'Lyall, can I have a word?'

'Course you can. The noo?'

Ryan was already heading towards the rear of the bullpen. Parker propped himself against a desk next to him.

'What's up?'

Ryan considered his words carefully. 'How much do we know about Sir Guy Haswell?'

DI Parker stiffened. 'Is this relevant?'

'Aye, actually; I think it might be.'

'Spit it out, man.'

Ryan rubbed the back of his neck. 'Look, I might be speaking out of turn, but he seems like he's got the Super jumping through hoops.'

Parker subconsciously squinted towards Connor's office door. 'Go on, laddie.'

Ryan explained his doubts about Connor's interference in the case, about the extent of Guy Haswell's input to it, and his concerns at the potential removal of crucial evidence.

'Evidence destruction? Aye, as a matter of fact, I do think you're speaking out of turn, now ye mention it. That's quite an allegation. Care to expand?'

Ryan was in too deep to stack his hand now. 'Terri Grainger. Connor authorised the disposal of her body. He knew we had ongoing concerns about the victim's identity, yet he signed the release forms.'

'That's his call, Ryan. You know it is. If the lassie's da' wanted her back, why prolong his agony?'

'Because it mightn't be Terri Grainger, that's why. Her dad might be cremating someone else's daughter.'

'Och aye; like, who's?'

'Howay man, Lyall. You know we had doubts about her identity.'

Lyall put an arm around Ryan's shoulder. The softly-spoken Aberdonian lowered his voice even further. 'I ask you again. Who else could it be?'

Ryan fixed Parker with a stare. 'The other file. The one with Restricted access. The one Hannah mentioned to you the other day.'

Something shifted behind Parker's eyes. 'Aye, I remember that, now you've reminded me.'

'The one that needed the Super's authority to access.'

'Aye, I did say that to DC Graves.'

'Lyall, the casefile's not 'Classified'. It's not 'Restricted'. Access doesn't need 'Authorisation.' It's bloody disappeared. It's as if it never existed.'

Parker blinked three, four times.

'Now,' Ryan continued. 'What do we know about Guy Haswell?'

**

The City and County CID, at least those under Superintendent Connor, were split into two commands. DCI Stephen Danskin led the Serious Crime team while DCI Rick Kinnear headed up what was colloquially referred to as 'The Hockers'; those allocated to ad hoc investigations.

Once the calls began to land in the Communications Centre in Ponteland, there were no distinctions. Every man-jack of Connor's team was deployed on following up leads referred to them by the Contact Handlers. These were the calls which mentioned key facts not revealed by Danskin during his press briefing; calls from red-heads, those who had received images which represented anything resembling a weapon or means of death, or messages sent by a Jim Smith.

Plenty fell into the first two categories, none into the latter.

Nonetheless, it was painstaking, routine, mind-numbing work. There was no opportunity for Ryan or Hannah or Lyall to do anything other than chase tails, no matter how vague or unlikely. Sir Guy Haswell was forgotten.

At five-forty, after eight hours without a break, Todd Robson dragged a bleary-eyed Ryan down three flights of stairs to the reception area where a public vending machine dispensed actual coffee.

Todd left Ryan to feed the machine a handful of pound coins and stack half a dozen cups onto a plastic tray while Robson nipped around the corner to collect the pre-ordered sandwiches.

Ryan was waiting for the last drink to dispense when a sandwich-less Todd burst back in.

'Leave them,' he shouted. 'We've work to do.'

'It'll keep, man, surely?'

'Not this, it won't. Upstairs. Now.'

'Ooh, you can be so masterful,' Ryan mocked.

'Give ower and get your arse into gear. Foreskin and Connor are ganna gan ape-shit.'

In his hand, Todd Robson held a copy of The Mercury.

**

The squad released a collective groan when Todd burst through the bullpen doors minus refreshments.

'Where's Foreskin?' Robson demanded.

'Where's me bait, more to the point,' Gavin O'Hara asked.'

'Sod that. Where's Foreskin? He's gonna lose his shit when he sees this.'

'I'm right behind you,' Stephen Danskin said. 'And, if you keep calling me Foreskin, I really will lose my shit.'

'Bollocks to that. There's an article in here about the serial killer.' He waved The Mercury as if it was a Roman standard.

'Robson, it may have escaped your attention, but I held a press briefing this morning; the whole point of which was to raise the case profile. I'd be pretty pissed off if there wasn't owt about it.'

'Shut up and listen.'

Danskin's eyes widened but, before he lodged his objection, he understood. He understood because Todd continued talking.

'Aye, but this article is different. It says the killer's sending messages to the victims telling them how they'll die.'

Danskin grabbed the newspaper from Robson's grasp. 'The public aren't supposed to know this. I kept it back from them so we could weed out the crank calls.'

The DCI's heart sank as he scanned the article. 'Fuck's sake, man. It says everything in here. Some of the victims are named. We've never released the names.'

He read on. 'Jesus, the red-hair, the significance of the messages, the fact they're sent twenty-four hours before he kills them: it's all here. It even includes the picture of the fucking Citroen. The only thing it doesn't mention is Jim Smith.'

'We've got a mole,' Hannah whispered to Ryan.

'Doesn't take a genius to work out who it'll be, does it?'

Connor's voice thundered across the bullpen. 'Danskin. Get your backside in here. Sangar – you too. You should be monitoring the web for stuff like this before it's in the public domain.'

'Shit,' Danskin swore. 'He's seen it.'

Stephen Danskin devoured the rest of the article in preparation for the bollocking headed his way. The DCI stopped at the final sentence. The report named the killer.

He was calling himself *The Lighthouse Keeper*.

CHAPTER TWENTY-ONE

Molly Uzumba was still in her thirties, but she'd been with The Mercury through thin and thinner.

She'd worked on the media outlet so long she was even there during its relative heyday, when its on-line streaming and interactive content set it apart from the competition.

That was before The Mercury's reputation plummeted on the back of its role in the notorious Tyneside Tyrant outrage. Now, it was just another regional newspaper struggling to survive.

Molly had always been in search of the Big One: the exclusive which would catapult her to fame. Throughout her time at the rag, she'd played second fiddle to Megan Wolfe. Whilst Wolfe was brazen, outspoken and a risk-taker, Uzumba was haughty, aloof and diligent.

Brazen saw Wolfe poached by the BBC. Diligent meant Uzumba remained unknown. Until now. The instant Molly Uzumba opened the e-mail, she knew this was her moment.

As any good, diligent journalist would, she fact-checked the details sent to her by the one called The Lighthouse Keeper. It didn't take long, with her contacts, to establish both Chelsea Birch and Jasmine Peters had indeed been murdered. Both girls had red hair. And, Jasmine had been mown down by a vehicle which appeared on her Facebook feed.

She didn't, however, have confirmation of the other two deaths. Nothing to back up The Lighthouse Keeper's claims. It was her call: publish and be damned, or publish and let the offers roll in.

The phone rang. This could be the first of those offers.

'You're speaking to Molly Uzumba of The Mercury.'

'And you're speaking to Detective Chief Inspector Stephen Danskin of the City and County police.'

**

'Oh,' She sounded disappointed. 'It'll be about my article, I suppose.'

'How did you guess?

'Interesting, don't you think?'

Danskin had already decided he didn't like the woman. Her voice sounded slightly hoarse. In anyone else, he would have found it sexy but, with the reporter, he just wanted her to cough out the chicken bone lodged in her throat.

'What I would find interesting is how you came by the information.' He was still in Connor's office. He didn't notice the Super wince when he asked the question.

'How else would I come by it? From the killer himself, of course.'

Danskin felt his arms turn to gooseflesh. 'What?'

'You heard me. From The Lighthouse Keeper.'

'Why do you call him that?'

He noticed the confusion in Uzumba's voice. 'It's not me who named him The Lighthouse Keeper. That's what he told me I should call him.'

Danskin's head spun. Connor waited for him to speak. So, too, Ravi Sangar. Instead, the next voice they heard was Molly Uzumba's.

'Hello? Are you still there, Detective Inspector?'

'It's Detective CHIEF Inspector, Miss Uzumba.' Her words made his thoughts snap into focus. 'Do you know someone by the name of Ferdie Milburn?'

There was a pause. 'Not to my knowledge, no. Should I?'

'He's the wildlife warden on St Mary's Island.'

'Oh, I see where we're going with this. You think he could be The Lighthouse Keeper, don't you?'

Shit. He'd just added to her story.

'Miss Uzumba, I think we should continue this discussion at the station.'

He expected the silence to be filled with her objections. Instead, she said, 'Great idea. I'd like to get an interview with you.'

Danskin frowned. That wasn't how it was supposed to work.

**

Superintendent Connor made a point of looking at his watch.

'How long does it take the bloody woman to walk down here from the Groat Market?' he asked. 'It's been best part of an hour now.'

'Depends,' Stephen Danskin said.

'On what?'

'Whether she was actually in The Mercury offices when I called. She could be working from home. Lots do, these days.'

'Oh, for heaven's sake. You didn't check?'

'You were there, sir. I called her immediately. You know I didn't have time to check.'

Connor breathed noisily. 'You're right, Stephen. Sorry. It's just I've had Sir Guy breathing down my neck. He's spitting feathers with this all being in the public domain and the by-election due…'

A uniformed constable opened the interview room door. 'She's here.'

'Thank fuck for that.'

The desk sergeant shepherded a tall, slim woman into the room.

Danskin was vaguely aware he'd met her before, during a raid on The Mercury offices during the Tyrant investigation. He hadn't taken much notice of her at the time. Now, he studied her as if she were a museum piece.

Molly Uzumba was younger than he'd expected. She had dark eyes which complemented skin the colour of hot chocolate. Her hair was braided into tight wads of black curls separated by tramlines the width of the A69.

Danskin felt her entire demeanour looked down on him. He forced a smile onto his face.

'Thank you for coming, Miss Uzumba.'

'Molly.'

'Molly, then. How did the killer…'

'…The Lighthouse Keeper,' she interrupted.

'…the killer; how did he contact you?'

'He sent me an e-mail. He told me he selected his victims carefully. Sent them messages. How they had to have red hair.' She spoke calmly, as if explaining why she preferred Pepsi to Coke. 'He gave me their names. Or, at least, two of their names.'

'When was this?'

She shrugged. 'Perhaps, ten o'clock?'

Superintendent Connor looked as if he were about to explode. 'And you didn't think to tell us?'

Uzumba stared at him. 'I'm sorry, you are?'

'Superintendent Connor,' Danskin said before the puce-faced Super could combust.

'I didn't tell you because I hadn't fact-checked the story. I didn't want to waste your time.'

'And after you did *'fact-check'* them – why not then?' Connor spluttered.

'I guess it was too late.'

Stephen Danskin knew it was because she wanted to wait until she'd run the story. 'You mean you wanted your five minutes of fame, don't you?'

Molly gave him a disarming smile. 'Detective Chief Inspector, I assure you it'll be more than five minutes.'

Somehow, Danskin restrained himself from wringing the journalist's neck. He took a sip of water. Noticed the plastic cup tremble in his hand. He took a deep breath.

'I need to see that e-mail. The one you got from a serial killer but didn't think important enough to alert the police.'

She shrugged. 'It's not like it contained any information you didn't already possess.'

Danskin hissed. 'Have you had any other contact with the killer?'

'No. At least, not yet.'

'Has he ever contacted you before?'

She shook her head.

'Are you sure?'

'I receive a lot of messages - it comes with the territory – but if he has sent me anything, he didn't call himself The Lighthouse Keeper, or say 'H*ey, look at me: I'm a serial killer*.'

Danskin scratched his head. 'You've had nee strange communications lately? Nowt out of the ordinary?'

'If you mean, has he sent me an image of an Uzi sub-machine gun anytime in the last twenty-four hours, no. But, then again, I haven't got red hair, have I?'

'That's a shame,' Danskin muttered.

She responded with a throaty laugh.

'How did you know it wasn't a prank?' Connor asked.

'I have my sources. And, before you ask, I'm not going to reveal them. Besides, I'd be a shabby reporter if I wasn't able to validate claims like that.'

Danskin and Connor exchanged glances. Slowly, reluctantly, Connor nodded.

The DCI exhaled a single, long drawn out breath. 'If the killer contacts you again, you'll let us know,' he said.

'I can. If you'll grant me an interview.'

Danskin barked out a laugh. 'It wasn't a question, Miss Uzumba. Or a request. If this *'Lighthouse Keeper'* gets in touch, you WILL tell us. Otherwise, you're an accessory. Now, piss off oot of my sight.'

'I will. I'll piss off and speak to Mr Milburn, I think you said his name was. Thank you for that information; you've been most co-operative, Detective Chief Inspector.'

She smiled her arrogance at him.

**

Ryan sidled up alongside Lyall Parker.

'What's going on, Lyall?'

'Stephen's having a wee chat with the reporter. He wants to know how she got her hands on confidential information.'

'Speaking of 'Confidential', have you found owt on Haswell yet?'

'Whisht, man. Keep your voice down.'

'Does that mean you think there's something in what I had to say?'

'As a matter of fact, no. All the same, I dinnae want folk shouting their mouth off when there's nae good reason.'

'People like Todd, you mean?'

'There's more brains in a Scotch Pie.'

Ryan laughed. 'You know fine well something's not right with the Terri Grainger thing, though. Ravi's been over her social media again and again and there's nowt there that's remotely linked to the way she died, let alone anything from Jim Smith.'

'Listen, Ryan. You're right. Far as I can tell, the case disnae match the profile. But it's not my case. Sue knows better, and she's happy enough to go along wi' it.'

'Exactly.'

'Son, you cannae go around saying things like that. And you certainly haven't enough to accuse a member of the government of…well, whatever you think he's up to.'

Ryan twisted his mouth.

'And don't you go looking like that, Jarrod. For what it's worth, I've asked the Markham woman for her opinion.'

Ryan's mouth fell open. 'Ah man, why? She was only brought on board after Haswell stuck his oar in.'

'You're unbelievable, d'ya ken that? First, the MP's up to something. Then, you wonder about DS Nairn. Now, it's the criminal psychologist. Anyone else you'd like to implicate?'

Ryan thought long and hard before answering. 'Where's Superintendent Connor?'

'What?'

'Haven't seen him for a while, that's all. Just wondering where he was.'

Lyall squinted at him. 'He's with the DCI, interviewing the journalist.'

'The Super is? I've never known him sit in on an interview in all my time here.'

Lyall Parker sucked in air. 'For what it's worth, laddie, neither have I. That's why I need to be sure afore I say anything.'

**

Dusk settled over the Glebe sports ground with the inevitable acceptance of a drunkard reaching for his White Lightning.

'So, I'm still not sure: is Lyall on board or not?' Hannah asked.

Ryan bent to unleash Spud and took Hannah's hand. 'He is and he isn't. I'm pretty sure he knows summat's not right, but I'm not convinced he'll bite the bullet. He's a lot to lose.'

'We all have. If we sit on this, we become complicit in whatever's up.'

'Yep. But, if we're barking up the wrong tree, we're finished in the force. Or, it's finished with us.'

She squeezed his hand. 'You don't think we're wrong though, do you?'

'I don't, no. But I'm not sure Lyall's going to help us. I think it's down to thee and me, kidda. We've a bit of homework to do on Guy Haswell and it's going to be tricky finding time. We're working all hours as it is.'

Lights began to twinkle in the houses peeking over the crest of the sports field's rise. Ryan whistled for Spud who was snuffling by a goalpost. The dog glanced up, circled the post one final time, cocked his leg, and pawed the turf where he'd sprayed.

'Better there than digging up the cricket wicket, I suppose, but the groundsman's still gonna love him for that. Good job the footie season's delayed, if it ever gets off the ground at aal.'

Hannah scoffed. 'It's only a park pitch. Nobody's going to be arsed about it, man.'

Ryan looked affronted. 'Divvent let me dad hear you say that. Whickham play here, man.'

'Like, a proper team?'

'Aye. The stand gives you a bit of a clue.'

'Stand? It's just a big shed, isn't it?'

'Hadaway. They're a canny team. In the pyramid, like.'

'Ry, I haven't a clue what you're talking about.' She looked towards the far touchline, barely visible over the field's slope. 'It'll be like playing on Kilimanjaro.'

Ryan laughed out loud. 'Me dad reckons it's their secret weapon. He saw them win the Vase at Wembley donkey's years ago. He says they only got there 'cos none of the opposition team ever came equipped with ropes and crampons.'

Ryan whistled again and waved a packet of treats in the direction of his dog. Spud scuttled towards him like an old codger crossing a busy street.

'Where do we start, Ry? With Haswell, I mean?'

He shrugged. 'More like, when do we start? Like I said before, we've a fair bit on at the moment, if you hadn't noticed.'

She grabbed his buttocks. 'And that's even before I redesign your bedroom.'

He gawped at her.

'What're you looking at us like that for? You didn't think I'd leave your house half done, did you?'

Actually, he did.

'The bed's going, for one,' she continued. 'And those flowery curtains. Not to mention the woodworm-infested chest of drawers.'

He shut his eyes. He'd better shift that ring from the *'woodworm-infested chest of drawers'* before she threw the baby out with the bathwater. He winced. Wrong phrase.

Hannah's phone rang, giving time to recover his poise and put melancholy thoughts aside.

She wandered away from him while she took the call. Ryan clipped Spud's lead to its collar and fed him a handful of treats. When he looked up, Hannah's expression had changed.

'You're not going to believe this,' she said. 'That was Todd. He's just heard from Lyall.'

'Don't tell me: he's got something on Haswell.'

'No, nowt like that. Stephen sent him to check out Ferdie Milburn. You know: Lighthouse Keeper, and all that. The name's a bit obvious, but it had to be checked out.'

'And?'

'And nothing. Milburn's not there. No sign of him. What's more, the Maritime Agency say he hasn't filed a report with them for a couple of days.'

'The only person we know who comes close to being a lighthouse keeper has disappeared.'

**

It was time to go shopping.

The woman in Boots had been ever-so-helpful but it was clear there was nothing available over the counter which would be suitable for his needs.

He'd have no trouble getting what he required on-line. He'd have to be careful, but care was his forte. He logged into the website, scrolled down and, within moments, he'd found what he was after. Twenty-four hour delivery, guaranteed. Just perfect.

The killer had already selected his victim. She was perfect, too. In fact, almost too perfect. Apart from the silky, dark red hair flowing over her shoulders like a fine claret, everything else about her was stunning. Why would anyone so beautiful leave her profile public? Especially after all the warnings. Especially with The Lighthouse Keeper actively seeking out an audience to hear the next part of his story.

He hadn't intended acting so quickly. He thought it would be fun to visualise Danskin and his friends jumping through hoops at every crank and nuisance call. Let them sweat for a while, then strike.

But then he found her. Or, rather, she found him. Once the urge took hold, there was no escaping it. All the memories, all the pain, all the relief, swept over him like a tidal wave.

The Lighthouse Keeper had watched her for four days. He knew what she'd be doing, and when she'd do it. More importantly, he knew her window would be open.

He'd checked the weather forecast on his phone not half an hour ago, but he checked it again. It still predicted tomorrow night would be clear with high humidity levels.

Yes, her window would be open.

Methodically, he tracked his order. He had a delivery slot already. He was impressed. Very efficient.

He opened his photo gallery. Let his finger caress the image. Then, he copied it and pressed send.

Tomorrow would be a good day. One of the very best.

A delightful tingle of electricity ran down his spine.

He let out a low, orgasmic moan.

CHAPTER TWENTY-TWO

Being male, Tomasz 'Tea' Potts was in a minority amongst the Call Handling team. Most of his colleagues were women; many, free and single. They flirted with him the way lots of women do with openly gay men, safe in the knowledge their approaches won't be taken seriously.

If truth be told, Tea enjoyed camping it up. He went along with their innuendo, joined in with most of it, even though he was under no illusions he'd be on a charge if the boot had been on the other foot. He knew diversity was all-too-often a one-way street.

He'd been at the job six months now, and he loved it. He was also good at it. He had a knack for calming folk down, a relaxed yet confident manner which the public warmed to. Until, that is, The Mercury ran the story on The Lighthouse Keeper.

The last twenty-four hours had been crazy, both in the Ponteland HQ where he was based and the force's other command centre in South Shields. Tomasz never thought human beings could be so hysterical. The only way he and the rest of the team got through it was with black humour.

'Here's a good one,' the colleague alongside him said from behind her perspex screen. 'I've just had a bloke on. I asked if he had red hair. He said he was bald. But, he was adamant he'd received one of the warnings. *'What is it?' I asked him. 'I've just had a message with a lion's head on. Someone's going to feed me to the lions,'* he says. So, I asked him who sent it. *'The Premier League'*, he says. *'They sent me an advert for the start of the season. It had their logo on. A lion's head.'*

Tea laughed. 'I think we should report it, all the same. I *luurv* the thought of The Lighthouse Keeper being Richard Masters.'

'Shitehouse Keeper, more like it,' the girl opposite said, though the poster stuck on the divider screen made it appear the voice had come from Alain Saint Maximin.

'Well, darling, I can beat that one,' Tea said. 'I had a woman telling me her new boyfriend had sent her a picture of his penis.'

'Never. How did she think he was going to kill her with that?'

Tea slapped her on the wrist. 'And you have to ask? Oh, my love – you've obviously led a VERY sheltered life.'

It all broke up the monotonous pressure of endless calls, one of which could be a life-saver, but never was. Every one of them was complete hokum.

The light on Tea's monitor flashed. He donned his headset and unmuted the mic. 'City and County Police – how may I help?' he said for the umpteenth time.

'H...hello?' The voice was young, timid, and frightened. 'I've just checked my phone. There's a message on it. They said on the news I should let you know.'

'Could I have your name?' Tea asked, stifling a yawn.

'It's Amy. Amy Aldridge.'

Tea knew the script by heart. He didn't need look at his screen. 'I'm sorry to ask, but how old are you, Ms Aldridge?'

'Twenty-three. Look, can you hurry, please?'

Tea bit back his annoyance. 'What does the message say?'

'Nothing. It's just a picture.'

'Of?'

'Gateshead Crematorium.'

One of the victims was found in Gateshead. Tea shuffled in his seat.

'By what means did you receive the message? By that, I mean was it a text, e-mail or something else?'

'Something else. Facebook. And, yes, before you ask, my profile is public. I know it shouldn't be, but it's a bit late for that now.'

Tea straightened. There was something about this call which made the hairs on his arms stand up.

'Ms Aldridge, could you tell me your hair colour?'

'It's black.'

Tea felt himself relax.

'But it's dyed. I'm a natural red-head.'

He swallowed. Took a sip of water. He raised his hand high above the screen. Waggled it limply. His supervisor spotted it. It was the signal for her to join the call. She dialled in his code, ensured her line was silent, and prepared to open up the channel to the City and County police in Forth Street.

'When did you receive the message, Miss Aldridge?' Tea asked.

The woman's voice quavered. 'I've just seen it. I don't look at social media very often. It arrived at ten yesterday. Yesterday evening.'

The clock on his screen showed eight pm. The woman on the end of the line might have two hours to live.

Tea ensured his voice remained calm and level. 'Is the sender amongst your contacts?'

The line remained silent. Amy Aldridge had either nodded or shaken her head. He knew which it was, but had to ask.

'Ms Aldridge?'

'S...sorry, no. He isn't.'

'How do you know it's a man?'

'Because it says it's from someone called Jim. Jim Smith.'

**

The Supervisor opened up communication channels with Stephen Danskin's team and the response unit simultaneously.

'We've got a potential hit. The caller names the sender as Jim Smith. Note the message was received at twenty-two hundred hours yesterday. Repeat, that's yesterday.'

'What's your address, Amy?' Tea Potts asked.

'15 Quarry View, Eighton Banks. It's a cu-de-sac off Mount Lane.'

The supervisor relayed the address. 'I need an ETA,' she urged.

A voice told her the first unit would be there in fifteen minutes. Danskin said he'd get someone there in twenty.

The supervisor cut back to the call. She heard Tea's voice, calm and reassuring, letting Amy Aldridge know a patrol car was on its way.

'Does that mean you think it's him?' The girl's voice was high-pitched with fear.

'It's unlikely but we're here to protect you so we'll make sure you're safe. Just don't go outside, just in case. Okay?'

'Okay.' She sounded neither reassured nor okay.

Even less so when Tea Potts said, 'And don't hang up. Stay on the line, yes?'

**

It was pure chance that Danskin was still in the office when the call came through.

He'd intended going home an hour ago, the same time Sue Nairn departed. She was the last of his team to leave, and Stephen meant to follow her out. Instead, he took a slug of Corsodyl and stood in front of the crime board.

He stared at Ferdie Milburn's photograph. Wondered where the hell he'd gone. Then, he studied the victims, one-by-one. The more he looked, the less he understood.

Something jarred; something out of place. He rubbed his forehead. Ryan was right. Terri Grainger didn't fit. So, why had Superintendent Connor made it fit?

The phone rang and the question was instantly forgotten. 'I'll have someone there in twenty minutes,' he said. He had no idea who, or how.

The Lighthouse Keeper

Again, he fell back on his two men south of the river: Lyall Parker and Ryan Jarrod.

**

He was already inside the house, waiting.

The window was unlocked, and he slipped in like an eel, dropping silently to the kitchen floor. He glanced at the time. Oh, it was close; so very close.

His fingers went to the vial in his pocket. He rolled it around his hand, savouring the smoothness of its lines.

The killer noticed she'd already placed the bottle, as open as his mother's legs for Uncle Jed, on the kitchen bench. He knew it would be there, but it was reassuring all the same.

He tiptoed towards it. He'd done his maths. He knew how much it would take. He tipped the required amount out of the vial into the wine and swirled the bottle in his hands until the cloudiness evaporated.

All he had to do was wait.

**

'I think I heard something,' Amy Aldridge whispered.

'Just stay whe...'

'Ssshh.'

Tea Potts shushed.

'I think he's here.'

'Stay calm, Amy. Someone will be with you any moment.'

'*How long?*' he mouthed to the supervisor.

She held up seven fingers.

He shook his head.

'*I know*,' the supervisor mimed.

'Amy, stay on the line, and stay where you are. Do you understand?'

Amy Aldridge made a noise. It could have meant '*Yes*' or '*Are you mad?*' but at least she was still with him.

The woman crept to her bedroom window, praying she'd see a fleet of flashing blue lights. Instead, she saw nothing but a black expanse across Springwell Quarry.

Another noise. She jumped. Squeaked like a mouse. Did the house always make these noises? Of course, it didn't; she'd have noticed. Wouldn't she?

'We're almost with you, Amy. You'll be okay.'

She peeked out the crack in the bedroom door. Across the corridor, the bathroom door stood ajar. Had she left it like it that? She couldn't remember. Her brain had shut down. She couldn't remember a thing.

Amy took a deep breath. She never left the bathroom door open. Never, ever. Did she?

Tea did all he could to soothe her, to keep her quiet and calm.

He knew he'd failed when he heard shout, 'Ohmygod, ohmygod, OHMYGOD,' as she dashed downstairs.

**

Ryan filled the inside of the Uno with obscenities for the entire journey. He hated callouts. He'd hated them with a passion ever since the night Hannah had been snatched whilst working undercover.

But, it came with the territory and he needed to focus on the one decision he had to make: to exit the A1 at The Angel, or stay on until the next junction. His Satnav told him to take The Angel, his brain to stay on the faster A1 and enter Eighton Banks from Springwell Village. He followed his brain.

He hated to admit it, but Hannah was right. He needed a new car. A more powerful one. The heap of dung he drove lolloped along at a snail's pace.

At last, he found himself on Mount Lane. He breathed easier because he could see a neon blueness lighting up the night sky. The squad car had beaten him there, but he didn't know what waited for him.

Lyall Parker waited for him, that's what. Lyall and two uniform units and a hyperventilating Amy Aldridge.

The Lighthouse Keeper

Parker walked away from Amy and intercepted Ryan. 'False alarm,' the silver-haired DI said. 'It was her bloody cat.'

The tension left Ryan's face. He took Lyall by the elbow and led him aside. 'What do you think? Did we stop it, or was it really just her cat? A false alarm?'

'I'm not sure. She's not a red-head, that's for sure.'

'She is. It's dyed.'

'Och, but I think it's the appearance he goes for. The appearance NOW, not what lies beneath.'

'Aye, but the message, man. A crematorium. From Jim Smith. Too much of a coincidence for me, like. I think he really has been in touch with her. Either something went wrong, or we've interrupted him.'

'You could be right. Let Forensics examine the house. See what they come up with.'

They stopped talking as a Fire Engine thundered by, drowning out their conversation.

'Anyway, I'm knackered, Lyall. I'm off to bed.'

Parker checked his phone. 'I wish you were, lad, but we're needed for a wee while longer.'

'Oh for fuck's sake. What now?'

'There's a suspicious fire just round the corner. Springwell Village.'

Ryan watched the shadows cast by the fire engine's lights flicker across open fields, inky-black in the darkness.

'Follow that cab,' he sighed.

CHAPTER TWENTY-THREE

The Lighthouse Keeper heard the key in the lock. He ducked out of sight. He knew she wouldn't put the light on. She never did. She was a creature of habit.

That's how he knew the exact time she'd return from her nightly tipple at The Guide Post Inn, and that she'd have the bottle of Merlot waiting in the kitchen to help her get off to sleep. Except, tonight, it would be a different sort of sleep.

He heard her kick off her shoes and pad over the hardwood flooring. He heard the cupboard door open, the clink of crystal as she removed the glass. Most satisfying of all, he listened to the rhythmic chug as the wine flowed from bottle to glass. A very large glass, by the sound of it.

He squirmed slightly in order to shift the erection which pulsed from his groin. This hadn't happened since the first one all those years ago, and he'd forgotten how good it felt.

The girl began to sing. A melodic, soulful sound. She picked her glass from the tabletop, the faint scratching noise it made on the surface sufficient to alert The Lighthouse Keeper. He held his breath. No way was he going to let this one slip through the net.

The young woman spoke to Alexa. Music as soulful as her voice filled the house. A saxophone, sexy and sassy, floated over gentle strings. This wasn't the music he'd expect her to listen to. Although he knew her so well, she was still able to surprise him.

He listened as cushions sagged beneath her weight. A faint luminescence glowed from the lounge as she flicked through her messages and trawled the internet.

He heard her breathing become laboured. He checked his watch. It had been twenty minutes. The Ketamine would be in her system and, in a few minutes more, she'd be as compliant as putty.

The thought made him want to explode.

**

God, for a dainty little thing, she was a dead weight. He struggled to drag her off the sofa and had even greater difficulty manoeuvring her splayed legs through the front door. He had to kick them out the way. Which was sad. He didn't want to hurt her.

Outside, the night was still and warm. Not as humid as forecast. Pleasant, he thought.

With his gloved hand, he pressed the button on the car key he'd lifted from the hook in her kitchen. The headlights flashed. He hoisted her into the driver's seat and, just to be sure, dragged the seat belt across her shoulder and clicked it into place.

He rearranged her hair, brushing it with his fingers. He stood back to admire the view.

'You're beautiful. So, so beautiful.'

Her eyes, an opaque blue, followed him. It was the only part of her she could control. She couldn't even show fear, although she was less afraid now than she had been.

When he'd first approached her, prone on the sofa, she knew what he'd done, and thought she'd known what he was about to do. The monstrous bulge in his trousers told her that.

But, he hadn't. And for that, she'd be eternally grateful.

Her eyes watched the man's lips as they moved.

**

'Mother must have panicked. Realised they'd find him. She knew that couldn't happen. If they found him, they'd take her away. She'd lose her little boy, and her little boy would lose his mother. Little did she know, that's exactly what her little boy wanted. More than anything, that's what I wanted.

She went back to that place. The place where she and Uncle Jed did all those things together. The place where he still lay, with the flies buzzing around what was left of his head.

The bitch couldn't stomach it. She threw up thick steaming puddles of vomit. It congealed on the carpet and the edge of the bed. The flies lapped it up. Some even left Uncle Jed to inspect it.

Then, she removed the pillowcase. I couldn't believe it. I really couldn't believe it. I knew she was mad, but to change the bed with Uncle Jed still on it? That was sick.

Of course, she wasn't going to change the bed. She pulled out a bottle. I thought it was vodka, or gin, but it was paraffin. She stuck the pillowcase in the neck of the bottle. Set it alight.

Mother dragged me down those bloody stairs again, out into the night. She didn't even let me stay to enjoy the bonfire.'

So, there you have it. That's why this has to happen.'

**

The beautiful girl with the beautiful hair watched the man open a bottle of lighter fluid. He walked to the front of the car and sprayed fluid over, around, and in, the windscreen washer jets.

He withdrew a disposable cigarette lighter. Flicked it on. He lengthened the flame to its maximum height and dropped the lighter onto the bonnet next to the nozzles.

The Lighthouse Keeper stood back and waited. Waited for the satisfying whoosh as lighter fluid and screenwash ignited. As soon as it did, he legged it up the drive and back to his car.

The bonnet of the girl's Corsa broke out in buboes as the heat buckled the steel. Paint bubbles blistered the surface. They pulsed and broiled like living organisms.

Inside the burning vehicle, the girl could do nothing but watch it all unfold. Watch, and wait. The wait wasn't long. Within seconds, the fire spread to the engine. Once the Castrol ignited, there was no stopping it.

The Lighthouse Keeper

The Lighthouse Keeper sped away, southbound; the opposite direction to which he'd eventually travel. Just in case anyone had seen him.

Planning. Detail. Contingency. He had it all covered.

He watched in the rear-view mirror as the petrol tank erupted in an explosion of crimson, scarlet, and orange. He turned a corner, the burning wreck no longer visible. Through the open window, he heard four loud detonations as the tyres popped one after the other.

It had been a most satisfying evening, even if his pelvis still felt strange.

**

The killer was on Washington Highway and beyond well before the fire engine arrived at the burning car.

A minute later, a convoy of two police cars and Lyall Parker's Kia Ce'ed, with Ryan's trusty old Fiat bringing up the rear, followed it into Springwell Village.

It was only a three-minute drive from Eighton Banks, but Lyall was already out his car by the time Ryan neared the scene. Parker stood in the middle of the road flagging Ryan down.

Ryan wound his window. 'What's up?'

'It's a vehicle fire. You don't need see it.'

'What? Is that all? Somebody's torched a car? Howay, man. I could be halfway home by now. They divvent need us for that.'

Something in Lyall Parker's face told him they did.

'What aren't you telling me, Lyall?'

'There's nothing for us to do. Not yet.'

'I don't know what you mean by *'Not yet.'* This isn't major. Kinnear's lot will pick it up, but it's probably not even for them. More a uniform matter.'

Nevertheless, for some reason Ryan opened the car door. DI Parker jammed his foot against it like a door-to-door salesman.

'Let us oot, man.'

'No, Ryan. I know about you and fire, remember. Trust me, you don't want to see this.'

Everything clicked.

'Shit.'

Parker nodded. 'Aye. I'm afraid so.'

'Jesus. Is he aal reet?'

Lyall didn't need answer.

'Shit, man,' Ryan said again, pulling at his hair so hard clumps came away in his hands. He looked down at strands of it hanging between his fingers. His fire-scarred fingers.

'Shit. Shit. Shit.'

He stamped his foot so hard he felt the vibrations right up to his groin.

'There's something else,' Lyall said. Even in his soft and soothing tones, Ryan knew it wouldn't be good news. 'It's no' a 'he'. It's a 'she.' Listen, Ryan, it's too early to say for sure, but I think we need to consider something.'

'I've got a feeling I know what you're going to say, but gan on.'

'Given the manner o' death, and the image sent to Amy Aldridge, I think we need consider whether The Lighthouse Keeper's been here, after all.'

Ryan looked to the heavens. The occasional red flare shot skywards like a Roman candle, and the acrid black smoke of burnt rubber filled the air and his nostrils.

'What sort of bastard are we dealing with, Lyall?'

'A sick one, that's for sure, son. I cannae get used to it, nae matter how long I've been with the polis. There's always someone out there who's worse than the last.'

'Aye, I know, man, but this bugger's something else.'

'He is, but he's on borrowed time. The psychologist woman, Markham, was right. He's started making mistakes. He sent the message to the wrong woman. If she's right about that, she'll be right about other things, too. Like, the fact we'll catch him – and soon.'

'I'm not so sure, Lyall. You know what? I don't think it was a mistake. I think he deliberately sent us to the wrong bloody address.'

His eyes stung with a cocktail of smoke and tears.

'He's playing games with his victims, and he's playing games with us.'

CHAPTER TWENTY-FOUR

If Stephen Danskin didn't already know the debrief was going to be difficult, the moment he stepped inside Superintendent Connor's office would have told him.

Connor had struck a pose. His Duke of Edinburgh one, where he stood with his back to the room, hands clasped behind him, while he looked out over the Tyne. It was his *'I'm really pissed off* stance.

'What happened?' Connor said without turning.

'We got a call at eight-oh-nine from an Amy Aldridge, a natural red-head, advising us she'd received a message from Jim Smith...'

He recounted every detail of the events to Connor, who remained impassive at the window.

'So,' the Super said, 'You fucked up, basically.'

'With respect, sir, we did everything by the book. It just happens the victim wasn't Amy Aldridge. It was a January Hope. She lived a few miles away.'

'You went to the wrong place.'

'We went to the address of the woman who reported receiving the message.'

'Which was the wrong place. As I said, you fucked up.'

Connor turned from the window. Stephen struggled to contain his shock. The Super had aged overnight. His face was as grey as morning fog over the Tyne. Worry-lines etched his forehead. His cheeks were sallow and sucked in. He looked like someone in the advanced stages of cancer.

For the first time since Danskin had known him, Connor was unshaven. Red streaks marked the sclera of rheumy eyes.

'Sir, you look like shit.'

The Super released a sigh. 'Probably because that's what I'm in, Stephen. All of us are in it.'

Before Danskin could respond, Connor gathered himself.

'Right, what's done's done. I want Parker in here. Now. I want Imogen Markham in here. Now. Most importantly, I want Ferdie-fucking-Milburn in here. Yesterday.'

He got none of them. What he did get was the sight of a man striding towards his office with the purposefulness of a bull in stud.

Sir Guy Haswell.

Connor's door slammed against the glass of the office wall as the politician barged in.

'Don't tell me what I'm hearing is true. There'd better not have been another one.'

'Sir Guy, please, take a seat,' Superintendent Connor offered wearily.

'Fuck the fucking seat,' Haswell hissed. 'Is it true? He's struck again?'

Danskin saw Connor wilt like a neglected plant. He spoke up on his Super's behalf. 'We did all we could to prevent it. We've got men there now.'

'NOW? That's no fucking good, being there 'now'. They should have been there yesterday.'

A muscle vibrated in Danskin's cheek. 'With respect, we were there yesterday…'

'Then you're even more incompetent than I thought.' Spittle sprayed from Haswell's lips in a way no face covering would prevent. 'You do realise the by-election's next week, don't you? And, I warned you what would happen if he struck again.'

Danskin struggled to contain himself. 'You were in this room when the criminal psychologist warned there'd be more casualties if we follo…'

'Right, I've had enough of you. Piss off and leave me with the organ grinder.' The thought seemed to please Haswell.

'What wouldn't I give to grind some organs right now,' he hissed, staring at Connor.

Stephen Danskin moved forward. Connor held up a hand. 'It's okay, Stephen. Honestly, it's fine. Go get Imogen Markham for me, please. Sir Guy and I could do with her input.'

Danskin's eyes shifted from Connor to Sir Guy. Reluctantly, he left them to it.

From his desk, he saw Haswell rage at Connor, arms waving animatedly. There was something about the man, apart from the fact he was an absolute twonk, that didn't sit right with the DCI.

Danskin picked up the phone. He'd call Imogen Markham, as Connor had asked. Then, until Lyall returned from the Gateshead crime scene, he'd have some time on his hands.

He decided he'd use it wisely.

He'd use the time to find out all he could about the Rt. Hon Sir Guy Haswell, KBE.

**

The quiet lane just off Peareth Hall Road remained closed to the public, and the driveway to number 7 lay hidden behind a blue, ten-foot high tarpaulin shroud.

Behind the tarp, the forensic team buzzed around the charred remains of January Hope's Corsa. A photographer snapped away, his camera's flashlight a redundant accessory in the morning sunlight.

Lyall Parker spoke to him. 'Jake, I want to check her phone messages. Is there any way I can get access to it?'

The photographer lowered his camera. 'Yes and no. It's in there, yes; what's left of it. You'd have more chance of retrieving The One Ring from the fires of Mount Doom.'

Lyall tisked. He turned to Ryan who stood well back, staring at the charcoal mound occupying the driver's seat. 'You okay?' the Scotsman asked.

'What do you think?'

'Och, it was a stupid question. I'm sorry.'

'No, I don't mean it like that. I meant, do you really think it was him? The Lighthouse Keeper?'

'Too soon to say for sure.'

'I guess. I said it last night, though, and I'll say it again: the message on Amy Aldridge's phone is too much of a coincidence.'

'Or, Markham could be right. He could ha'e made his first mistake.'

'What – a random mistake who just happened to live a couple of miles away?'

'Let's not jump to conclusions. You know what Danskin would say: *Don't see what you expect to see.*'

They ducked under a flap in the tarpaulin and breathed air that seemed fresher, as if the screen had been an invisible barrier which blocked all sense of normality. Beyond a second cordon, a single TV van and a couple of reporters still lurked, hoping they'd discover something new.

'Like bloody vultures,' Lyall said. His phone rang. 'Ravi, how's it going?'

Parker covered the mouthpiece and spoke to Ryan. 'It's Sangar. We don't need her phone. Ravi's got in remotely.'

Ryan moved closer as Lyall shifted the phone from his ear so Ryan could hear.

'I've checked the victim's messages,' Sangar was saying. 'Nothing for six hours before the attack.'

'What about twenty-four hours? That's the key.'

'Nothing.'

'Not even social media?'

'Na. Nothing specific to her, and nothing that is any way linked to the MO.'

Lyall thought for a moment. 'Ryan's here and he and I have a couple of wee thoughts. One, the killer made his first mistake, just as Markham predicted.'

'Or,' Ryan interjected. 'He deliberately misled us. Have you discovered anything to back up either theory?'

'Howay, man. Give us a chance here, will you? I've only just started.'

'Aye, sorry Ravi. I'm getting ahead of myself.'

'There's one thing you do need to know, though,' Sangar said.

'Yes?'

'The lass who got the message, Amy Aldridge? She knows the victim. She's on January Hope's contact list.'

**

Amy Aldridge was still shaken even though it was the day after the night before. On the other hand, Hendrix, the cat, didn't give a toss.

He was more concerned about the woman detective eyeing him suspiciously from the armchair opposite. Hendrix hadn't understood the cops when they said someone would be over in the morning to check on Amy, and he didn't much take to Hannah Graves.

For both their sakes, it was a relief when he uncoiled himself and strode towards the kitchen, tail aloft.

'Do you know if it's him?' Amy asked. 'Did the serial killer send me the message?'

'It's too early to say for certain, Amy,' Hannah said, offering a smile she hoped was reassuring. 'Do you mind if I ask you some questions?'

'Not at all. If I'm honest, I'm happy for the company. Besides, you'll keep The Lighthouse Keeper away.'

Hannah thought it unlikely seeing as she'd arrived in her Renault and not a full-liveried patrol car, but she kept the thought to herself.

'Do you know anyone called January?'

Amy replied, 'No,' instantly.

'Are you sure?'

'Absolutely. I'd remember a name like that.'

It wasn't the answer Hannah had expected, and it threw her off track in much the same way as the ensuing silence perplexed Amy Aldridge.

'Don't you want to ask me about the message?' Amy finally said.

'I'll get to that in a moment, but this is important. Are you sure you don't know a January Hope?'

'I've already…' Her voice trailed off. 'Hope? Jan Hope? Yes, I know Jan. I didn't know it was short for January. Wait until I see her again,' she laughed.

Hannah didn't laugh. 'Did January, Jan, tell you if she'd met someone new recently? A date, perhaps?'

Amy giggled again. 'Let's just say, Jan likes to play the field. And it's a big field. She's a stunning girl so she's never short of company. She's not shy talking about it, either; I can tell you. She's broadminded and very open when it comes to letting us friends know about her love life, if you know what I mean.'

Hannah did. Girls will be girls. 'So, you think she would have told you if she'd met someone a bit unusual?'

'I think she would, yes.'

'Did she date on-line?'

'I very much doubt it. She can have anyone she wants, with her looks.'

'Never mentioned anyone following her?'

'Nothing comes to mind. Why all these questions about Jan? Oh my God, has she received a message from …'

Amy froze mid-sentence. *'Did Jan date on-line,'* the detective had said. *Did.* Past tense.

Shaking, Amy pulled out her phone and scrolled through her contacts. Before she could make the call to Jan's number, Hannah gently lifted the phone from her hand. Amy saw the sadness in the detective's eyes.

'No. No, no, no. She can't be.' She looked at Hannah Graves again, and knew she was.

'How?' she spluttered through a sob.

'I'm sorry to say, she was murdered.'

'By…' she couldn't begin to say the dreaded name. Settled for 'Him?'

Hannah took Amy's hand. 'I know it's difficult, but please try to concentrate. If we're to catch the person who did this, I need you to answer some questions. Is that okay?'

The girl gave several short, sharp nods.

'Good. Have you and Jan ever swapped phones? Perhaps by mistake? Possibly, pick the wrong one up off the table in the pub and use it before you realised?'

'No. Never. I'd have known.'

'I see. Can you think of any reason why someone might have mixed the two of you up?'

A bubble formed at the end of Amy Aldridge's nose. She burst it with a sniff, wiped her nose with a tissue, then dabbed her eyes with the same sheet. 'Hardly. Like I say, she's… was, beautiful. Gorgeous. And, well, let's be honest, I'm not. No-one could mistake me for her. She wanted to be a model, you know…'

Hannah didn't know, but Amy Aldridge did. She knew, because she'd arranged it.

'Oh. My. God.'

'What is it? Hannah asked.

'There was an ad from a Model Agency. Jan said it was probably right dodgy, but I thought it looked genuine. I did some digging, and discovered it WAS genuine. I didn't want to build her hopes up, so I gathered some selfies from her Facebook and Instagram accounts, and I set up a phoney Facebook profile for Jan from my iPhone. Then, I sent the Agency a link to it.'

'I see. Do you have the name of the Agency?'

'I'll have it, somewhere. I can get it for you.'

'Please.'

The full realisation hit Amy. 'I've done this to her, haven't I? Oh God, it's all my fault.'

'Try not to worry. I'm sure the Agency is genuine, but we have to check these things out.'

The woman sobbed a 'Thank you.'

The Lighthouse Keeper

'What happened to the fake Facebook profile, Amy? Did you take it down again?'

'No,' Amy said. 'I forgot all about it. It's probably still live.'

Hannah knew there was no *'probably'* about it. It was still live. Live, and public. And, The Lighthouse Keeper had tracked her through it. Hannah wouldn't tell Amy Aldridge.

Amy had already stored up enough guilt to last a lifetime.

CHAPTER TWENTY-FIVE

By the time Lyall Parker had been briefed by Hannah on her Amy Aldridge interview and got back to Forth Street, Stephen Danskin and Imogen Markham were already in Superintendent Connor's office.

Parker took the last available seat; the one next to the attendee whose presence most troubled him: Sir Guy Haswell.

The MP reeked of Dior's Ambre Nuit. 'So,' Haswell said, marginally more composed than before. 'We have another dead girl. Tell me again how you let this happen.'

Lyall Parker directed a question at Superintendent Connor. 'Is this no' police business, sir?' He was astonished Sir Guy was in on the discussion, never mind leading it.

Haswell looked down his nose. 'I think my Minister of Justice status trumps your Detective Inspector, DCI, and Superintendent combined, don't you?'

Connor shifted uncomfortably. 'Let's press on, shall we?'

'We received a message from the wrong girl,' Stephen Danskin explained for the fourth time. The killer sent his message to the victim's friend.'

'Why would he do that?' Haswell looked at Imogen Markham.

'I did say the killer would make mistakes as he ramped up his activity.'

Lyall stopped her there. 'We think the killer was misled, no' mistaken.' He told them about the fake profile Amy Aldridge set up.

'So, really, neither the City and County Police nor your psychobabble sidekicks have any idea what's going on. Admit it.'

'We have an APB out on Ferdie Milburn. I know Ms Markham thinks the killer is too smart to use a name with an obvious link to his identity, but until we speak to him, we can't rule it out,' Danskin said, more calmly than he thought possible.

'But you don't know where he is.'

'No. We don't.'

Sir Guy snorted. 'Right. In the meantime, if you can't apprehend, what do you intend doing to prevent another incident, especially before next week's vote?'

Imogen Markham could hide no longer. This was her territory. 'The killer stalks his targets. It's almost certain he starts with social networks. All the girls have public profiles…'

'Except Terri Grainger,' Danskin said. Lyall stared at him. Had Jarrod spoken to the DCI, he wondered?

Markham continued unabated. 'The girls have Facebook or Instagram accounts, or both. The accounts all contain numerous pictures of themselves. They all have red hair, and their profile pictures show several similarities. They are taken in close-up, looking downwards, and pouting. The pose attracts the killer. They look submissive. Wanton.'

Danskin laughed. 'Wanton? Does that word actually exist these days?'

Imogen's look froze him to the spot. 'Yes, it does. It means frivolous and lustful. The same as it always has. It's a look the killer both abhors and craves.'

'Interesting,' Haswell said, 'But what does the information give us?'

'It tells us precisely the kind of victim our killer will target next.'

Stephen Danskin rose from his seat. 'I've had enough of this shite. Just about every young lass I know poses like that for her profile picture. Do you want us to put a tail on every 'wanton' lass on Instagram? There'll be thoosands of them, man; and that's just the red-heads.'

'Sit down, Danskin,' Haswell ordered. 'Let Ms Markham finish. Imogen, please, you were saying?'

'I wasn't about to suggest taking action to prevent the killer attacking again. On the contrary, I was proposing we lure him in. He's fallen for a fake account before. He'll do it again, if we pitch it right.'

Sir Guy rested his chin on a fingertip. 'What are you getting at?'

'I suggest we lay a trap. Set someone up…'

Stephen Danskin exploded from his seat again. Lyall Parker followed suit. 'You've really no idea what you're saying,' Danskin shouted. 'I agreed to that once before. I nearly lost one of my officers. One of my BEST officers.' His voice broke with emotion at the memories of his stepdaughter held hostage during a similar set up.

'It's no' happening,' Parker agreed. 'No' in a million years will anyone in this department go along wi' your idea.'

'Connor?' Haswell asked.

The Super sat, hamstrung. Danskin and Parker waited. The longer the wait, the greater the tension. Stephen felt the oxygen suck out the room.

'Decision time, Connor. I say we do it,' Haswell pressed.

Would the Emperor raise his thumb or lower it?

'I say no. Final answer. Now, get out my office and leave my men to get on with what your department pays them for.'

**

Stephen Danskin sat in the breakout area. His fingers trembled with adrenalin dump as he tore the wrapper off a Mars bar.

'I thought Connor was going to go along with it for a minute there.' He almost took his fingers out as he bit into the chocolate bar.

'Aye. I did, too,' DI Parker agreed. 'The Super's no' daft, though. He wouldnae agree to it. Not after the last time.'

Danskin wiped sweat from the nape of his neck. 'There was a time when I would've known that but, just lately, I sometimes wonder.'

Parker drifted in the tide of silence. He took in air, then spat it out. 'Listen, I really shouldnae say anything but...'

'You think the same as me, don't you? There's something fishy about this Haswell character.'

'You've been talking to Ryan.'

'Jarrod? What's he got to do with it?'

Lyall exhaled through his nose. 'Him and Hannah asked me to do a bit of homework. On Haswell and, if I'm honest, on the Super as well.'

Stephen dipped his head. 'Aye, Jarrod's hinted at a couple of things, now you mention it. Odd, though.'

'What is?'

'You, Ryan, Hannah, and me – we all think something's not right. In any other situation, we'd follow it up.'

'So, why don't we?'

'Cos he's a bloody member of the Government. If it goes tits up, we're shafted up to our prostate.'

'Doesn't have to be official,' Parker said.

Danskin squinted at the DI.

'If we're careful, and it's only us.'

Stephen balled up the chocolate wrapper and tossed it into a waste receptacle.

'Ah, bollocks. We've got a serial killer out there, Lyall. Let's focus on getting him off the streets.'

There was no way he was going to put Lyall, Ryan, or Hannah's career on the line. No, he'd do the groundwork himself. The others could concentrate on The Lighthouse Keeper.

Until, of course, he found something. Or, more accurately, found even more.

**

DCI Stephen Danskin spent the afternoon pursuing Ferdie Milburn.

He despatched Sue Nairn to St Mary's Island for another scout around, only for the DS to suggest she and Gavin O'Hara were better served liaising with DCI Kinnear's mob. Danskin agreed, so the task fell to Nigel Trebilcock.

Meanwhile, Ravi Sangar set about tracking down Milburn by other means. He established the mobile phone registered to Milburn was last used in the days leading up to the murder of the florist girl, Dorothy Jackson. The call was made from Whitley Bay town centre, somewhere between The Victoria public house and The Fat Ox. The phone no longer emitted a signal and was untraceable.

Ravi checked the number Milburn had dialled. It belonged to an unregistered device. It, too, was switched off. Danskin chewed the fat with Sangar before they both decided the information was of low value. If Milburn was their man, he wouldn't be using his own device for The Lighthouse Keeper's activities. Imogen Markham was right: he was too intelligent to fall for that one.

Ninety minutes later, Trebilcock reported back with the news that there was no news. Milburn's cottage remained unoccupied and lifeless.

Trebilcock said he'd fed some mouldy bread to the seagulls, and a tin of mackerel to an unimpressed bull seal. The Cornishman mentioned he'd enjoyed the trip out, though, so it hadn't been a waste of time.

Danskin didn't see it that way. He asked Lyall to man the fort while he grabbed an early finish. Parker asked if he was okay, and Stephen told him he was.

What he didn't tell him was, he had bigger fish to fry.

**

In one of the smaller apartments on the Great Park estate, Stephen Danskin loaded an Americano pod into his Tassimo and spread a thick layer of pate onto a slice of toast while his PC booted up.

Stephen chose to unwind with his usual country music. 'Alexa, play Crazy.'

Alexa misunderstood his command. Instead of Patsy Cline's rich contralto, CeeLo Green's vocalisation of the Gnarls Barkley song filled the void in Danskin's apartment.

Hmm, come on now, who do you
Who do you, who do you, who do you think you are?
Ha ha ha, bless your soul
You really think you're in control?
Well, I think you're crazy
I think you're crazy
I think you're crazy
Just like me.

Danskin shuddered. It was as if his Echo device had morphed into the spirit of medium Doris Stokes, allowing The Lighthouse Keeper to taunt him through its choice of lyric.

He ordered Alexa to piss off.

'I'm sorry. I'm having trouble understanding you right now.'

'Aye, you and every woman I've ever known.' He fingered the remote and shut her up that way.

For once, he welcomed silence.

A crumb fell from the toast onto the keyboard. He brushed it aside and entered his keyword search into Google.

Sir Guy Haswell + Conservative Party.

Next, he added the phrase which intrigued him most from his preliminary research back in Forth Street; the phrase he feared may be picked up by the force's inbuilt security monitoring programme should he delve deeper at work.

He typed:
+1997 Deselection.

Even as the results filled the monitor screen, DCI Danskin's phone rang.

'Ah, bugger and hell, man.'

He closed down the screen.

CHAPTER TWENTY-SIX

Tomasz Potts preferred early starts. He liked to arrive at his workstation first thing, have a protein shake and a granola bar, and share a bit of banter with the girlies before he logged on.

Whenever he found himself on the evening shift, like today, everything felt rushed. The lines remained red-hot, and the intensity unremitting, so there was no opportunity to ease himself in gently. He had to hit the ground running, as his supervisor never failed to remind him.

As it happened, there was no-one for Tea to communicate with, apart from frantic or paranoid members of the public, because everyone in the Communications Centre was already engaged on calls.

Tea just about had time to sanitise his hands and wipe down his desk, tuck his man bag beneath his chair, and make sure his personal headset didn't spoil his hair, before the first call arrived.

He made the obligatory introduction and, within seconds, had his arm raised above his head.

Tea Potts couldn't believe it. Why did it have to be him, again?

**

The girl emerged from the steam of the shower like a mirage. Pink skinned and aglow, she felt her flesh pucker in the relative cool of the bathroom.

She wrapped herself in a skimpy white towel, wiped at a film of condensation on the mirror, and admired herself in the streak of exposed glass.

'Nice,' Jessica said, tugging the towel a little lower until it barely concealed her erect nipples.

She padded barefoot to the lounge, passing her laptop which sat open on a glass-topped coffee table, and straightened a framed poster hanging on the far wall. The poster portrayed the shirtless torso of a black man cradling a tiny infant in his arms.

Jessica turned, fluffed her hair and, head lowered, cat walked back towards the sofa with an exaggerated sway of her hips.

She perched on the edge of the seat with her knees clasped together. Which was just as well, for a light on the frame of her laptop glowed blue.

Someone was watching and recording.

Her fingers danced across the keyboard as she typed in her mobile number and password. She smiled at the humorous comments on her newsfeed. A box at the top reminded her it was Morag Richardson's birthday.

She typed, *'Happy birthday, babe. Pity we can't party like last year. Miss you x'* and posted it to her friend.

Jessica quickly reknotted the towel around her, nearly revealing all but actually showing nothing. At the top of the screen, she noticed she had three messages.

She switched windows. The first message was a typically rude comment from her boyfriend. She laughed out loud and replied with a lol.

The second notified her of a friend's new address.

Jessica scrunched her hair and opened the third.

'See you soon,' it said.

The words were typed beneath a stock photograph. A photograph of a petrol-motored hedge trimmer.

**

'When was the message delivered?' Tea asked, following the script.

'I don't know, exactly. Give us a second.'

The caller held the phone a little too close to her mouth. Her breath rasped like Darth Vader before it stopped completely.

'Hello? Miss? Are you still there?'

The breath she'd been holding exploded from her. 'Yes, I'm here,' she said her voice thin and reedy. 'Yesterday. The message came yesterday. Twenty-three hours ago.'

'Are you sure of the time?' Tea asked.

'Yes, I'm looking at it right now. Does...does that mean it's okay? You know, that it would have happened by now?'

'We'll send someone over straight away, miss. Can I just confirm the exact address in Preston Grange? Did you say number th...'

Tea heard the sound of breaking glass, a whimper, a scream – then the line died.

**

The moment the call came through, Stephen Danskin forgot all about Sir Guy Haswell.

Uniform were already on route to the scene, and armed response had been scrambled. Danskin checked his watch. It'd take him twenty minutes to reach the location. It'd be over by the time he got there.

He immediately mobilised the officers on the stand-by rota: Todd Robson and, he noted with a pang of conscience, Ryan Jarrod. Again.

The DCI knew Ryan was at Hannah's. He'd make it in half the time it'd take Danskin to arrive. Todd, too, was around ten minutes away. It was a toss-up which of them would get there first.

Whichever it was, he hoped to hell armed response made it quicker.

**

The moment she heard the glass break, Jessica vaulted over the sofa and took refuge behind it. In the process, she hit her wrist against the back of the seat, jarring her phone from her grasp.

She watched it somersault away from her in a series of slow loops. It came down on the edge of the coffee table, spun across its glass surface, and rattled against her laptop.

The phone deflected onto the carpet, in full view of the open lounge door.

Her mobile's screen flickered and died.

'Shit.'

Jessica peeked round the edge of the sofa. She could see out into the corridor, along to the entrance hall. There was no-one in view. The front door remained intact. Which meant the sound of breaking glass came either from the kitchen to the right, or her bedroom to the left.

She shrunk behind the sofa, propped her back against it, and tried to slow her racing heartbeat.

Jessica edged to the other end of the sofa. Her entire body tensed, ready to bolt past anyone entering the lounge. She peered out once more.

The apartment remained eerily quiet.

She forced herself to breathe slowly. *Okay*, she thought, *whoever is in here doesn't know my phone's deactivated. He'll be wary. Cautious.*

The police knew she was in trouble. They'd be on their way.

Jessica clutched her towel. The *what-ifs* haunted her. What if they didn't arrive in time? What if they thought it was a hoax? My God, what if that's what they thought?

Her laptop still lay open on the coffee table. Could she use it to contact the police? Let them know The Lighthouse Keeper really was coming for her?

Cautiously, she glanced out. There was no-one there.

On all fours, she crawled cat-like towards the laptop. Jessica touched the keyboard, once. The sound of finger on key didn't set off an alarm bell, no siren sounded, thunder didn't rumble. The noise was imperceptible, even to her only an arms-length away.

The Lighthouse Keeper wouldn't hear her.

She typed in *City and County Police*. Only, her trembling fingers recorded it as City and Country, with an added r.

She got the wrong results.

'*Fuck, fuck, fuck,*' she said in her head.

Jessica deleted the errant letter.

Got it.

She stopped. Was that a floorboard creaking? She was in no-man's land, midway between open door and hiding place.

No-one came. No-one fired up a petrol hedge-trimmer.

She entered the City and County website. Prayed there'd be a Live Chat window on the menu.

There was no chat facility. The nearest she found was 'Contact Us.' All it gave was the Forth Street address and telephone number.

Fat lot of fucking good that was to her, without a phone and with The Lighthouse Keeper in her apartment.

She heard a creak. Then another. He was coming.

Everything happened in a fast-forward blur.

A figure dressed in black filled the doorframe.

Took a stride into the lounge.

She heard the wail of approaching sirens.

Saw a puff of blue smoke and heard the explosive burr of the implement's motor firing up.

Jessica screamed.

She got to her feet.

The towel unfastened and fell to the floor.

And the man with the hedge trimmer stepped towards her.

**

The patrol car zig-zagged its way into Cambo Place and screeched to a halt across the cul-de-sac's only exit point.

'Where's the others?' Warren Gill asked.

'Somebody's got to be first,' the driver and senior partner, Tom Bone, said.

'Reet, we'd better get in.'

Tom held Warren's wrist. 'Not without back-up. You know the drill.'

'Hadaway, man. We haven't time.'

Warren climbed out the car. Tom beat him round the front of it.

'Had your horses. I'll gan round the back,' Tom said. 'See what I can make out. You hear me? You're not to go in. Understand?'

'I'll give you two minutes.'

'That's all it'll take. Just stay here, reet? Back-up's on its way.' Tom disappeared down a cut at the edge of the street and veered right around the back of the property.

Warren heard the girl scream.

He made towards the front door. Hesitated at the gate. Tom Bone was the senior partner. Warren knew the protocol: he was duty-bound to follow his colleague's instructions.

But, Tom Bone was also overweight, forty-five, and had a gammy knee from his rugby days. He, on the other hand, was twenty-one and fit as a lop.

He was also keen to make a name for himself.

At training college, Warren had been inspired by the instructor recounting the example of a young officer who had rose to prominence in three short years, from Special Constable to one of the most promising detectives the City and County force had ever recruited.

If Ryan Jarrod could do it, so, too, Warren Gill.

He was going in.

**

Hannah was right. Ryan did need a new car. He'd borrowed her Renault and it powered him along the Coast Road as if it were jet propelled.

The car cornered the junction between John Spence College and the Swimming Pool on two wheels and flew along the A192 towards the scene. At the mini roundabout by Morrison's he swung right into the estate, just as a patrol car heading towards him passed the Tynemouth Community fire station and followed him in, left.

The mustard-coloured Renault skidded to a halt behind the single squad car already at the scene. Ryan leapt from the vehicle with its engine still running.

A uniformed officer by the gate to a property turned to face him.

'You're not allowed in here,' the cop shouted. 'Get back behind the car or I'll have you arrested.'

'Give ower, man. I'm CID.' Ryan flashed his ID at the kid.

Warren made out just enough to recognise the badge and backed down.

'What we got?' Ryan asked.

'Girl is still alive. Or, was until seconds ago. I heard her scream,' Warren said.

'Is there just you?'

'Me colleague's round the back.'

'But no armed response, yeah?'

'Negative,' the young cop replied.

They both turned at the blues and twos drawing to a halt behind their cars. Not armed response.

'Ok,' Ryan said. 'Who am I with?'

'PC Warren Gill.'

'I'm DC Ryan Jarrod. Are you good to go in with me?'

Warren Gill's face lit up. 'Wow. Ryan Jarrod. Bloody hell. Yeah, you bet I am.'

**

Ryan and Warren raced to the door. It was locked from the inside.

Ryan took a step back and charged it. The door bowed as his shoulder made contact, but it didn't give.

'Stand back,' Warren Gill said. He flew through the air like Bruce Lee and his heavy boots thudded against the lock. Bolts sprang, wood splintered, and the young cop felt the air burst from his lungs as he landed flat on his upper back inside the hallway.

Ryan hurdled him. 'Police! Get down! Get down!'

He sprinted towards the open lounge door. Warren eased himself to his feet and followed.

Inside the doorway, a man dressed entirely in black looked first at the intruders, then at Jessica, and back to the cops. A Scream mask covered his face.

He turned his body towards Ryan and PC Gill, the hedge-trimmer held out at arm's length; the blades a whirring shadow. Behind him, a naked girl cowered against the arm of a sofa.

Warren Gill's eyes lingered on the nude woman. It was only for a second, but enough for the man in black to take a step towards him.

'Freeze! Armed police. Put your weapon down. Now!'

Three armed officers in full protective garb blocked out light from the entrance. They had their weapons trained on the man's torso.

'Don't shoot.' The man raised his arms skywards. 'Don't shoot. I'm unarmed.'

He saw their eyes focus on the object in his hands.

'Oh. Okay. Apart from this. I'm switching it off.' He released a finger from the safety catch. The motor died. 'Do you want me to put it down?'

'Too fucking right, pal.' Todd Robson stepped over the debris into the crowded room. The moment the hedge-trimmer hit the floor Todd kicked it away. 'Now, you get on the deck, an' aal.'

One glance at the massive frame and battered face of Robson terrified the masked man more than the armed cops. He prostrated himself, face-down.

The armed response team crept forward until three weapons hovered inches from the man's head.

Tom Brown had followed Todd into the room and he dropped an arthritic knee into the small of the man's back. He cuffed the man's hands behind him and hauled him to his feet.

Jessica fumbled with the towel and covered herself. She whimpered in fright.

'It's okay. You're safe now. We've got him,' Ryan said, softly.

'You don't understand…' the man began to say from behind the Scream mask.

'Shut it!' Todd shouted.

The man shut it.

Ryan moved forward. Gripped the man's mask in both hands. 'On second thoughts,' he said, 'Would you like to do the honours?'

'Me?' Warren Gill said. 'Wow. Yeah.'

The young cop ripped the mask from the man. The face behind it was young. Little older than Warren, let alone Ryan. His face glistened with sweat, his forehead red and raw from the friction of the mask. His eyes showed fear and dread.

'It's a mistake…'

'Shut the fuck up!' Todd screamed at him.

Todd studied the man's face. He glanced from assailant to victim. Jessica cowered behind her towel as Robson glared at her.

'What are you staring at?' Jessica said, wrapping the towel tighter.

Todd let his eyes linger, a curious expression on his face.

'Want a better look or summat?' Jessica asked. 'Here you are, then. Cop an eyeful then leave me alone.' She grasped the edge of the towel and held it wide open.

Tom Brown's mouth gaped like a cartoon character.

'Todd, man,' Ryan said. 'Leave the lass alone. She's been through enough, for God's sake.'

Robson sneered. 'Divvent flatter yersel, pet. I've got bigger tits than those.'

'Todd!!' Ryan bellowed.

The Lighthouse Keeper

It was too late. Robson was walking towards the girl. He took a handful of the girl's flowing red hair. She twisted away from him.

'Todd, man. Have you gone mad? Get off her.'

Todd didn't. Instead, he pulled at the girl's hair.

The wig came away.

Jessica's hands shot to her short, spikey blonde hair. The towel lay in a heap at her feet.

'You didn't think it through, did you?' Todd said, his eyes at waist level. 'It's bloody obvious you're not a natural redhead.'

'Bloody hell,' Ryan mumbled.

Todd took a couple of strides to the man in black. 'Just one more thing,' he said in his best Colombo voice.

He jerked his knee into the man's groin.

The man in black jack-knifed and thought he'd ruptured a testicle.

CHAPTER TWENTY-SEVEN

As soon as Stephen Danskin despatched Todd and Ryan to the scene and established armed response and uniform support were on their way, he made a beeline to Forth Street.

He ensured all parties kept communication channels to him open, and he reported the successful mission to Connor. The Super told him he was on his way in, and under no circumstances interview the suspect without Imogen Markham's presence.

Danskin objected long and loud, but Connor was insistent. 'We need someone inside the lunatic's head,' were his exact words.

Markham arrived thirty minutes after Stephen. She was dressed in a loose-fitting T-shirt and tight leggings, wore no make-up, and had a serious case of bed hair.

To his horror, Danskin found the look slightly alluring. He shuddered at the thought. Her words soon brought him to his senses.

'There's something wrong with all this,' she said.

He scratched eyes itchy from lack of sleep and stared at her, blankly.

'Are you listening?' she persisted. 'It's not him.'

'I'm listening. It's the believing-what-I'm-hearing bit I'm having trouble with. He sent a message to the victim. He sent a picture of the weapon. He was caught, in her apartment, with said weapon in his hands. Of course, it's fucking him.'

'I've read the report of the arresting officers, PCs Brown and Gill. I've seen what DC Jarrod said. I've even made sense of DC Robson's illiterate scrawl…'

'Leave it, Markham. Just leave it, okay? It's him.'

Imogen swung her seat away from him and sulked at the pile of papers in front of her.

Danskin saw his face reflected in the black of his lifeless monitor. In it, he saw a smidgeon of doubt. Just the merest hint of it, but sufficient to make him wonder.

'Look,' he said, 'If it helps, you can be in on the interview.'

'I have every intention of being there anyway.' She continued to look at the papers, unaware they were upside down.

Danskin sighed. *'Women. There's nee pleasing them,'* he thought.

Superintendent Connor entered, haggard but smiling. 'I believe we have reason to celebrate!'

Both Stephen and Imogen turned to face him.

The smile faded. 'What is it?'

'We don't think it's him,' Markham said.

'SHE doesn't think it's him,' Stephen corrected.

'Why not? It matches the MO, I gather.'

She shook her head. 'When the police arrived, he was in the room with the hedge-trimmer running. The girl was alive. He had plenty of time to kill her.'

'Perhaps the motor didn't start. Perhaps he'd just got the thing fired up when we got there.'

'I don't believe a killer as meticulous as The Lighthouse Keeper wouldn't have checked he could start it before he attacked her.'

She saw the Super ponder on it. Danskin, too. She ploughed on.

'The killer was dressed in black, like the Milk Tray man. He wore a Scream mask. I ask you: really?'

Danskin clung to the belief they'd caught The Lighthouse Keeper. He had to, for the sake of his sanity. He heard CeeLo Green in his head: *'I think you're crazy, just like me.'*

'The man's a psycho. Maybe he wants to be Jason when he grows up.'

Imogen Markham snapped her fingers. 'You said it; '*When he grows up.*' The lad we caught was barely out of his teens. Our killer's older than that. Considerably older.'

Connor sat down. 'Thank God I didn't tell Haswell.'

'Hang on a minute. We haven't even interviewed the bugger yet. Let's not jump to conclusions,' Danskin pleaded.

'You're kidding yourself, DCI Danskin,' Dr Markham scoffed. 'The message was different. '*See you soon*', it said. None of the other messages contained words. The girl wasn't a red-head, either.'

'She wore a wig, for Christ's sake. A red one. He wouldn't have known.'

Imogen Markham looked at him with genuine sadness. 'If DC Robson knew, The Lighthouse Keeper would have known, too, if it had been him. Trust me, he'd have known.'

Silence inhabited a room devoid of air. Finally, Superintendent Connor spoke.

'So, we have a copycat.'

'It's a possibility, but one thing I'm certain of: it's not The Lighthouse Keeper. He's still out there, somewhere.'

**

Kane Weston was petrified. He'd thrown up in the holding cell and his gut ached, partly as a result of the retching but mainly because of his dislocated nuts.

The uniform cops had kept his hands cuffed when they moved him, and blood oozed from scrapes and abrasions on his wrists. They left him alone, in a dull and lifeless room painted cirrus grey, to stew in his own juice.

He sat on a chair one side of a table, a Perspex screen between him and two vacant chairs on the opposite side. The room was cold, the lighting harsh.

Kane's eyes filled with tears.

The door behind him opened. Three men and a woman walked in. The woman took a seat against the wall to his rear, and the man in uniform stood alongside her by the door.

The other two men walked to the other side of the table and took their seats. He recognised one of them from the night before. The other one, the bald one with a look of Alan Shearer about him, recited a series of words he'd often heard on TV – 'You have a right to remain silent,' and all that.

'I'm Detective Chief Inspector Stephen Danskin. This is Detective Constable Ryan Jarrod. The woman behind you is Dr Imogen Markham. She's a criminal psychologist.' He managed to keep the disdain from his voice. 'Personally, I think it's a psychiatrist you need, but we'll get to that.'

Weston felt the man's eyes look inside him, and felt the woman's do the same from behind.

'What's your name?' the DCI demanded.

'K…Kane Weston. Kane Daniel Edward Weston.'

The cop stared at him with dark, lifeless eyes, as if Kane were nothing but dogshit.

'Kane, why did you attempt to kill Jessica Lonsdale?'

'I didn't! It was a joke. Jessica's my girlfriend. It was just a joke gone wrong.' His words came out high-pitched, as if his voice hadn't yet broken. 'If you'd listened to me when I was arres…'

'Jessica is your lass?'

'Yes!'

'And, you tried to kill her for a laugh?'

'Yes. No. I didn't try to kill her, but it WAS a joke.'

'Hilarious,' Danskin said.

Ryan spoke up. 'She didn't seem to see the funny side last night.'

'I don't think she thought your lot pointing those guns at me was much to laugh about.'

'But you taking her head off with a hedge-trimmer is amusing, I suppose.'

Kane Weston made eye contact with Ryan. 'We do it all the time.'

'Okay,' Danskin said. 'Tell me what happened.'

'I was in the flat when she had a shower. I got the hedge-trimmer out the shed. She knew about it. I sent her a message…'

'You admit you sent her a message?'

'Of course. That was the whole point.'

Danskin stood up. The chair screeched on the floor. Kane jumped at the sound and almost wet himself.

'Mr Weston. Kane. You know there's a serial killer on the loose, one who sends messages to his victims letting them know how they're going to die.'

'Yes, I do. I mean, everybody does. It's been on the news and in the papers.'

'And you think it's funny to scare the shit oot of your lass?'

'Yes. Sort of. She was in on it. Part of the fantasy.'

Danskin sat back down. 'Like, sex play, you mean?'

'No. Not like sex play at all.'

'Then, like what?'

'Call her. Just bloody call her and ask.'

Danskin slammed his hand on the table. 'I've had enough of this. You sent a message. You attacked Jessica Lonsdale with a hedge-trimmer, you killed Chelsea Birch, you killed…'

'No! It was a fucking joke, if you'd only listen.'

The interview room door opened. Ravi Sangar's head poked through the gap.

'Can I have a word, guv?'

'Now? Really?'

'Yes, sir, really now.'

'Interview suspended.'

Danskin stormed out the room, Ryan and Imogen trailing behind him.

**

Ravi typed in the web address and waited for the screen to load.

'What are we doing here, Sangar?' an impatient Danskin enquired, fingers drumming the desk.

'You'll see.'

Ryan recognised the logo immediately. 'YouTube?'

'For fuck's sake, Sangar. You interrupted us to show us, what? Someone's cat skateboarding? Some acne-scarred fat lass giving out beauty tips? Jesus Christ, man.'

'No, sir. Turns out Kane Weston has another name. So has Jessica Lonsdale.'

'And?'

'Together, they're known as Kanye Weston and Jessica Rarebit. Look.'

A paused video appeared centre-screen. It showed a teenage Jessica Lonsdale. She stood behind a young-looking Kane Weston who was sat on a wooden stool set in a tiny garden.

'What're we watching, man?'

Ravi hit play. Jessica tipped a bucket full of ice-cubes over a startled Kane Weston.

'Ice-bucket challenge. Big deal.'

'Watch, sir.'

Another video followed. The players were reversed, Lonsdale seated, Weston behind. He emptied the bucket over the girl's head. Iced water drenched her – along with a dozen crabs, some of which clung to her long blonde hair. The girl screamed and performed a manic, stompy dance while Weston doubled over with laughter.

'I get that,' Danskin said. 'That's funny. A hedge-trimmer at the jugular isn't.'

The video streamed seamlessly into another: Jessica spreading chilli powder inside a sandwich. Kane biting into it, then pouring a jug of water down his throat as his face glowed furnace red.

Next, Weston was filmed replacing the contents of Jessica's water bottle with neat vodka. Shaky footage of the girl kneeling over a toilet bowl followed.

'And, so it goes on,' Ravi said. 'Until we get to the point where she unpicks his trouser seam and his arse bursts out of his pants when he runs for a bus. His backside's pixelated, but the number of hits quadrupled. They discovered nudity – albeit blurred out – always resulted in a spike in the number of followers. So, that's where their focus lay from that point on. Right up to Jessica and her towel, or lack of.'

'Bugger me.'

'Sir, I'm sorry to say it, but Kane's right. It was a set up. They prank each other, each one more outrageous than the one before. You see, Kanye Weston and Jessica Rarebit have their own YouTube channel with close to a hundred-thousand subscribers.'

'Fuckity-fuck-fuck. You sure?'

'Aye, I am. The moment Ryan, Todd and co hauled Weston out the building, Lonsdale tried to upload the footage. If it hadn't been for YouTube monitoring the content and flagging it up as dubious, it would've been all ower the net already.'

'Are you absolutely positive?' Ryan sounded disbelieving. 'I mean, how'd they do it? There was nobody else around.'

'I'm sure, Ry. I've seen the footage. Everything's covered. There's a camera facing the sofa to make sure Jessica's nakedness is shown in all its glory. I guess they used her laptop's webcam.'

'Of course.'

'There was a second camera, as well. Shooting forward, taking in the lounge and the corridor beyond.'

A vague recollection of a picture on a wall came into Ryan's mind. It must have housed the second camera.

'Trust me; they captured the whole thing. Including Todd kneeing Weston in the balls.'

Danskin groaned.

'Don't worry. That bit's been deleted and we've an injunction to stop the rest of it being aired.'

'You've got to admire them, in a way,' Ryan said, grudgingly.

'Aye,' Ravi said. 'You mightn't be so gracious if Lonsdale's upload had sneaked through, though. You'd be world-famous by now.'

Danskin and Ryan gawped at each other with fish's mouths.

'We've been had,' Ryan said. 'Well and truly. It should've been obvious Even Todd suspected summat. I should've seen it.'

Connor looked a beaten man. 'Release him, Stephen.'

'Like fuck I will. I want Jessica Lonsdale in here, an' aal.'

'On what grounds?' Connor said, wearily.

'Any grounds, sir, as long as the pair of them are detained. Obstruction. Perverting the course. Being a couple of knacker-heeds; owt, really, just keep them off the streets. They're publicity seekers. The moment they're out of here, they'll be selling their story. That's what they do. We can't have it. Not again. There's too much at stake.'

Stephen Danskin could just about tolerate the smug look on Imogen Markham's face. He didn't give a toss whether Sir Guy Haswell spontaneously combusted.

The one thing he couldn't stomach was the thought of another Molly Uzumba exclusive.

CHAPTER TWENTY-EIGHT

Life for Molly Uzumba changed overnight the day The Lighthouse Keeper first contacted her. Her exclusive story on him in The Mercury, in which she described details not even released by the City and County police, catapulted her to fame.

She saw her words quoted in high-profile broadsheets, she was referenced on Newsnight, received requests for interviews from magazine editors, and took a number of congratulatory phone calls from respected investigative reporters.

Most satisfying of all, she was interviewed live on TV by Megan Wolfe. Wolfe had clearly been instructed to fawn over the wunderkind and she conducted the entire interview through her perfectly polished, but gritted, teeth. It had been Molly Uzumba's sweetest moment.

Unfortunately, Molly found fame far more addictive than she ever imagined. Within two short days, the calls dried up. And, when they did, she needed another fix. Sadly for her, it wasn't one she could buy from a hawker in the toilets of a Bigg Market pub.

Instead, she went straight to the horse's mouth. Molly Uzumba sent an e-mail to The Lighthouse Keeper.

When he didn't reply, she wrote again. And a third time. She sat with her browser open for hours on end, the window minimised then enlarged, minimised and enlarged. She'd been sure he'd respond. When he didn't, she opted for a different approach. Still nothing.

Left feeling like she'd been used for a one-night stand, Molly resolved to move on. She was certain there was plenty of mileage in the story, but she needed to find a new angle.

The Lighthouse Keeper

Which is how Molly Uzumba ended up at January Hope's funeral. She wasn't allowed in the church, of course, but she loitered in the grounds while the girl's remains were interred in front of the statutory thirty mourners.

January's mother was in a trance, staring blankly at the coffin. Her father remained stoic until the moment the casket was lowered into the grave, at which point he dissolved into a fit of sobs.

Molly thought she was prepared for the emotion of the occasion. Thought she'd steeled herself for it. She'd even rehearsed a few headlines.

'January's parents left without Hope' was too tabloid, *'A loving mother weeps at the graveside of her daughter'* too obvious, and *'The Lighthouse Keeper spreads more darkness'* overly clichéd.

It didn't matter. When she witnessed at first-hand the desolation of January's parents, she knew she couldn't write the story.

As the solemn cortege left the cemetery, Molly Uzumba sat on a bench beneath a beech tree heavy with leaf. Sun and shade dappled her face.

Light and darkness.

Darkness and light.

Perhaps her final headline wasn't so clichéd after all.

A young woman took a seat on an adjacent bench. She clutched a small posy barely visible amid a handful of damp and snotty tissues. The girl snuffled constantly and stared at the grave with bloodshot eyes.

'I'm sorry for your loss,' Molly said.

The girl bobbed her head in thanks.

'Are you a relative?'

'No,' the woman said. 'Just a good friend.'

'I'm sorry,' Molly repeated.

'So am I. Although, you know, I think Jan would've found all this funny.'

'I'm not with you.'

'The funeral. The burial. She had a wicked sense of humour, did Jan. I think she'd appreciate the irony. You know, the fact she'd been both cremated and buried?'

The young woman gave a bitter laugh which morphed into a sorrowful wail.

Molly gathered her bag from her feet, stood, and brushed herself down. 'Take care,' she said.

'I thought he was going to kill me instead, you know,' the young woman said.

Molly sat down with a thud. 'What?'

'The killer sent me a message.'

Caution kicked in. The woman could be an attention seeker, a lunatic or, quite possibly, both. *'Check your facts. Check your sources. Check your facts again'*, Molly told herself.

'He sent me this,' the woman was saying. 'He thought I was Jan, you see.' She was holding up her mobile phone.

Molly leaned across the gap between the seats. The image could be interpreted as a warning, that's for sure. Not many people are sent random pictures of a crematorium.

'Can you enlarge it for me, please?' she asked.

'Sure.' The woman placed two fingers on the screen and dragged them apart.

From her seat, Molly Uzumba could see the image more clearly. She could also see the sender's name.

Her heart almost broke free from her chest when she saw the name, 'Jim Smith.'

'Do you want to talk about it?'

**

The Mercury landed on the streets the following morning. Its editor, a local lad called Dennis Cherry who had succeeded the owner, South African magnate Marcus Vorster, made the decision to keep Uzumba's exclusive off The Mercury's web feed initially.

His plan was to maximise physical sales and keep the copy out of their competitor's grubby mitts. He knew fine well they'd be monitoring the web for anything with Uzumba's name attached. She was hot property, even if the spotlight had faded.

While that part of the plan worked, Cherry didn't succeed in keeping it away from the ears of Sir Guy Haswell, who arrived at Forth Street within minutes of the first issue hitting the streets.

'Divvent tell me the fucker's back again?' Todd Robson groaned. 'Has he got a season ticket, or summat? He can have my seat if he loves it here that much.'

This time, Haswell didn't even wait for Connor. He launched into a frenzied tirade the moment the bullpen doors swung open.

He brandished The Mercury above his head. 'How did this get out?' he demanded.

'You're ahead of me there, sunshine,' Haswell heard a voice say.

'Sunshine? SUNSHINE? Who the hell called me that? Don't you know who I am?'

'It was me,' Todd said. 'And think yersel' lucky I was so complimentary. Aye, I know who you are, but in here you're a nobody.'

'Where's Connor? Where's Danskin?'

'I'm here,' Danskin said from in front of his office door. 'The Superintendent's gone sick. He won't be in today.'

'Very convenient,' the MP sneered. 'Well, you'll have to do, I suppose. Don't think you're going to get away with this.'

'With what?' Stephen said, controlled and calm.

'We'll talk in your office.'

Stephen closed the door and took a step into the bullpen. 'No, we'll talk here.'

The rest of the squad took cover behind their desks. Ravi Sangar hid in the tech room. Ryan and Hannah raised eyebrows at one another and followed him. Gavin O'Hara and Nigel Trebilcock buried their heads in casefiles. Todd and Lyall Parker remained standing.

Haswell blinked and swallowed down his rage though he couldn't disguise the tremor in his voice.

'There's a report in here.'

'Yep. That's what's usually in newspapers.'

Haswell's jaw dropped open at Danskin's temerity. He recovered in time to explain himself.

'It says you were at the wrong house in Gateshead.'

'Well, it's right. You know we were at the wrong house. You were here spitting feathers aboot it, remember?'

'Don't you realise how that looks? It makes you look incompetent.'

Danskin shrugged. 'We know that's not true, though, don't we? It was the killer who made the mistake, not us. He's the incompetent one.'

Haswell spluttered like a kettle boiled dry. 'Oh great. That's all right, then. I'll give this reporter her next headline, should I? *Incompetent murderer roams the streets*. Or, even better, '*Shit police protect a perfectly safe girl.*'

'How, man,' Todd intervened, 'Calm your tits, will you?'

Haswell lost every pretence of urbanity. He glared at Robson.

'Calm my tits? You've really no idea what's at stake, do you? Any of you?'

'I think we do,' the DCI said. 'I think we know the female population is at risk. I think we know there's a serial killer on the loose. I think we know perfectly well what's at stake.'

'Ha! That's where your wrong. You're wrong because what's at stake is a seat in the house. That's what's at stake.'

'Oh, of course,' Danskin said. 'You mean the by-election.'

'Yes, I mean the bloody by-election.'

Stephen Danskin put his hands on his hips. 'Remind me, again: what constituency's up for grabs?'

'Hadrian and Tynedale.'

'Uh-huh. So it is.' He grinned at Sir Guy Haswell, but the smile never reached his eyes.

'Hadrian and Tynedale, Hadrian and Tynedale; now, why does the name sound familiar?' Danskin tapped a finger against his lips as he stared absently towards the ceiling.

He snapped his fingers. 'Ah yes. I remember now. That's the seat you were deselected from four weeks before the 1997 General Election, isn't it?'

Sir Guy Haswell's bravado crumpled like tissue paper.

'We can talk in my office now, if you want. Or would you prefer to have this discussion out here?'

**

Stephen Danskin closed the door behind them and pulled at a drawstring. The blinds at the window closed on the faces gawping in.

Haswell was already seated, legs crossed at the thigh. He waggled his foot nervously. The politician appeared smaller than before, looked like a man in his fifties rather than the carefully cultivated younger image he liked to present. Gone was the scent of expensive cologne, replaced by the pungent sweat of a man at toil.

For his part, Stephen Danskin fought to appear calm. Inside, his heart raced. Blood thundered at his temple. Pitch this wrong, and he was finished. He decided to remain silent.

So, too, Haswell.

They played it like a game of chess, each man running down the clock before making his move.

Tick. Tock.

Tick. Tock.

Tick...

Sir Guy moved his pawn. 'You're finished, you do realise that, don't you?'

'Are you sure it's me that's finished, Sir Guy? Are you absolutely positive?'

Haswell didn't respond. He just sat there, perfectly still apart from the vibrating foot.

'You should be out there catching a murderer,' Haswell finally said.

'It doesn't need me to do that. I've a perfectly capable team out there doing it for me.'

Haswell gave a nasal laugh. 'Could have fooled me.'

'Well, perhaps we would have caught him by now if we hadn't been thrown off the scent. I wonder who could have done that?'

'Look, Connor's as incompetent as you. The fact he hid the file's got nothing to do with me.'

Danskin tried to remain impassive as he sat down opposite him. 'What file would that be?'

'The Saltwell Park case file.'

'Really? Now, tell me: how on earth would you know about that?'

Checkmate.

**

Sir Guy Haswell stayed tight-lipped, no matter how much Danskin pressed him. He had no desire to talk and, with his ministerial status behind him, no obligation to do so.

He wasn't being charged with anything and knew he never would. The only ones who'd come out of this as losers were Connor and Danskin.

Stephen Danskin knew it, too, which meant the discussion was brief and perfunctory. After little more than ten minutes, the conversation dissolved into a staring contest.

Danskin lost. He grabbed his jacket from the back of his chair, stalked out the room, through the bullpen, and into the elevator. He couldn't help feeling he'd just made one almighty balls-up.

Sir Guy Haswell plonked his feet on the DCIs desk and pulled out his mobile phone. Purely as a precaution, he chose to make a call.

'Mayberry, Pollock and Everett Legal Services,' a disembodied voice said.

'Evelyn. It's Sir Guy here. Be a good girl and patch me through to Rueben, would you?'

The girl called Evelyn replied to Sir Guy.

'No, no. It's nothing urgent,' Haswell said. 'Don't disturb him on my account. It's nothing I can't handle at this end. Just ask him to be on stand-by for me, will you?'

Evelyn asked a question.

'Look, Evelyn, I'm not going to discuss what it's about with you. If Reuben wants to know, you can tell him to give me a call when he's free.'

He stuffed one hand in a pocket. 'Thank you, dear.'

Haswell terminated the call and sauntered through the bullpen whistling *Always look on the bright side of life.*

CHAPTER TWENTY-NINE

The minute Ryan arrived home, the tiredness hit him. More than tiredness. Sheer, absolute exhaustion. If he'd been Jack Reacher, he'd have made himself a pot of strong, black coffee and be ready to roll without sleep for another week.

He wasn't Jack Reacher; he was Ryan Jarrod, and life didn't work like that for him. Instead, he stumbled around the kitchen like a zombie and, when he realised he'd forgotten how to fry bacon, decided to hit the sack.

Ryan rolled into bed just after six and was in a comatose sleep by five past. He dreamt he was on an island, somewhere hot. Hannah was with him, and she wore his grandmother's engagement ring. In fact, she wore six of them – but they were all around her neck like a Myanmar tribeswoman.

Hannah pointed up at something. He followed her finger towards a snow-white lighthouse standing proud on a rocky outcrop. Ryan craned his neck and looked up at it. Flecks of cloud swirled in a brilliant blue sky. They circled faster and faster, like water drawn to a plughole.

Ryan became dizzy as he watched them rotate around the lighthouse. He felt himself falling…

'Ryan. Ry – wake up, man.'

He opened one eye. Hannah gazed down on him. Not the dream Hannah with the rings around her elongated neck, but the real one.

Ryan smiled. 'Mmm, hello, gorgeous. I was just dreaming about you.'

She looked embarrassed. 'We haven't…'

He flipped back the sheet to reveal his nakedness.

'Look who's pleased to see you,' he said.

'A-hem.' A polite cough came from the doorway.

Stephen Danskin stood at the foot of the bed.

'Jesus Christ. Sir. S...sorry, sir.'

Ryan leapt from beneath the covers. Realised his mistake and dived back into bed, sheet pulled up to his chin.

Hannah dissolved into fits of laughter. Ryan blushed, furiously. Stephen Danskin said, 'I can see why Hannah wants to do this place up. Looks like something out of Balamorey.'

'What's gannin' on?' Ryan asked. 'It's the middle of the night.'

Hannah chuckled. 'It's only half six, man.'

Disoriented, Ryan managed a 'What?' before Stephen Danskin spoke again.

'Get dressed. We're going for a walk.'

**

They headed into the Bucks Hill fields at the foot of Ryan's estate. To their left, long fan-tails of barley danced in the gentle breeze while, on their right-hand side, maize hung rich and heavy, ripe for harvest.

Hannah perched on top of a wooden fence above a swathe of nettles, Ryan sat on a path of rutted earth, while Stephen rested his back against a five-bar gate and sucked on a grass stalk.

'Off the record,' the DCI said, 'I know we all have our suspicions aboot Haswell and his interference in the case. Well, I've discovered something about him which I think is worth following up. Trouble is, I think I've put me foot in it. I might have tipped him the wink.'

Ryan began to speak.

Danskin shut him down. 'Just listen for a minute, yeah? Please?'

Ryan nodded.

'Okay. Look, Haswell knows more about the Saltwell Park case than he should. He knows there was a second Miss Per file. He knows it's disappeared. He knows the Super's involved.'

Ryan sucked in air. 'I didn't want to believe Connor was implicated but I knew he was. Why'd the Super do something like that?'

'I can only think of one reason. Haswell's put pressure on him. Threatened to slash the budget. Merge us with the Prince Bishop force. Ship Connor out. Who knows – it could be any or all of those things, but I've known the Super long enough to realise he wouldn't hide evidence unless someone was squeezing his balls so tight they squeaked.'

'And that 'someone' is Sir Guy Haswell?'

'Give that man a coconut.'

They sat in silence, the hum of distant traffic from Whickham Highway floating over the farmland like a bee at work.

'Where do we go from here? Hannah asked.

'Like I say, I think I've made a bollocks of things. Haswell will be watching me like a hawk. Your mission, should you choose to accept it, is to do the dirty work for us.'

'No change there, then,' Ryan mocked.

Stephen snickered and threw a pebble at Ryan. 'Cheeky git.'

'I'm up for it. Hannah – what aboot you?'

'Aye, I'm game. Like I said a few weeks ago, you and me make a canny team, Ry.'

Stephen Danskin looked at both of them. 'Are you sure? You know there'll be repercussions if it goes tits up and we're wrong.'

'Sir, we're not wrong.'

'Thank you. Right, this is what I know about Haswell. He was always seen as a bit of a high-flier in Tory party circles. He was first selected as a candidate for parliament when he was in his late twenties. He was due to sit in the 1997 election, the year Tony Blair took office. Then, just weeks before the election, the local party chairman deselected him.'

'I know nowt about politics,' Ryan interrupted, 'But can he do that, off his own bat? I mean, if Haswell was so highly thought of…'

'Exactly my point, Ryan. It can't be anything minor.'

Ryan joined the dots. 'You want us to find out why?'

Stephen smiled. 'Aye, I do.'

'Okay. Where do we start?'

'You're going to Corbridge to talk to a Harold LeRoux. He was chair of the constituency party at the time. Find out why the bugger dropped Haswell like an arseful of curry.'

Ryan looked at Hannah. She inclined her head. 'Sounds good to us, sir,' Ryan said.

'Excellent. Oh, and just for good measure: the constituency which deselected him? It's Hadrian and Tynedale. The one Haswell's losing his shit over.'

**

The sun arrowed in at an angle low enough to make driving treacherous. Ryan had a taste for Hannah's Renault now, but the seat position wasn't set for him and he hunched over the wheel, squinting into the sun.

It spoilt what would have been an otherwise idyllic drive to the scenic village of Corbridge set deep in Roman Wall territory.

They exited the A69 onto Stagshaw Road and meandered past the Wheatsheaf Inn and a Craft Gallery, both of which struggled to stay afloat and solvent in a COVID-secure world.

A quick right turn took them directly to Dovecot Cottage. Nestled on the banks of the Tyne beneath Corbridge Bridge, it was chocolate-box perfect.

This was a different River Tyne to the one which lurked menacingly behind the Forth Street station. Here, salmon-rich waters sparkled and gurgled like a contented infant.

Ryan took a moment to breathe in the scents of lavender, rose and honeysuckle before he turned to Hannah. 'You ready for this?'

She put her hand on the latch of a wooden gate and pushed it open. 'I'm ready.'

The solid wood door at the end of a crazy-paving footpath contained matching adornments; a lion's head knocker and a similarly designed door handle.

'Nice pair of knockers,' Ryan said as he rapped on the door.

Hannah was still smiling as the door inched open until caught by the safety chain.

'Yes?' a croaky female voice said.

'Good evening, madam. We're Detective Constables Ryan Jarrod and Hannah Graves, City and County Police. We were wondering if we could have a word with Mr LeRoux? Harold LeRoux?'

'Let me see,' the woman behind the door commanded.

Ryan passed her his ID through the gap. It must have proved satisfactory because they heard the chink of metal as the woman released the chain and swung open the door.

'I'm his wife. Mildred. Harold's out on constituency business, I'm afraid, what with the by-election and all.'

'Oh, I understood he'd retired.'

The woman, a wrinkled Dot Cotton lookalike, cackled. 'Harold will never retire. Not from politics. It's his life, you know. He's not chairman anymore, if that's what you mean, but he's still active.'

'Actually, it's politics we're here for, in a way.'

The woman's brow adopted even more furrows. 'Is there something wrong with the Polling Station? I knew we should have used the school.'

'No,' Hannah said. 'It's nothing like that. Do you know when he'll be back?'

'I'm sorry, I don't. Can I help?'

Ryan shook his head. 'I doubt it. It's about a constituency matter from a long time back.'

The woman folded her arms across her. 'You mean Guy Haswell, don't you?'

The Lighthouse Keeper

Ryan and Hannah looked at one another. 'As a matter of fact, we do; yes. How did you know?'

Mrs LeRoux snorted. 'Bound to come out one day. Should have happened years ago but Harold wouldn't have any of it. *'No,'* he always said. *'It'll bring shame on the party.'* Never mind our shame, I say.'

'I'm really sorry, madam,' Hannah said, 'I don't know what you're talking about.'

'Haswell, I'm talking about. Twenty-nine he was. Twenty-nine. Having sex with our granddaughter.'

Ryan's brain went into overdrive but failed to find the right gear.

'Your husband deselected Guy Haswell because of an affair?'

'An affair, is that what you call it? That's not my word for it. He used her, that's what he did.'

'You mean, your granddaughter was forced into it?' Hannah's eyes boggled.

'Look, you'd better come in. I can't talk about these things on the doorstep. But yes; of course she was forced. Our Sally didn't have any choice.'

The woman inhaled through her nose, lips trembling.

'She was only fourteen years old.'

CHAPTER THIRTY

The interior of Mildred and Harold LeRoux's cottage was expensively furnished, and the elderly couple proved to have surprisingly modern tastes.

Ryan caught Hannah looking around and wondered if she was seeking inspiration for the next phase of The Drive's transformation. As long as they didn't include the giant-sized signed portrait of Margaret Thatcher, he was cool with it.

The young detectives sat next to each other. They'd donned their plastic visors rather than cloth face masks to limit the communication barriers between them and the elderly woman.

Hannah sat with a rose-patterned teacup balanced on her knees. She didn't know why she'd agreed to have one – she couldn't drink it with her shield on – but that's what people did, didn't they? They made tea.

'Tell me what happened to Sally,' she asked.

'She went away. Harold couldn't be doing with her here.'

'But, she was only fourteen. Where did she go? And, what about your daughter? Her mother? Where was she?'

The old woman laughed. 'A piece of advice, young lady. Ask one question at a time unless you want a politician's answer.' Hannah looked suitably chastised. 'But, for you, I'll try to answer all of them.'

Mildred LeRoux stared at the ceiling, almost as if she were travelling back in time.

'Let's start with the last one first. Sally's mother, my daughter, is at peace.'

Hannah immediately regretted her question, and it showed in her face.

Mrs LeRoux leant forward and touched Hannah's knee. 'It's alright, dear. It was a long time ago. Ninth of February 1990 to be precise.'

The woman took a sip of tea. The cup wavered slightly in her hand. 'It was a dreadful shock at the time, of course. There was no warning. Angela went to bed one night and just didn't wake up again. Harold and I were told it was an adult version of cot death. Extremely rare, but it happens.'

She stared out of the cottage window for what seemed an eternity. Then, as if coming out of a hypnotist's trance, she sat upright.

'So, Harold and I were left to bring up a seven-year-old. If I say so myself, we did a damn good job. Until Guy Haswell arrived.'

Ryan listened as the woman's tale unfolded. He let the information settle in his head. He tried not to judge or interpret or put his own slant on her story. He vowed he wouldn't *'see what he expected to see.'*

Hannah did all the talking, woman-to-woman.

'How exactly did Sir Guy become involved with your family in the first place?' she asked.

'That, my dear, is a mystery. All I know is, Harold took a telephone call one evening. He never told me who it was, and I never asked. The upshot was, though, that creep Haswell was foisted upon us.'

Ryan saw a shudder course its way up the woman's body, from waist to head.

'He was a bright young thing. A star in the making. Set for party greatness. He needed somewhere to stay while he prepared for the election. An address in the constituency is always key to election success, you know; so, we took him in.'

She laughed bitterly. 'Or he took us in, more like.'

Quietly, with as much compassion as she could muster, Hannah asked. 'Where's Sally now?

The woman's reply was brusque. 'We're not in touch. All I can tell you is, we sent her to live with Harold's cousin. Over Gateshead way.'

Ryan spoke for the first time. 'I'm sorry, but I don't understand why she had to go away. Couldn't you sort it out, somehow?'

'Young man, you've no idea, have you? Of course, we couldn't *'sort it out'* as you put it. It could never go away.'

She saw the puzzled look on Ryan's face.

'Do I have to spell it out for you? Our fourteen-year-old granddaughter was pregnant with Guy Haswell's baby.'

**

'Oh, you silly, silly girl.'

The Lighthouse Keeper sat in darkness. Blackout curtains, blinds, and shutters at the windows banished all hint of daylight from the room. Only the glow of the monitor illuminated his features, cast ghostly shadows against the wall, and high up across the artexed ceiling.

He reached for a screen wipe. Caressed it over the keyboard, the screen and, in particular, her face.

'What DO you think you're doing?'

He'd ignored her at first. It wasn't difficult. He did things on his terms, no-one else's. But she'd proved persistent. He admired that much about her, although it made it obvious she had no idea who she was up against.

Now, in a last, desperate measure, she'd sent him a link to her social media accounts.

'Tut, tut, tut.'

She didn't think he'd fall for it, surely? The hair was wrong, for starters. She'd dyed it a strange plum colour. It wasn't red at all. Nor was there enough of it. It sprouted from her scalp like the coiled springs of a car's suspension.

The germ of an idea began to form in his mind. She didn't deserve to hear the end of his story, but that didn't mean he couldn't have some fun with her.

He glanced down at the number on the corner of the page. It was a struggle to make it out in the dim light, but he was sure it said, Six.

The Lighthouse Keeper dipped his hand into a large cardboard box beneath the table. He counted as his fingers fished around inside it.

'One. Two. Buckle my shoe.'

This wasn't the way he did things, but he was enjoying the excitement of something new.

'Three. Four. Knock on my door.'

Outside, the only things which troubled his door were the sounds of nature. A crashing tide. The caw of seabirds. A strengthening wind.

'Five. Six. Pick up sticks.'

On the count of six, his fingers closed. He brought out a device, opened its casing, and slotted in a fresh SIMcard.

Sometimes, random suited him just fine.

The man raised his eyes to the screen. Took in every nuance, every flaw, every perfection of the woman's profile picture.

He chuckled. She'd got one thing right: she gazed up at him with doleful, subservient eyes.

The look made him think.

'I wonder.'

Bluff, or double-bluff?

'Which shall it be?'

**

The drive back to Newcastle was hushed, bordering on awkward. Ryan and Hannah had plenty to discuss but said nothing. Each consumed their own thoughts in silence.

What conversation there was, was muted and monosyllabic. They agreed on two things: one, they'd update Danskin in the morning, in private. Two: Sir Guy Haswell was a sleaze-ball of the highest order.

They'd reached West Denton before either addressed the elephant in the room.

'You okay?' Ryan asked.

'Yes. Why wouldn't I be?' The words came out more defensive that she'd intended.

Ryan said nothing.

'Come on, Ry. Why wouldn't I be?'

'I saw your face, Hannah. When Mildred LeRoux mentioned the pregnancy.'

'She was fourteen, man. It's disgusting. Of course, I was upset. So were you.'

'I was disgusted by the pervert.'

'And?'

Ryan took his eyes off the road. 'And you were upset at the thought of the pregnancy.'

Hannah stared straight ahead. 'Fourteen, she was. No-one should be a mother at that age.'

'Fine, if you're sure that's what it was.'

They turned onto the southbound A1 in renewed silence. They were on the Blaydon Bridge when Ryan heard the sniffles. He took his hand off the wheel and laid it on Hannah's thigh.

'It's not fair,' she sobbed. 'Sally didn't want to have a child.'

Ryan thought, *'Neither did you, really,'* but he wouldn't say it.

'Ah shit, Ryan. Let's get home.'

His eyebrows raised slightly.

'To YOUR home,' she qualified. 'Don't get your hopes up, kidda. You know where I stand on that one.'

'It's been a long day,' he said. 'We'll be back in a couple of minutes. Let's leave it.'

He got no argument from her.

**

The day had been busy. Busy, and successful.

She'd taken a dozen or more calls, caught up with over a hundred new e-mails, and pinged off almost as many herself. There'd been three video conferences with colleagues and her regular catch-up with her boss. He'd been fulsome in his praise. She'd even made time to squeeze in some on-line shopping.

Yes, it had been a good day. Now, it was time to unwind in a warm bath.

The woman stripped off, folded her clothes in a neat pile, and draped a silk kimono over a milkmaid-style, three-legged stool.

As the tub filled, she lit a couple of candles and set them afloat on the surface. They bobbed like skiffs in a harbour, at mercy of tide and tempest.

With her fingers flat and together, she massaged her breasts with a circular motion. Satisfied there were no lumps, she lowered herself gently into the hot, fragrant water.

She closed her eyes and let her mind drift to her happy place.

But not for long.

'Damn.' She should have left her mobile downstairs.

The woman climbed out the tub. Dried her hands. Neglected the bathwater which ran down her legs, dripped from her slender frame, and pooled on the bathroom floor.

The glanced at her phone's screen. *'Caller ID unknown,'* it screamed at her.

She accepted it, anyway.

'You're through to Molly Uzumba.'

CHAPTER THIRTY-ONE

'Listen, our focus has to remain on The Lighthouse Keeper. We all know that. We should hand over what you discovered about Haswell yesterday to Rick Kinnear. His lads will deal with it.'

'Sir, with absolute respect, that's not gonna happen,' Ryan said. 'Ask yourself one thing: if this case landed on wor desks with nothing else going on, would a child abuse investigation involving a VIP fall to us? If it would, then we should run with it.'

Stephen Danskin's eyes roamed his office walls in their search for inspiration.

'Borderline,' he said.

'Bollocks, man. Especially because, somewhere in there, there's links to our case. We know he's got the Super's knackers in a sling. We know he has inside knowledge of the Terri Grainger case and the missing file. We can't let this one go.'

The DCI scratched the back of his neck. Outside, Lyall Parker cupped a hand around his face and peered in. He pointed at his wristwatch. The rest of the squad were gathered around the crime board, looking towards Danskin's office.

Stephen sighed. 'You've got half an hour, Jarrod. Thirty minutes to come up with something definite, or I'll have to hand it over to Kinnear. Remember, Haswell knows I suspect summat, so I need to be cautious here.'

'You don't need be involved, sir. Not yet. Leave it with Hannah and me.'

Stephen Danskin saw the expectant faces staring in at him.

'I've a briefing to run. You're excused, Jarrod. Hannah, not you. Let's not raise suspicions out there.'

The Lighthouse Keeper

He pushed his arms through his jacket. 'DC Graves, follow me. Jarrod; I'll be half an hour. Let me know what you find.'

**

Ryan didn't need half an hour. He didn't need Stephen Danskin or Hannah Graves. He didn't even need Ravi Sangar's technical wizardry to find what he wanted.

All he needed was access to the electoral roll and Ancestry.co.uk.; and even he knew how to do that.

The LeRoux lineage was lengthy and distinguished. They had a heritage rich in landowners dating back to the middle ages. They were countrified gentry. It didn't take a genius to locate a family member's whereabouts in Gateshead. There was only one.

Harold LeRoux's cousin turned out to be a Lesley Moffat. The electoral roll gave her address as the Mount Pleasant estate, in Gateshead's Deckham suburb.

Ryan gave a low whistle. Mount Pleasant was as far removed from the rural splendour of Corbridge and the rest of the LeRoux clan's abodes he could imagine.

He'd worked with a lad from there, in his Civil Service days. Ryan had visited him once. He was struck by the tight-knit, supportive community spirit – but, esoterically speaking, 'pleasant' was the last adjective he'd use to describe Mount Pleasant.

Neither the electoral role nor 192.com listed anyone else living at the address. He checked for a Sally LeRoux. It, too, produced no results.

'Bugger.'

On a whim and a prayer, he tried *'Sally Moffatt.'*

192.com gave him twenty-three hits. Hope sprung within him.

The nearest lived in Barnsley and Rotherham.

'Double bugger.'

There was only thing for it. He sifted the surface of Danskin's desk for a post-it note, scribbled something on it, and affixed it to Danskin's PC.

It said, *'Gone fishing.'*

**

Ryan turned onto Sunderland Road and crawled his Uno downhill. Trees and allotments lay on one side of the road. He checked off street names on the other.

He passed Moore Street, Howe Street, and onwards. He almost missed the entrance he needed. He spun the wheel and the Fiat swung across the path of a number twenty-seven bus. The driver pointed to his temple and shook his head in the exaggerated, time-honoured tradition of frustrated bus drivers the world over.

House number nineteen looked the same as all the others. An unremarkable terraced house with small front garden laid to unkempt lawn. An old, damp mattress lay across the narrow path; the only thing that differentiated the house from its neighbours.

Ryan rang the bell and adjusted his face-shield while he waited for someone other than the three yapping mongrels to answer.

When the door did open, it jammed a few inches in. The occupant hidden behind it struggled to lift the door over the frayed carpet.

'I'm not interested, ta,' the woman said. 'Whatever your selling, it won't be owt I want so fuck off.'

Ryan checked the door number. Was this really a LeRoux speaking?

'You misunderstand,' he said before the door could slam shut. 'I'm DC Ryan Jarrod of City and County Police. I'm looking for a Lesley Moffat.'

'Oh aye, like. What's that nosey cow next door reported me for now?'

Ryan forced a smile. 'Nothing like that. I wondered if I could come in for a moment?'

'Na.'

The smile remained glued in place. 'Are you Mrs. Moffat?'

'Look, I've got a pan of soup on and I'm burstin' for a piss. What do you want?'

'Actually, if I'm honest, it's not you I want to speak to at all. Not really. I'm seeking information about a Sally LeRoux.'

'Oh, for fuck's sake, man. She buggered off years ago with her fella. Now, will you do the same?'

'I understand she had a child. Do you know where I can find her?'

Lesley Moffat considered the question for a moment. 'Come in. Divvent let the neighbours see you, though. I'm gannin to the bog. Find somewhere to sit if you can.'

It was more of a challenge than Ryan imagined. He shifted unwashed laundry from one side of a two-seater sofa onto a unit stained with mug rings. He dumped a pile of magazines from the other onto the floor, and wiped crumbs off the seat before sitting down.

A mangey looking black and tan dog joined him. The mutt nibbled his ear, then hopped down to join his two mates somewhere out back when he realised the stranger hadn't come bearing gifts.

The toilet flushed and Lesley Moffat returned without having had time to wash her hands.

'Looker, I divvent knaa what you want, but I've nee idea what Cheryl's been up to, reet?'

'Cheryl?'

'Aye, Cheryl.'

'Who's Cheryl?'

'Are you fuckin' simple or what? Sally's lass. That's the thing I thought you wanted to taalk aboot her.'

The woman was Geordie as broon ale and stottie cakes, but she had the EastEnders affliction: 'thought' came out as 'fort', 'thing' as 'fing.'

'Ah, thank you,' Ryan said. 'I wasn't aware of the child's name.'

Lesley gave a mocking laugh. 'Child? I reckon she'll be aboot the same age as you.'

The woman had a point.

'I'd be really grateful if you could tell me where I might find Cheryl.'

'So would I. She owes me two month's rent.'

Now we're getting somewhere, Ryan thought. 'She lives here?'

Lesley gave another humourless laugh; a sharp bark more befitting one of the dogs. 'When she can be arsed. Comes and goes as she pleases, that one.'

'When was she last here?'

'Two, three months ago, mebbe? Not sure, really.'

'And, you don't have any contact with the mother, Sally?'

'Not for years.'

This was a dead-end, and Ryan knew it. Stephen Danskin was right – they needed to focus on The Lighthouse Keeper.

'Thanks for your time, Mrs Moffat. I'll leave you to it.'

'Aye, me soup's aboot done now.'

Ryan stepped over a posse of dogs.

'Did her faatha put you up to this?'

'I'm sorry?'

'Cheryl's faatha.'

Ryan stood still, his back to Lesley Moffat. 'What makes you think that?'

'Just 'cos he's been asking aboot her, an' aal.'

'Mrs Moffat. Please, see to your soup. I'll wait here, then we can talk some more.'

**

'What do you know about Cheryl's father?'

Lesley Moffat shrugged. 'Not a great deal, to be honest. He's a posh get, and a scruffy bugger to get a bairn up the spout the way he did.'

'You don't know his name?'

'Looker, you might find it hard to believe, but I divvent really care. I know he's rich as fuck. I see nowt of it, like, but he makes sure Cheryl's well-cared for. Sends money to her every month. Shitloads of it, too, by the look of the expensive clothes and rings and all the other shit Cheryl wears.'

Ryan looked around the shabby, cramped room. 'I'm sorry if this sounds rude, but if her father is as caring as you say towards her, financially like; why does she stay here?'

'Because that's part of the deal. Her faatha says he'll cut her off as quick as me gas and leccy if she ever talks about it.'

Ryan was missing something here. Something so clear and transparent he was looking straight through it.

The silence lingered so long, Lesley Moffat asked, 'Are you finished with us?'

He wasn't sure. He didn't think so, but he didn't know where else to go with it.

'You say Cheryl hasn't been here for a while. Does she often go missing?'

'Oh hell, aye. Wouldn't you, if you had all that cash but had to live in a shithole like this? She was always off on holiday, staying in fancy hotels. I reckon she'd probably be away more times than she was here. Not for a long spell at a time, mind. She couldn't risk her sugar-daddy finding out, could she?'

'So, she's never gone away for this length of time before.'

'Na. Never. If you ask me, I divvent think she'll be coming back now. At least, I hope not. That's her mattress I've chucked outside. If she's not back soon, I'm gannin to get mesel a new lodger.'

She smiled at Ryan with sharp, blackened teeth.

'I divvent suppose you're looking for somewhere to live, are you?'

**

Ryan made his excuses and left. Left with more questions than answers, but at least he had something to justify his time away from Forth Street.

The Fiat struggled to start. Not a good sign. He must get a new car. At the third time of asking, the engine fired. He backtracked onto Shipcote Terrace then Durham Road, heading north to Newcastle City.

He was more certain than ever Guy Haswell was a nonce of the highest order, but he wasn't quite sure what else he'd proved.

At least the creep had made sure his daughter was financially cared for, even if Cheryl did have to spend most of her time in Lesley Moffat's dump of a house to earn it.

But, never mind: Haswell's stipend, his bursary, his bribe; give it whatever name you wanted, it enabled Cheryl to get away and enjoy the fineries in life.

Ryan drove past Valley Drive on his left, noticed for the first time a street with a similar name to his right. It was called, simply, The Drive. He wondered whether Hannah had formulated her plans for the bedroom in a street with the same name, only a few miles away.

His mind began to turn to the brief he'd give Danskin on his arrival back at Forth Street when, in a flash of blinding white neon, everything fell into place.

It was the sign which did it; the brown sign adorned with four simple words:

'Pet's Corner
Saltwell Park.'

'Jesus Christ! Of course. Of course!'

It explained everything. He knew, with absolute conviction, why Sir Guy Haswell was so interested in The Lighthouse Keeper.

It was so obvious, so transparent, Ryan had indeed looked straight through it.

They all had.

CHAPTER THIRTY-TWO

Ryan remembered to breathe. It's about all he did remember.

He knew Haswell's profile was such he had to tread carefully. He knew he still harboured doubts about a number of his colleagues. For both those reasons, he was conscious he needed to report what he'd discovered to Stephen Danskin without drawing attention to himself.

He realised he'd failed the moment he strolled into the bullpen, as cool as he could muster.

'What's the matter with you?' Todd Robson asked.

Ryan's heart beat faster still. 'Nowt.'

'Hadawayandshite. Summat's up.'

'Why? What makes you say that?'

'The look on your face, man. I can tell.'

Ryan tried to play it casual.

'What look's that, like?'

'The *'I've just creamed me pants but hope nobody'll notice'* look.'

Ryan managed a laugh, but the blush gave the game away.

'Where's the DCI? And Ravi?'

'Ravi's in the tech room. Foreskin's in his office with Lyall. Says they're not to be disturbed.'

'Any idea how long they'll be out of commission?'

Todd shrugged. 'Piece of string, mate.'

Ryan settled for Ravi and the tech room. Fortunately, no-one else occupied it.

'You busy, Rav?'

'Do Russians drink vodka?' Sangar replied without looking up. He heard Ryan sigh through his nose. 'What can I do for you, though?'

'Cheers, Rav. I'd like you to do a social media check for me. It's linked to The Lighthouse Keeper,' he said by way of explanation.

'Isn't everything, these days? Howay, then. Who is it?'

'Name's Cheryl Moffat. If it helps, she lives in Gateshead, although divvent bother checking electoral roll. I've already done that and she's not on there.'

Ravi typed the name into his program. 'Where, specifically?'

'Deckham. Mount Pleasant, to be exact.'

They waited.

'I've got another name if that doesn't show owt.'

'Okay. Fire away.'

Ryan hesitated. 'Can we see what this one brings up first?'

'Sure. Just it'll save duplicating effort, that's all.'

'I'd rather not.'

'Suit yersel'.

Ravi hummed some ridiculous made-up tune while they waited. Ryan checked his watch.

'Here we go,' Ravi said.

Ryan scooted his chair next to Sangar's.

'Bingo. Print it out for me, will you?'

Ravi hit print.

'I'll be back for it after I've had a word with the DCI.'

**

'They're not to be interrupted,' Sue Nairn warned.

Ryan ignored her.

'I'm sorry, Ryan. I can't let you in.'

'Don't worry. You're not letting me in. I'm going in mesel'.

He weaved past her and marched into the DCIs office without a knock.

Stephen and Lyall sat, grim-faced and silent, facing each other. A sheet of paper lay between them, sideways on so both could read it.

They looked up and offered Ryan no hint of a welcome.

'You shouldn't be in here, Jarrod.'

'What's up? Divvent say The Lighthouse Keeper's struck again.'

'Nowt like that. It's the Super.'

Stephen handed Ryan the sheet of paper from the desk. 'You may as well know.'

Ryan skim-read the letter, handwritten on City and County Police headed notepaper. It was addressed to the Commissioner, and cc'd to Danskin and Rick Kinnear.

'Dear Ma'am' it began.

'I write to inform you that as of this date I give notice of my retirement from my role as Superintendent with City and County Police.

I have held this role since October 2009 and it has been an honour and a privilege to do so. I take genuine pride in the work of the officers who have served under, and alongside, me. Together, we have achieved many things.

I am also proud of my own personal achievements, of which there are several. However, of late, there are acts I regret bitterly; acts which may cause embarrassment to colleagues I respect. For that reason, I feel my position has now become untenable.

For the benefit of those I leave behind, I must place on record my criticism of the increasing bureaucracy, cuts in frontline resources, and political interference which they now face. Despite what the Government may say, this job is now all about numbers. This is not why I joined the police force, nor is it the way it should be.

I wish all the colleagues I leave behind, of every rank, all the luck in the world. They will always have my utmost respect, and I shall miss them dearly.

Finally, I wish to convey my deepest gratitude to Detective Chief Inspectors Stephen Danskin and Richard Kinnear, who have been unswerving in their support.

To the government I have nothing good to say whatsoever.

Regards'

The letter bore Superintendent Connor's unmistakeable sweeping signature.

Ryan noticed the letter shake in his hand. He handed it back to Stephen.

'We know who this is aimed at, don't we?' Ryan said.

'That's just what the guv'nor and I ha'e been discussing,' Lyall said.

'Right. Well, we'll have to make the bastard pay for it, won't we?'

Ryan gestured towards the crime board.

'Give me ten minutes with Ravi, then join us out there.'

'What've you got?'

'You'll find out.'

Ryan then said the most cliched, Hollywood statement he'd ever heard slip from his lips – yet, it came from the heart.

'Let's do this for the Super.'

**

Ryan corralled the team around the crime board.

'There's been developments,' he told them.

He ripped Terri Grainger's photograph from its place alongside the picture of the partly decomposed remains recovered from Saltwell Park and replaced it with a photograph of another young woman.

'This,' he announced, 'Is Cheryl Moffat. Twenty-three years old, lived with her aunt in Mount Pleasant. That's Deckham. Gateshead,' he spelt the exact location out specifically for Trebilcock's benefit.

He rapped a knuckle against her picture.

'Cheryl Moffat is our girl, not Terri Grainger.'

'Had on,' Gavin O'Hara said. 'I know you've had your doubts about Terri Grainger all along, but are you sure you're not just making this fit because it suits you?'

Ryan didn't need defend himself. Ravi Sangar did it for him.

'I think Ryan's right. Remember, we were worried about the fact Terri Grainger didn't receive any warning messages? Well, there's no such worries about Cheryl Moffat.'

He stepped in front of Ryan and appended a second photograph to the board.

'Jeez, will you look at that?'

'Aye, Todd; exactly.' Ryan pointed to the image. 'This is a message received by Cheryl Moffat. She received it around the time the forensic bods reckon the victim was buried. Now, look at its relevance. Remember, our victim was buried alive, yeah?'

The photograph was a still lifted from a movie promo. It showed an arm protruding from a freshly-dug grave - the closing scene from Carrie.

'Tell them who sent her it, Rav.'

'Divvent bother. It's our Jim Smith, isn't it?'

'It is, Todd.'

Sue Nairn took the revelation personally. The Grainger case was her baby. 'Terri Grainger's father identified her, though.'

'Because he wanted closure. I said that all along.'

DS Nairn persisted. 'Deckham's in the top ten percent of the UKs most deprived boroughs. The girl in Saltwell Park wore jewellery worth thousands. How'd a girl from Deckham afford it?'

Ryan glanced towards Stephen Danskin. The DCI nodded. He was ahead of Ryan, and the bow was Danskin's way of granting Ryan permission to reveal all.

'Because, Sue, she didn't pay for it. Her father did.'

'Oh, so he was one of Deckham's many millionaires, I suppose?' she scoffed.

'No, Sue. Her father isn't from Deckham. Her father is Sir Guy Haswell.'

After a moment's stunned silence, Nairn and O'Hara laughed.

'Here him out.' Danskin's voice.

'Thanks, sir. Haswell lodged with a family by the name of LeRoux while he prepared to sit in the 1997 election. He never contested the seat. Why? Because he shagged the

LeRoux's granddaughter, Sally. Harold and Mildred LeRoux had brought her up. LeRoux was constituency party chairman. When he discovered Haswell had got Sally pregnant, he deselected Haswell.'

'Bit harsh.' Todd pulled his best John Wayne impression. 'A man's gotta do what a man's gotta do, and all that.'

'Not when Sally LeRoux was fourteen years old, he hasn't.'

In the heat of summer, the room turned ice cold. Not even Todd had an answer for that one. Apart from, 'The dirty bastard.'

Ryan ploughed on. 'Here's what I think happened. No, here's what DID happen. Sally was sent away to live with a distant relative. She adopted the aunt's name; hence, Moffat. So, too, did Cheryl. It's all very Victorian, but it's also true. I know, because I've spoken to the aunt.'

Ryan checked the room, making sure they were all still with him.

'Haswell supplied both Sally and Cheryl with blood money to keep schtum. Sally trousered the cash and did a runner, but the kid continued to benefit. Until our friend The Lighthouse Keeper turned up and got his hands on the perky little red-head's Facebook profile.'

'Whoa, whoa, whoa. Slow down. Surely, if she'd disappeared off the face of the earth, someone would have reported her missing?' DC O'Hara protested.

'They did,' Ryan explained. 'Guy Haswell did. When his money went unspent, he reported it.'

'So, how come there isn't a file?' Gavin O'Hara again.

'There is. Or, was.'

'What do you mean: *was*?'

Again, Ryan glanced at the DCI for advice. Danskin shook his head. *'Keep the Super out of it'*, the look said.

Ryan shrugged. Made something up on the spot. 'Mistakes happen. It was lost. But, we know it existed. There's a reference number for it on record.'

The Lighthouse Keeper

They took five minutes out to digest what they'd heard. When they returned, they reached a consensus. Ryan's theory was a plausible one. Even Sue Nairn confessed it explained Haswell's interest in the case - *'Interference,'* Danskin corrected.

Ryan was on a high. This was his finest hour. Until the DCI, of all people, brought him down like a sack of spuds.

'None of it helps us catch The Lighthouse Keeper, though.'

Ryan's face sagged. He realised he'd lost sight of the endgame.

Seeing him flounder, Danskin sent in the cavalry. 'Here's what we do,' Stephen decided. 'Lyall and me will scoot off for a less-than-quiet word with Haswell. I'm sure a child abuse charge won't go doon well with the PM.'

'They're probably aal at it,' muttered Todd.

'A touch cynical there, Robson. Not like you at all. Anyway, somebody needs to speak to the aunt. Jarrod, that's your job. See if you can find where the kid's mother's got to. She deserves to know, even if she did bugger off and leave the poor kid in bloody Deckham.'

Stephen searched out Hannah. 'DC Graves – you inform the LeRoux's.' He allocated tasks to the rest of the squad, leaving Sue Nairn until last.

'You can tell Malcolm Grainger he's cremated the wrong lass. Then, see if you can find his daughter for him. She's still out there, somewhere.'

CHAPTER THIRTY-THREE

Like a humbug mint, a soft centre lurked beneath the crusty exterior shell of Lesley Moffat

She'd refused to believe Ryan when he'd first told her. Cheryl was having the time of her life at Guy Haswell's expense, she was sure of it. She only began to harbour doubts when he'd unsealed a plastic evidence bag and asked her to inspect a gold bangle, four high-carat gold rings, and a ruby pendant.

'Where'd you get these?' she asked suspiciously.

'Do you recognise them?'

'Course I do. They're wor Cheryl's.'

'Mrs Moffat, are you absolutely sure?'

'Why aye, man.'

'Thank you. I'm really sorry to say, it confirms what I've just told you. These items were found on the body of a young woman discovered in Saltwell Park.'

Lesley Moffat tapped the cushion beside her. The black-and-tan mongrel hopped up next to her. She picked the dog from the seat and cradled him in her lap. The woman's hard face folded in on itself. Tears welled in her eyes even as she said, 'Somebody could have robbed them off her.'

Ryan didn't need tell her that wasn't the case. Lesley knew she was kidding herself.

'Mrs Moffat, have you heard of someone who goes by the name of The Lighthouse Keeper?'

'Hasn't everybody? It's in all the papers… hang, on, you don't think – shit, man: you do, don't you?'

'Have you any recollection of Cheryl introducing you to someone new?'

'Na. She wouldn't, anyway. I mean, let's face it, would you bring somebody back to a dump like this?'

The Lighthouse Keeper

Ryan remained silent while a summer storm broke outside. Rain hammered against the windowpane. Lesley Moffat's face regained its rigidity. She stared at the rain squirming down the glass. 'Divvent think I'm gannin to get me washing oot the day, like.'

'I'd be really grateful if I could have a look through Cheryl's things. There could be something there that'll help us find whoever did this.'

Lesley released a forlorn sigh. 'I wish I could. There's nowt here.'

'What? You mean Cheryl took all her belongings with her?'

'Nah, man. But, like I said last time, I thought she wasn't coming back. I was gannin to rent her room. I chucked her bed oot. All the rest of her kit I hoyed into storage.'

Ryan breathed a sigh of relief. 'So, they're still intact?'

'Aye, most of it. Before her mother buggered off, she hired a storage unit doon the Old Fold. Near the Stadium. She kept the stuff her and Keith didn't need there. I've got a key for it, so I shipped Cheryl's belongings there, an' aal.'

'It would be really helpful if I could borrow the key. It's possible we might find a clue to where Sally went, too, if her gear's there. She needs to be told.'

'I divvent give a toss about Sally.' Tears flowed down the woman's face, rivulet-for-rivulet with the rain outside. 'But, God, I wish I'd kept some of the bairn's stuff with me. I could do with her here right now.'

She kissed the mongrel's head and pointed to a cracked vase on the fireplace. 'Key's in there, if you want it. Bring us summat of Cheryl's back, will you?'

Ryan promised he would.

**

When the heaven's opened, the beaches cleared.

Whereas the Gibraltar Rock pub and the bars and restaurants either side of Tynemouth Front Street would normally fill to overflowing, COVID restrictions meant there was nowhere for anyone to go, except home.

The angled parking bays on Sea Banks resembled the starting grid at Le Mans as day-trippers raced to escape the deluge. All of which gave Lyall Parker the opportunity to slip into one of the vacated spots overlooking the North Sea.

Parker and Danskin emerged from the car and turned their backs on the water. A concave landscaped area separated the two detectives from the row of Victorian houses on Percy Gardens.

Parker whistled in awe. 'Noo, there's terraces, and there's terraces. This is a terrace.'

'Aye, but you didn't expect Haswell to live in a colliery row, did you?'

'Och nae – but these are like hotels.'

'Most are split into a few apartments. Or, *maisonettes*, as the folk who live here call them. Haswell, though; he's got one of the few that remain as single houses. Five or six bedrooms, just for him. And this is just his constituency home.'

'Probably classifies it as his office. All on expenses, no doubt.'

'More than likely. Howay; let's give him a knock, Lyall. I'm getting drenched here.'

'Just a wee while,' Parker said. He turned so he was facing in the same direction as the view from Haswell's windows.

The curvature of the building's façade gave an outlook over Tynemouth Priory and King Edward's Bay, though most of it was hidden beneath a curtain of sea fret. Lyall moved to the edge of the pavement and looked in the opposite direction, northwards.

'What's on your mind?' Danskin asked.

'He cannae see the lighthouse from here.'

'Don't tell us you were thinking Haswell might be The Lighthouse Keeper?'

'Well, if he was sick of paying up for his bairn. If she'd threatened to spill the beans on him for extra cash. Blackmail, ye ken?'

'So, he decided to bump off a few others just to throw us of the scent? Send them all dodgy messages? Kick off in front of everybody in the station?'

'Stranger things have happened, sir.'

'We're in the realms of fantasy now, Wilson,' Danskin said in his best Captain Mainwaring impression. 'Let's get over the road and see what he's got to say for himself, though.'

They climbed half a dozen stone stairs in front of the property. Four stories towered above them. When Danskin pressed the doorbell, a distant chime acknowledged their presence.

'I bet he's got a butler,' Parker said.

Sir Guy Haswell himself opened the door.

'Wrong again,' Danskin said.

'I'm sorry?'

'Nowt. I was talking to DI Parker.'

From the top stair, Haswell looked down on them. 'What do you want?'

'Can we come in? I'm like a drowned rat here.'

'I don't recall you being in my social bubble, Detective Chief Inspector so, no; you can stay where you are.'

Danskin wiped his nose with his hand and ran his fingers down the polished surface of the door. 'If that's what you'd prefer,' he said.

'Yes, I would. Now, what are you after? Come to apologise, I trust.'

Rain spat through the doorway onto the wooden flooring within. It saved Stephen Danskin the trouble.

'Okay, if that's the way you'd like to play it, we'll get doon to business. The Saltwell Park case: why did you order the destruction of the file on the second missing girl?'

'This is really most tiresome, Danskin. I had nothing to do with any missing file, and you'll have a damn hard job proving otherwise.'

Haswell knew Danskin had no chance of proving it. So, why was the cop looking so cocky?

'Okay. Let's try another one. When did you know the body was that of Cheryl Moffat?'

Haswell blinked rapidly. Swallowed hard. Said nothing.

'Why did you not tell us your daughter had been murdered? I mean, it takes a pretty sad bastard to front that one up, don't you think?'

Still, the politician refused to speak.

'Are you going to let us in, or do we have this conversation on the doorstep?'

Haswell straightened as if a curtain pole had been shoved down his shirt.

'You mean, you're not taking me down the station? You can't be so sure of yourself after all, Detective Chief Inspector, can you?'

Danskin narrowed his eyes. 'Oh, I'm quite sure, don't you worry about that.'

A nerve twitched in Haswell's cheek. 'You can prove diddley-squat but, yes, it was Cheryl, and she is my daughter. Why do you think I was so interested in the case?'

Lyall Parker spoke up. 'So, you are human after all? I was beginning to wonder. If you want to see the killer locked up, you'd better start answering our questions.'

'Listen, Jock,' Haswell hissed, 'If you catch him, all well and good. But, not because of Cheryl. Her and her mother were just a drain on my resources. I never saw them so why should I care for them? No, I want him caught because of the election, that's why.'

Danskin couldn't believe what he was hearing. 'You're a bastard and a half, Haswell. You do realise we know, don't you? Know that the lass was only fourteen when you got her up the duff.'

Haswell smiled. 'Evidence? There is none. Cheryl's not around. I know she was cremated so there's no DNA. Her mother's disappeared off the face of the earth. Her father isn't named on her birth certificate. You've nothing but hearsay. Unless, of course, you are recording this conversation, which even you know is illegal.'

Danskin chewed on the inside of his mouth as Haswell continued. 'I have instructed Reuben Mayberry to prepare a case of defamation against you, just so you know. I thought you'd want to be aware before doing anything silly like charging me.'

The rain slanted down. Plastered Lyall Parker's hair to his forehead and ran slickly over the shaven scalp of Stephen Danskin.

'Have it your way,' Danskin said. He turned to leave. Sir Guy Haswell grinned like a Cheshire cat.

'You cannae walk away...' Lyall began.

Over his shoulder, Stephen asked, 'When's the election again?'

'Day after tomorrow,' Haswell replied, nonchalantly.

'Of course. Just in time for the papers to run a story on a child molesting member of the Government who withholds evidence in a murder enquiry and threatens senior members of the City and County police.'

'You wouldn't...'

'Good day, Sir Guy. I'm sure the PM shall have a very interesting conversation with you.'

Stephen Danskin pulled out his mobile and was already dialling his press contacts.

**

Sir Guy Haswell wasn't to know Danskin's call would go unanswered, but it did. It did because the call went to Molly Uzumba and she was otherwise engaged.

The frisson of excitement which ran through her when The Lighthouse Keeper finally deigned to call her surpassed anything she'd ever experienced in her life.

His words were brief, simple, and to the point. 'I am sorry for not replying sooner,' he'd said. 'I have been rather busy – but you know that already, don't you? I thought your article on me was excellent. Thank you for giving me a voice. It's rare

I find one who truly understands. I'd be delighted to tell you more.'

The Lighthouse Keeper terminated the call before she had an opportunity to speak.

Uzumba never really thought through the implications when, still naked from her bath, she dashed off her e-mail response.

'I'd be thrilled. Call me to arrange.'

The call never came. Instead, eventually, she received a message from him. Again, the number was withheld.

'Tomorrow. Six-thirty. Be alone if you want to hear my story. This is your moment, Molly Uzumba, but come alone. No photographers. Leave your phone in your car. You cannot record or photograph me. I shall be watching. If you're accompanied, you shall suffer. I can trust you, Molly, can't I?'

The tone was unmistakably threatening but it wasn't accompanied by an image. She read the message four times. There was no overt warning. It wasn't like the others. And, it would be broad daylight. There'd be others around. Wouldn't there?

She typed a single word: 'Where?'

The reply came back instantly, as if he had it already typed out.

'The lighthouse. Where else?'

**

Molly Uzumba parked up on the clifftop and walked across the causeway to St Mary's Island.

It was reassuringly busy. She sat on a bench. No-one approached her. She stood by the doorway to the phallic tower. People hustled on by. She waited outside the closed coffee shop. The only approach came from a middle-aged woman who told her, 'It's closed, pet.' Wherever she went, no-one followed.

She ambled to the easternmost point of the island, little more than exposed and barnacle-encrusted rocks. She looked out to sea. A grey curtain hung over the waters; a sure sign of a sea storm.

Molly turned to her right. Tynemouth had already disappeared beneath an invisibility cloak of cloud, mist, and rain. People were taking heed of the portents. They began leaving the island in their droves.

A trio of Labradors yelped excitedly in the frisky waters as their owner urged them to her. From a volcano-shaped rock twenty yards out to sea, a single seal basked like a fat slug. Soon, it would be the only thing left on St Mary's Island.

Molly Uzumba looked up at the lighthouse as the first smattering of rain fell. She'd been well and truly had. She trudged back along the causeway feeling foolish yet relieved – but, mostly, disappointed.

From inside the bird hide on the North car park, the man with the binoculars trained on the girl plodding along the causeway smiled.

'Good girl,' he said to himself. 'I knew I could trust you. Next time, my dear, I promise you, you'll hear the end of my story.'

CHAPTER THIRTY-FOUR

The lock-up lay in the shadow of Gateshead International Stadium, on a patch of semi-industrial wasteland just off Nelson Road. It seemed to be joined to a Screwfix depot, which led Ryan to miss it at first.

He drove around for a while, becoming lost in a maze of units which all appeared identical apart from having different signage, until he eventually located it.

He tried the key given to him by Lesley Moffat but the padlock wouldn't budge. There was a phone number on the side of the unit. He dialled it.

'Yup?' a voice said.

Ryan introduced himself. Explained what he wanted.

'Which unit?'

'What do you mean? The one I'm standing outside. Next to the Stadium.'

'Ah knaa that, man. But which one? There's twenty individual units inside the warehouse.'

That explained the failed entry. Cheryl Moffat didn't tell him he'd need to get inside the warehouse first.

'I don't know. Look, can someone let me in, please?'

'Give us half an hour.'

'Where the hell are you, like?'

'At home. In bed. I expect my customers to have their own keys.'

'Get here as soon as you can. This is urgent.'

While Ryan waited for the owner of the voice to get his act together, he checked in with Forth Street.

Todd Robson answered.

'Any developments?' Ryan asked.

'Not really. Ravi's doing some checks on the phones from some of our earlier suspects. Foreskin and Lyall are having a day oot doon the coast. Sue'll be getting it in the neck from Malcolm Grainger any minute now when she tells him he's spent a fortune cremating the wrong lass and she still doesn't have the foggiest where Terri is.'

'Have you a spare hour or so? I'm at a lock up in Gateshead. It's got Cheryl Moffat's gear in, but it's also got stuff belonging to her mother. I could do with a hand sifting through it.'

'Why aye. Even if we don't find anything to do with the killer, I'll be like a pig in shit if there's summat in there to nail that Tory nonce.'

Ryan gave Todd the co-ordinates and rang Hannah just because he could. He invited her over for a Chinese and suggested she bring enough things for a couple of nights. Hannah said she was already at her apartment and would pack a bag. She'd see him back in Whickham when he was done.

Todd and the warehouse owner arrived within minutes of each other. The owner – Charles Yorke - was a stocky guy in his mid-forties with shaven head and bushy beard.

'Jesus Christ. Are we in an episode of Storage Wars here?' Todd muttered.

Ryan laughed. Todd's observation was as sharp as ever. 'We'll soon find out.'

Once Yorke was satisfied with their ID, he unlocked the chain looped around the doorhandle and needed two further keys to open the door itself.

A series of naked bulbs hung on cords dangling from metal beams across the warehouse's roof. They sprang to life as Charles flicked a switch. It didn't make much difference. Inside remained dark, dank, and musty.

'Which one you after?'
'Sally Moffat's.'
'Which one's that?'
'You mean you don't know?'
'Nope.'

Ryan looked at the array of metal cages, each covered by a navy blue tarp. 'Guess it's trial and error, Todd.'

Charles Yorke stood vaping by the warehouse entrance while Ryan fiddled with each lock in turn. Fortune favoured him. The sixth lock yielded, and he and Todd entered Sally Moffat's den.

A mountain of cardboard boxes stood piled against one wall. There were a few items of furniture dumped in a corner, and several bin-liners stuffed full of clothes sat upon three sturdy crates in the centre.

'Where do we start?' Todd asked.

'That lot, there.' He indicated the cardboard mountain with a nod of his head.

'Right. Let's get cracking.'

An hour later, the best they'd come across was an old photograph album. It contained pictures of Sally Moffat through the ages. Her first day at school. Christmases with LeRoux's, friends' birthday parties. Then, three photographs of her as a young teenager in school uniform.

'Bastard,' Todd spat. Ryan knew what he meant.

Ryan turned the page. The series of photographs showed the same fresh-faced girl with a belly distended by different stages of pregnancy.

The next page showed her bloated, blotchy face gazing down on a new-born Cheryl cradled in her arms.

Ryan turned the page. It was blank. So was the next, and the one after that. It was as if Sally Moffat's life ended with Cheryl's birth.

'There's nowt here, Todd.'

'What did you expect? A picture of her and Haswell in the act? A giant poster with dartholes through the eyes? Something saying *Yoo-hoo: it's me. I'm a serial killer*? A collection of pubes snipped from his victims?'

'Aal reet, Todd. You've made your point, okay?'

'Listen. You take that stuff over there and I'll start on this lot.'

Ryan had Cheryl's belongings. Todd seemed to have Sally's bloke's. There wasn't much in any of them.

'What do we know about the fella?' Todd asked.

'Not much. In fact, nowt at all. He's called Keith.'

'Keith who?'

'Don't know. Lesley Moffat never met him. I got the impression Sally might have been round the block a couple of times. He as probably one of many.'

'Well, I think Keith Whatsisface might be a decorator.' Todd held up a white boiler suit splashed with red paint.'

Ryan sifted through Cheryl's belongings. 'No photographs here. Got a couple of bank statements but there's nothing to implicate Haswell.'

'Here's another fine mess you've gotten me into, Stanley.'

'Hmmm?' Ryan glanced up to see Todd with a bowler hat on his head.

Todd flung it towards Ryan like a frisbee.

'How, man. Give it a rest, Odd-Job,' Ryan laughed, and went back to Cheryl's horde.

He found a couple of soft toys and popped them into a bag. He'd drop them off for Lesley Moffat.

The coastal rain had made its way along the Tyne and hammered on the corrugated metal roof of the warehouse like a woodpecker on speed.

'Shit; listen to that, man.'

Ryan picked up an address book. It was amongst Cheryl's gear but it had *Sally Moffat* written across it.

'This could be useful,' he shouted to Todd above the deafening rattle from the roof.

'What is it?'

'An address book.' Ryan opened it at a random page. Flicked over a couple of leaves. Nothing. He went to the page headed 'H'. He didn't expect to see the name Haswell so he wasn't disappointed. He tried 'G' for Guy with a similar lack of success.

'Sally's bloke was a cricketer, if that helps.'

Ryan looked up. Todd wore a cricket box on his head.

'Yukk. That's gross. You don't know where it's been.'

'Oh fuck. I do. Good point.' Todd dropped it to the floor.

Ryan went to the beginning of the address book. A name caught his attention.

'Bloody hell.'

'You got summat, Ry?'

'Aye, I think. You'll never guess who's in here.'

'Gan on, then.'

'Remember the perv from Walkergate we interviewed about Chelsea Birch?'

Todd thought for a moment. 'The artist bloke?'

'The very same. Ahmed Nuri knew Sally Moffat.'

Todd's phone echoed shrilly in the confined space. 'What is it, Ravi?' he answered.

Ryan wasn't listening. How could Sally Moffat know Ahmed Nuri? Coincidence, or connection?

His thought processes were disrupted by Todd's voice.

'Looks like all the boys are back in town. That was Ravi. He's traced Ferdie Milburn.'

**

The Sun Wah Express turned out to be a contradiction in terms.

Thirty minutes after the allocated delivery time, Ryan and Hannah's meal still hadn't arrived. Once it did, they forgave and forgot.

Chinese wasn't Ryan's favourite cuisine but, by the time it landed, he could have eaten a scabby horse. Perhaps he was, but he didn't care – it tasted delicious, even if he feared the aromas would linger long in the new furnishings of his house.

He let Hannah select a movie from Netflix on the understanding it was his choice tomorrow. Seemed a good deal until she chose Dare to Dream.

'Seriously? Of all the movies in all the world, you choose one based on a self-help book.'

'Shut up and watch it. You can always just stare at Katie Holmes if you get bored.'

'I'm bored with it already and it hasn't even started yet.'

She whacked him over the head with a cushion.

'Howay, man. You'll get Hoi Sin all over me new soft furnishings.'

'Soft furnishings? Hark at Lawrence Llewellyn-Bowen here.'

'Who?'

'Never mind. So, I take it you're quite happy with my interior design skills now you've got used to it?'

'I suppose. Divvent push your luck, though.'

They settled down to watch the movie. At least, Hannah did. Ryan watched Katie Holmes. Within half an hour, they'd both turned to long snogs and cheap wine for entertainment.

They were in bed by nine-fifteen, but it wasn't like the movies because, an hour later, they were discussing the case.

'Imogen Markham's been spouting off again,' Hannah said.

'Stephen's in charge now, in the Super's absence. I'm not sure he'll take much notice of her.'

'No. Probably not,' Hannah agreed with a laugh.

'I know you want me to ask: what's she been saying?' He traced a finger around the curve of the dragon's tail tattooed on her midriff.

'Stop it,' she giggled. 'You know I can't concentrate when you do that.'

He ignored her and moved his hand upwards until it cupped her breast.

'Do you really want to know what she said?'

He licked her throat. 'Not really.'

'Well, just for that, I'm going to tell you. She said he's due to strike again. OUCH! Stop it!'

He released her nipple from between thumb and index finger while she slapped him gently between the legs.

'Get down, Shep.'

'Spoilsport,' he sulked.

'Anyway, as I was saying, Markham reckons we should prepare ourselves for another victim any day now.'

'Great. I hear Ravi's tracked down Ferdie Milburn? That should rule one suspect out.'

'Probably. Stephen wants an update from him first thing.'

Ryan shook his head. 'I still can't get over how you switch between calling him 'Sir, Guv, the DCI and Stephen', but never Dad.'

'I've hardly ever called him that, and neither of us could work together if anyone found out. Remember, you and I can't if one of us gets promoted, never mind me and…well, Stephen.'

'I know.'

'Oh, and he wants an impact analysis from you on the connection between Sally Moffat and Nuri, as well.'

'I knew he would. I'll be ready.'

Hannah propped herself up an elbow. 'And now, I'm going to take some measurements.'

'Remember to add an inch or two on, just to flatter my ego.'

She tossed back her head and laughed. 'I'm talking about the room size. I've got plans for it and need to know what I'm up against.'

She climbed out of bed and went in search of a tape measure.

'You're a funny one, Hannah Graves,' Ryan said to himself. 'I never know what you're going to do, or when you're going to do it.'

With that in mind, he reached into the bedside drawer and tucked his grandmother's ring into his jacket pocket.

'Can't be too careful.'

CHAPTER THIRTY-FIVE

Coffee. They had coffee!

They queued from the vending machine, through the bullpen, and out into the elevator lobby. The odd squabble broke out between Danskin and Kinnear's crew as if they were refugees jostling around a Red Crescent relief convoy.

'Wise move, Acting Superintendent,' Lyall Parker whispered.

'Well, I thought they'd appreciate it a bit more than a few extra whiteboard markers. And let's not get ahead of worse!' – the Commissioner's only asked me to man the fort for a couple of days 'til she can bring somebody else up to speed. As far as the lads are concerned, Connor's still just sick and the coffee's down to him.'

The squad congregated around the crime board, cups in hand. The mood was as upbeat as Danskin ever remembered. He opened the briefing by asking Ravi Sangar for an update on Ferdie Milburn's movements.

'I got a call from a big cheese in the Marine Maritime Agency. I'd asked them to contact me the minute they heard from Milburn, and this McCormack bloke told me they'd had word he'd be back 'soon.' When exactly that is, he didn't know.'

'Do we know where he is, now?' Danskin asked.

'No, sir. McCormack said all Milburn told them was that he'd had to take himself off for a few days. Too many people around for his liking in tourist season. Said he needed some solitude until he got his head around things.'

'What things, I wonder? Innocent young gingernuts? Sounds like he could be back in the frame.'

Nigel Trebilcock asked, 'What does the criminal psychologist make of it? She was dead sure it wouldn't be Milburn, so she was.'

'Markham's off the case,' was all Danskin said.

'How did Milburn let the MMA know? Did he e-mail them? Might trace him from there.'

'Negative, Lyall. A phone call, apparently. No way we'll trace it, before you ask,' Sangar replied.

'So, we have to hang around until he gets his shit together, basically. I'm not comfortable with that. O'Hara; I want you to check his background and identify places he might be.'

Stephen picked up a whiteboard marker and planted an asterisk either side of Ferdie Milburn's photograph before circling his name in red.

'Now, somebody else has crept out the woodwork.' The DCI rapped the butt of the marker pen against another photograph on the 'Suspect' side of the board. 'Jarrod, tell us about Ahmed Nuri.'

Ryan cleared his throat. 'Ahmed Nuri was the first suspect in the Chelsea Birch killing. He had an alibi which holds up. However, yesterday, Todd and I came across an address book belonging to the mother of Sir Guy Haswell's dead daughter. Nuri's in there. It's an old address, but it's him alright.'

'You've spoken to him?'

'Aye. He denied all knowledge of her at first. Said he didn't know any Sally Moffat.

'What was his reaction when you told him he was in her address book?' Danskin asked.

'Surprised. No, stunned, I think's a better description. In fairness to him, that's because he didn't know her as Moffat. He knew her as Sally LeRoux. Turns out he went to school with her. Says he never knew what happened to her. She was at school one day, then never came back.'

'Hang on. She'd kept his address all these years? Why?'

Ryan shrugged. 'Doubt we'll ever know unless we find Sally Moffat. I'm not sure we should read too much into it. I checked out a couple of other names in the book. She kept the addresses of four or five kids from her class, both male and female. They all back up Nuri's version of events. As far as anyone was concerned, she just left school without a word. She might have their addresses, but none have heard from her since she was fourteen.'

'Helluva coincidence, Jarrod.'

'I know, but it looks like that's all it is.'

Danskin checked his watch, and his empty cup.

'I don't know about you lot, but I could do with a top-up. I've got a couple of calls to make. You lot get on with your tasks. I'll be in my office if you need me.'

Danskin made sure he went to the room with his nameplate on, not Connor's. He still didn't want the others to know the Super wouldn't be back.

It would prompt too many questions he hadn't the heart to answer.

**

'Do you still want an interview with me?'

Molly Uzumba pondered over the question. After yesterday's let-down, she needed a pick-me-up and she guessed it would keep both her name and The Lighthouse Keeper in the spotlight.

'Why the sudden change of heart, Detective Chief Inspector?' Uzumba asked, treading warily.

'Let's just say I think we could be of mutual benefit to one another.'

'Okay. Where do we meet?'

'I'm not sure we've got time for that. Let's just do it now.'

'By phone? That's a bit risky on your account, isn't it?'

'Like I say, there's not much time. There are conditions, though.'

'*Here's the catch*,' she thought. 'I'm not sure I can agree to any conditions, Detective Chief Inspector.'

Danskin fought down the urge to strangle the woman. 'Do you want the fucking story or not?'

'Fire away,' she said, an obvious smile in her voice.

'One: this hasn't come from me. If anything appears which could link me to the story, you'll be charged with so much shit about your Lighthouse Keeper stories you won't know your snots from your toenail clippings.'

'I never reveal my sources, Detective Chief Inspector. You, of all people, should know that.'

'Okay. Second condition: you run the story in two parts. You print one tonight, the other runs continuously on the web tomorrow.'

'I don't have that sort of editorial control.'

'I'll say it again: do you want the fucking story or not?'

Molly Uzumba was delighted she'd agreed once he started talking. Her eyes widened as Sir Guy Haswell's secret was relayed to her in all its glorious deviancy.

'With the election due tomorrow, I'm as certain as I can be that my editor will be only too keen to run with it!' she told Stephen.

'He'd better.'

'What do you want in return?'

'Nothing I haven't already asked,' Danskin said. 'If The Lighthouse Keeper contacts you again, you WILL let me know.'

'What do you take me for?' the reporter replied. 'Of course.'

Not.

**

She put the call in to Dennis Cherry. 'Do you think we can run it, and on the terms my source demands?'

'Do fat dogs fart? If your source has evidence to back it up, we're not turning down a story like this. Not on the eve of the by-election, or any other time. Molly, if you were here, I'd kiss your feet. Or any other part of your anatomy you choose.'

Molly grimaced. 'Feet will do.'

'I want the copy within the hour. On top of your Lighthouse Keeper story, the nationals will be beside themselves knowing we've got this one as well! Sky News, ITN, Laura Kuensberg: they'll all be suicidal. Molly, this is mahoosive!'

As an afterthought, he added, 'Well done.'

**

She was in the final throes of completing part one of the Haswell expose, with fifteen minutes until deadline, when her phone rang.

She picked it up without checking and, in her rush to keep working, dispensed with her normal, professional introductions.

'What?' she snapped.

'Dear, oh dear. That's not very polite, is it?'

Something triggered deep within her. 'You're playing fucking games with me,' she said without thinking. 'I'm busy.'

She heard an intake of breath, like the fizz escaping from a lemonade bottle.

'Speaking of games, Molly dear, you are playing a dangerous one, speaking to me in those terms. Never mess with The Lighthouse Keeper.'

'Look, I'm sorry. I'm up to my eyes here. What do you want?'

'You. That's what I want.'

A shiver ran up her spine. She stopped what she was doing, deadline or no deadline.

'Oh, not in the sense you're thinking. I didn't mean to frighten you. At least, providing you're as good a girl as you were yesterday, I don't.'

Molly regulated her breathing while she checked through her social media profiles. She found no messages. Nothing from Jim Smith. 'You were there all along?'

A quiet chuckle crossed the airwaves. 'Yes, I was there. I watched you every step of the way. In fact, you walked right by me to get to your car.'

Every hair on Uzumba's body stood upright. 'You didn't approach me.'

'No, I didn't. I needed to know I could trust you. Now I know I can, I'm ready for you.'

She caught her breath. What did he mean by that? 'So?'
So? Is that the best I can come up with?

'So, let's try again. Tomorrow. Same place. Same arrangements. Alone. No-one may know. The island was rather busy when we were there, and I wouldn't want anyone to overhear us. We should make it later. Eight-thirty.'

Uzumba's head throbbed. 'Why should I trust you? You mightn't turn up again.'

'That's the whole point, Molly Uzumba. You can't trust me. That's why we both enjoy this so much, isn't it?'

The room began to spin around her. 'I've got to go.'

'No! You go when I say. Understand?'

'S...sorry. Yes, I understand.'

'Good. I would hate it if you were to miss the end of my story. You'd forever regret it. I shall see you tomorrow. You may go, now.'

**

Ryan and Hannah devoured every word of Molly Uzumba's article. It stopped short of the really juicy bits, but it was enough to throw the local TV news channels into a frenzy.

On the eve of a crucial by-election, a historic story about a prominent Government minister was always going to be newsworthy, especially when it involved internal party machinations with a bit of sex and scandal thrown in.

But, not half the nationwide scandal there would be when the story was brought up to date tomorrow, and the age of Sir Guy Haswell's consort was revealed.

Happy days.

The Lighthouse Keeper

Hannah lay stretched out on the sofa, her head resting in Ryan's lap as he poured her a glass of wine with one hand and fiddled with the TV remote in the other.

'Showtime,' he said as the opening titles rolled.

'What you chosen?' she asked.

'I thought we'd go retro tonight. It was one of me grandad's favourite movies. Quite cutting edge at the time, apparently.'

'Divvent tell us it's black and white, man. You've got a nerve after last night, if it is.'

'Nah, man. It's not that retro. Seventies, I think.'

In less than twenty minutes, Hannah knew it wasn't for her.

'This is crap. What's it called, again?'

'A Clockwork Orange.'

'Do we have to watch it?'

'Give it a bit longer, should we?'

Hannah gave it until Malcolm McDowell and his Droog mates began cutting through Adrienne Corri's red catsuit.

'I'm going to bed. This is horrible.'

Ryan stroked Hannah's curls. 'I know. That catsuit clashes with her ginger hair summat awful.'

Hannah didn't laugh. 'Are you coming to bed or not?'

'Nah. You get yersel up. I won't be long. I'll just watch this a bit longer.'

A bit longer turned out to be another hour. In a corner of his mind, a thought lurked like a bat in a darkened cave. He tried to tease it out but it stubbornly refused to budge.

Ryan's attention waned. As a man on screen picked up a copy of The Daily Mail with the headline, *'Murderer Freed: Science has cure'*, Ryan's hand scrabbled for The Mercury they'd discarded on the floor.

He re-read Molly Uzumba's piece, scanned the back page, and was about to head upstairs, when the soundtrack music hit him like a two-ton truck.

Colin Youngman

'I dream of living in a lighthouse, baby
Every single day
I dream of living in a lighthouse
A white one by the bay.
I want to marry a lighthouse keeper.
And polish his lamp by day.'

CHAPTER THIRTY-SIX

Ryan woke early. It wasn't a surprise: he'd hardly slept a wink all night.

He'd tossed and turned, his mind racing, as his thoughts repeated in a continuous loop. He did his best to determine whether he was seeing what he wanted to see, but he remained unconvinced.

When Hannah elbowed him in the ribs for the sixth time and rolled to the edge of the bed, he crawled downstairs and decided to watch it again.

Hannah found him lying on the sofa in nothing but a pair of boxer shorts. She had a sheet draped around her shoulders like a toga.

'You're not watching that rubbish again, are you? Once was more than enough.'

'Watch for a bit.'

'Must I?'

'Yes, you must.' He pointed the remote at the screen and unpaused the movie.

Erika Eigen began singing her little ditty again. '*I wanna marry a lighthouse keeper.*'

'And?' Hannah asked.

'I wanted to be sure.'

'Sure of what?'

He groaned like a dog's snore. 'I'm not sure.'

She wrestled the control from him and switched to the breakfast news.

The screen showed a middle-aged man with a blanket over his head being smuggled into a limo. Scores of paparazzi mobbed the car. Two fell to the ground and rolled away from the vehicle's tyres just in time as the chauffer sped away.

The picture changed to library footage of a man raising a query at PM's Questions. Those around him slapped their thighs and waved rolled up papers. It was easy to lip-read the ribald chorus of 'Here, here's'.

Another shot of the same man followed. It was archive footage from inside Downing Street and showed the man shaking hands with Metropolitan Police Commissioner, Cressida Dick. Also in shot was the Minister of State for Families and Children.

Finally, and most damning of all, old footage of a Conservative party gala day with a young-looking Sir Guy Haswell posed with his arm draped around the shoulder of a teenage girl with pixelated face.

'One-nil!' Ryan said, punching the air.

In the studio, a man with coiffured hair held a newspaper to the camera.

'Government Minister fathers child to underage girl,' the headline screamed.

'Two goals in a minute', Ryan said.

Finally, across the foot of the screen, the newsreel banner read:

'BREAKING NEWS: PM sacks Justice Minister on day of Hadrian and Tynedale by-election.'

A second headline followed: 'Police investigate allegations of historic sexual abuse.'

'Yes, yes, YES,' Hannah squealed, Meg Ryan-like. The two young detectives hugged each other.

'I feel it in me bones,' Ryan said. 'Today's going to be a good day.' He pulled on a pair of pants, donned an unironed shirt, and shrugged his jacket over his shoulders.

'Now, I just need to find a serial killer.'

**

Rush-hour traffic on the A1 was always a bugger from as far back as Kingston Park right up to The Angel. Ryan only had to endure it for a fraction of the distance, but he'd been on

The Lighthouse Keeper

the road almost half an hour and was still to reach the Team Valley, barely four miles from The Drive.

The fact the A1 was down to two lanes as workmen tossed a stream of traffic cones onto the carriageway in preparation for yet more roadworks made the situation worse.

'You know what it is; starting this in rush hour is madness,' he said to himself.

All around him, folk with knackers for brains picked up their phones and began tweeting about the council's lack of forward planning, while others texted their bosses, wives, loved ones or all three, to let them know they'd be late. If he'd been uniform, Ryan could have doled out his monthly quota of tickets in quarter of an hour.

Instead, he settled for calling Todd Robson - hands-free, of course. In the background, Ryan heard laughter, Stephen Danskin talking animatedly; even the normally quietly-spoken Lyall Parker's voice carried over the speaker.

'Sounds like quite a party down there,' Ryan commented.

'Aye, you're missing oot, bonny lad. Foreskin's even stuck some posh coffee in the machine today. Caramel macchiato or summat.'

Ryan chuckled as Todd continued. 'Mind, Haswell's posh solicitor gadgee's trying his best to put a dampener on things but the DCI's not having any of it.'

'He doesn't need to, Todd. The press coverage is doing it all for him.'

'What time you joining the party?'

'I'll be a while yet.'

'Owt I can help with?'

The traffic crawled forward a few yards. A hazy sun, pale and low, hung in the sky like a melon ball. Drivers flicked down their sun visors or donned shades.

'That's why I'm ringing.' He paused, unsure where to start. 'I'm on my way to Mount Pleasant to see Lesley Moffat.'

'Again? You're not shagging her, are you? She's more GILF than MILF, I reckon.'

Ryan laughed out loud. 'No, man. Listen, you remember you said you thought Sally Moffat's bloke was a decorator, yeah? The boiler suit with paint on?'

'Aye.'

'How sure are you it was paint?'

'I didn't really inspect it, to be honest.'

'Right.' Ryan almost cheered out loud as he actually managed to get up to second gear. 'Could it have been blood?'

Ryan heard Todd tell the boisterous crowd behind him to shut their gobs. 'You onto something, mate?'

'It's going to sound daft, but I might be; aye.'

'Howay, man. Get it out.'

He took a deep breath. 'Have you ever seen a film called A Clockwork Orange?'

'Why aye. It was on the box last night.'

'Good.' He took care not to plant any ideas into Todd's head. 'The main character, Alex, and his mates. Think about them.'

'The Droogs? What about…' He stopped mid-sentence. 'Shit the bed, man.'

'You're with me? Bowler hats, boiler suits, codpieces like cricket boxes?'

'The stuff in the lockup.'

'Exactly.'

Ryan could almost hear the cogs creak and grind inside Todd's brain.

'I see the connection, but not where you're going with it, Ry.'

Ryan took in air. 'What if Cheryl Moffat wasn't the only victim in the family? What if Sally Moffat was first?'

The silence was palpable as Ryan concluded, 'What if she was first because she wanted to marry a Lighthouse Keeper?'

**

The Lighthouse Keeper

'Oh. You again,' Lesley Moffat said after winning a battle with the door.

'Yeah. I've got a couple of Cheryl's things I thought you might like.'

'You'd better come in.'

Even by Lesley's standards, the house was a disgrace. Three mugs sat on the coffee table, their clay cold contents at various levels of sludge. The wrappings of a fish and chip supper lay shredded across the floor where the dogs had feasted on it, and an empty wine glass stood perched on the arm of a chair.

Ryan zipped open his bag and removed a stuffed elephant and bright pink knitted sheep. 'I wasn't sure what to bring.'

Lesley stared at them with dead eyes. 'Ta.'

'How are you?'

'Aal reet, I suppose. Hasn't sunk in yet.'

Ryan inhaled noisily. 'Look, there's no easy way of saying this. I'm afraid Cheryl's already been interred. I'm terribly sorry. There was a case of mistaken identity. We originally believed Cheryl was someone else and so, it seems, did the other girl's parents.'

Ryan saw a glimmer of hope in her eyes. 'No. It was definitely Cheryl.'

Lesley Moffat made a noise, halfway between a snort and a laugh. 'At least I divvent have to fork out for the funeral. Although I guess the MP would have done that. I saw it on the news. It was him, wasn't it? Cheryl's dad?'

'I can't comment, Mrs Moffat.'

'Aye, I know you can't, son.'

Ryan passed across one of the photographs he'd come across in the lock-up. The one of Sally on a maternity ward bed, Cheryl in her arms. 'I thought this might remind you of both of them.'

She put it next to the wine glass without glancing at it.

'Mrs Moffat. Lesley. Is there anything you can tell me about Sally's partner?'

'Keith? Nah; nowt, really. Why like?'

Ryan didn't answer. Instead, he asked another question. 'Do you think Sally may have been unfaithful?'

A puzzled expression twisted her face. 'I thought this was aboot Cheryl, not Sally.'

'Where do you think Sally may be?'

Lesley Moffat clutched the pink sheep to her breast. 'I divvent care. I know she had a tough time of it, God; I really do. But, she was a handful. To answer your questions, son, she could be anywhere and, aye, she could've put it aboot a bit.'

Ryan reached down and stroked one of the dogs who'd curled up alongside him. 'This Keith: do you know if he was the jealous type? Was he ever violent towards Sally?'

'Looker, I don't know owt. Seriously, they've both been away for yonks, man.'

Ryan stood. The dog leapt up and took his place on the sofa. 'I may need to speak to you about Sally again some time.' He didn't want to worry her unnecessarily. Not until he knew for certain. 'If you do think of anything, give me a call, yeah?'

'Aye, I will.'

'Look after yourself, Lesley. I'll ask one of my Family Support colleagues to check in on you.'

The woman sniffed. 'Family? What bleedin' family's that, like?'

**

Ryan's phone rang even before he'd fastened his seat belt. He'd left his mobile in its holder, stuck to the windscreen by a suction cup, while chatting with Lesley Moffat. It showed three missed calls. Shit.

'What's up, Todd?'

'Where've you been, man? Foreskin's been trying to get hold of you.'

'You know where I've been. Lesley Moffat.'

The Lighthouse Keeper

'Oh aye. Get your arse back to Forth Street. The guvnor's got something to share but he wants everyone to hear it.'

'I already know.'

'How come, like?'

'Long story but let's just say I've seen the Super's letter.'

'What's Connor got to do with it?'

Ryan saw his windscreen fog over with body heat as the blush hit his face. Robson didn't know. He'd just put his foot in it.

'You'll find out. Just don't say owt, please, and I'll be there as soon as I can.'

'Don't worry. We're waiting for Lyall as well.'

'He already knows.'

'Knows what, man?'

'Never mind. Just keep quiet for now.'

He took a deep breath. No harm done, he supposed. They'd all learn of Connor's resignation soon enough. There was no need to beat himself up about his mistake.

The first thing he did back at the station was treat himself to a coffee. The posh stuff had long since gone, but a good, honest latte hit the spot. He took a sip and joined the rest of the team clustered in the breakout area.

Ryan dug into his pocket for a tenner in readiness for the Super's collection.

'Just waiting for Lyall now then I'll say what I've got to say, and we can get on with things.'

Parker hurriedly joined them. 'Sorry I'm late, sir. Traffic's awful again.'

'Ravi – over to you,' Danskin said.

Ravi? What's he got to do with it? Ryan thought.

'A quick update. I've had McCormack on from the MMA. He's had word from Ferdie Milburn. Apparently, he's been holed out on one of the Farne Islands. Just him and a few kittiwakes and fulmars and a few tons of guano. He told McCormack there's nothing to keep him there now the last of the puffins have gone so he's ready to return.'

'Nice work if you can get it, coming and going like that,' the DCI commented.

'McCormack's not best pleased. Told him if he wasn't back by tomorrow, he could stay where he was.'

'And?'

'Milburn said he was tempted but he'd checked the tides and would be back by eight tonight.'

Danskin turned to Parker. 'He's your mate, Lyall. Go and meet him.'

'Och, come on, sir. If the tide's wrong, I cannae spend another night on there wi' him. I'll go nuts. Unless you've good reason to believe he really is The Lighthouse Keeper, it'll wait, surely. I'd prefer to watch the news coverage of Haswell, if I'm honest.'

'For the eighth time,' Ravi said.

'Aye. And it's still no' enough. Besides, I cannae wait to see the Tories get stuffed in the vote because of him.'

Stephen Danskin considered it. 'I guess Milburn's not going to harm anyone at that time of night even if it is him. There'll be nobody on the island, and he's hardly likely to advertise the fact he's back if he was planning an attack.'

'Sir, I don't mind going.'

'Thanks, Jarrod, but Lyall's right. It'll keep.'

'We've had no alerts from the Communications Centre, have we?' Ryan asked.

'No. Another reason for it not to be urgent.'

'All the same, I'll do it. Listen, I don't think Milburn's The Lighthouse Keeper, but I'm certain he's tied up in it, somewhere along the line.'

Danskin's brow furrowed. 'You're up to summat, Jarrod, aren't you?'

Ryan tried to force a natural laugh, but it came out false and exaggerated. He didn't want to share his theory that, rather than Milburn be The Lighthouse Keeper, The Lighthouse Keeper might want him.

'Let me talk to him first,' Ryan said. 'There's a logic behind my train of thought, but I don't want to see what I expect to see.'

They were the magic words for Stephen Danskin. 'That's good enough for me, Jarrod.'

'Sir, I'll go with him.'

Ryan shook his head. 'Not necessary, Todd.'

'Are you sure?' Todd knew the stakes.

'You heard him, Robson. If it's not necessary, I'm not paying you overtime.'

Stephen Danskin brought the meeting to a conclusion by saying, 'I've got to recover the cost of the coffee somehow.'

CHAPTER THIRTY-SEVEN

Molly Uzumba arrived early. Unaccompanied, of course, apart from a face taught with tension.

The island was busy when she arrived but, as the tide inched across the causeway, her company evaporated.

By the time the water was knee-deep, she was alone. Alone, except for the birds, the seals, and The Lighthouse Keeper.

This wasn't like yesterday. She felt it in her bones. He was here, somewhere. She sensed his presence. Wanted to run but running was impossible. She'd have to swim.

Every ounce of her being told her this was wrong. She pulled out her phone. Checked her twitter feed, her e-mails, Facebook, and Instagram accounts. She checked everything she could, but Molly Uzumba found nothing out of place.

Apart from the cold steel of the barrel pressed into her ribcage.

'Hello, Molly.'

His voice was little more than a whisper, his breath warm and hostile against her cheek.

She whimpered. Swallowed hard.

'Don't be afraid. You're about to hear something very few have born witness to. You are so fortunate, Molly Uzumba. Oh, and please don't worry. I have no wish to harm you.'

She closed her eyes and sighed in relief.

'But I may have to. Let's keep our options open, shall we?'

He grabbed her wrist.

'You wanted my story and you shall have it, one way or another.'

The barrel of his gun forced her forwards. Forwards to the lighthouse itself.

**

The Lighthouse Keeper

Ryan battled against thigh-high water. A strengthening wind had whipped the tide across the causeway at a rare angle. Five minutes after he set foot on St Mary's Island, the causeway became impassable.

Ahead of him, the white tower of the lighthouse rose from the rock like a stalagmite. By its side, Ferdie Milburn's cottage stood abandoned. No sound came from it, no lights showed within it. It was as deserted as the island itself.

There should have been daylight but a heavy mass of cloud brought darkness. There should have been a gentle tide, but the elements brought a rushing cascade. And there should have been life, but nothing stirred. Even the gulls fell silent.

Ryan shivered. Buttoned up his jacket and thrust his hands in his pockets. Milburn hadn't turned up, and he was stuck on a godforsaken lump of rock until the tide turned.

He trudged towards Milburn's cottage, icy seawater squelching from his shoes and dripping from his trousers. At least he'd find warmth and shelter inside. He picked up a rock, drew back his arm, and prepared to throw it at the window when he heard it.

At least, he thought he had.

Was it a voice? He listened intently.

Ryan heard nothing but the snore of the tide.

He brought back his arm once more.

Another sound, almost metallic.

It came from high above him.

Ryan stared into the gathering gloom. There, he saw him.

Ferdie Milburn stood with his back against the gallery rail which circled the lantern room.

Ferdie Milburn was there after all. And he wasn't alone.

**

The lighthouse door stood before him, a tiny portal to a mammoth edifice. Ryan tried the handle. It turned. The door swung open of its own volition.

This was the moment where, in every slasher movie he'd ever watched, he yelled, *'Don't go inside!'* at the screen.

And, like every slasher movie he'd ever watched, he went in.

He found himself in an entrance lobby and looked up towards the dizzying centre of the lighthouse.

Ryan saw the decay of a building weathered by an unforgiving North Sea. The remnants of faint and fading daylight slanted through small windows casting eerie spotlights on the paint-peeled walls.

Those same windows - wood-framed and ajar – allowed a ghostly cascade of noise to penetrate. The swell of the ocean, the occasional shrill cries of seabirds, and a whispering wind masked the echo of his own footsteps as he inched his way up the tightly-winding stone staircase.

Ferdie Milburn didn't concern him. His mystery companion did.

At every turn, he hugged the wall and listened intently before edging around the bend. The ascent was gradual to begin with, but it soon steepened.

Ryan knew there were one-hundred and thirty-seven steps. He counted them as he climbed, partly so he knew how close to the summit he was, mainly to keep his mind off what waited.

By step forty-two, his legs felt heavy with tension and effort. By step sixty-five, his breathing became laboured. The battle to remain silent was infinitely harder than he imagined.

At step ninety-five, Ryan paused for recovery. While he waited, he gathered his thoughts.

He knew Ferdie Milburn was on the gallery. He knew he wasn't alone. He was as sure as he could be that Milburn wasn't The Lighthouse Keeper, ergo the person on the gallery with him was the killer.

Ryan pressed pause on his thoughts. It made the rampant beat of his heart more evident. He regulated his breathing.

The Lighthouse Keeper

Brought his pulse rate down. Once he'd regained control of his body, he risked a glance upwards.

The narrow staircase spiraled towards a small door. He had an unobstructed view up to it. The staircase was clear. Milburn and the killer remained outside on the gallery, one-hundred and twenty feet above razor-sharp rocks and a thrashing tide.

Ryan's thoughts turned to the one known as The Lighthouse Keeper. Ryan was confident he'd worked it out. He knew who the man was.

The killer's name was Keith. He was the ex-lover of Sally Moffat. And now he was here, intent on wreaking revenge on the one she intended to marry.

The Lighthouse Keeper stalked the lighthouse keeper.

Imogen Markham had been right: the killer was a man with a violent past. The memorabilia from A Clockwork Orange confirmed it.

Sally Moffat had red-hair – the link to the other victims – but why murder innocent women? They hadn't cuckolded him. The mystery remained.

Apart, of course, from the fact he was a psychopath.

Which made him more dangerous.

Ryan thought of the other victims. January Hope. Dorothy Jackson. Jasmine Peters. Chelsea Birch. And Sally Moffat's daughter, Cheryl.

Time to move on. Ryan shifted his weight and started to climb once more. As he did so, he stopped dead; perfectly still, totally exposed, in the centre of the staircase.

He couldn't help it.

He'd been struck immobile by the realization he knew The Lighthouse Keeper.

They'd already interviewed him.

**

Todd Robson pulled into the Southern car park alongside Ryan's Fiat. The car park stood cold and lonely; a Billy-no-mates car park. Only four bays out of one hundred and fifty were occupied.

'Are you sure about this, Todd?' Hannah Graves asked. 'I mean, do we need backup?'

'If I was sure, we'd have more backup than the OJ Simpson chase. All I know is Ryan's pretty sure The Lighthouse Keeper isn't Ferdie Milburn.'

'So, why the rush? He'll be okay in that case, won't he?'

Todd pulled out a pair of binoculars. Trained them on the island. 'Aye. As long as the real killer doesn't get there first. He reckons The Lighthouse Keeper's after Milburn's guts.'

'Why'd he murder all those girls if who he's really after is a bloke?'

Todd's bins roamed the island. ''Cos Milburn nicked his lass. That's why he wants him. Why the girls? Who knows? Because he's a fucking loon, I suppose.'

'Do you see owt?'

'No sign of life.' He winced as he said it. 'Can't see anybody,' he corrected.

If he'd raised his binoculars to the tip of the lighthouse, he'd have seen enough to warrant backup. Instead, he focused on the island itself.

'Hannah, I reckon I should get over there, just in case.'

She started down the winding clifftop path. 'Not without me, you're not.'

'Had on,' he said. 'You've forgotten summat.'

'What?'

'We need a boat first. Tide's in.'

**

Ryan had to call it in. He should have done it as soon as he saw two figures on the gallery. He'd been caught up in the moment.

He reached into an inside pocket of his jacket. The object he touched puzzled him. It wasn't his phone. He realised what it was. Had forgotten he'd put it there. Ryan fished his mobile out the other pocket.

The Lighthouse Keeper

'Shit.'

No signal from within the solid concrete confines of the lighthouse tower.

He was on his own.

Ryan risked another peek around the final bend. He had an unobstructed view of the climb to a thick white door at the head of the staircase.

He did a quick calculation. Forty-two stairs to mount. Fifteen seconds, maximum. He made a bolt for it and reached the door in ten.

Ryan ducked low. Reached up for the handle. Quietly, slowly, he turned it. The door eased open an inch.

Where he should have heard the roar of the ocean and the howl of the wind, he heard neither.

He'd got to the door in ten seconds, rather than fifteen, because this wasn't the top.

Ryan put his eye to the crack in the door. He was looking into a circular room. An antechamber. The walls were covered in nautical charts, and display cabinets containing sextants and compasses and other nautical memorabilia.

A thick wooden table lay against one wall. Sandwiched between its wooden surface and a glass covering, maps and old newspaper cuttings told the story of shipwrecks through the ages. An old, upright metal storage unit stood next to it.

The room didn't contain Ferdie Milburn or The Lighthouse Keeper. Ryan crept in, keeping low.

Ahead of him lay the final dozen or so steps, more akin to a ladder, which arched towards the exterior door, behind which lay nothing but sky above, sea below, and fate somewhere between.

Ryan was on the third step when the door of the storage cupboard rattled open. Ryan half-turned at the same moment as the thick, knotted hawser rope looped around his throat like a noose.

The Lighthouse Keeper hauled it tight until the world of Ryan Jarrod spun into a black hole.

CHAPTER THIRTY-EIGHT

'Christ, that Grace Darling lass must've been built like Dolph Lundgren.'

Todd hauled on the oars and the ancient boat moved forward two lengths and was washed back three.

Foamed spray flecked the deck, and drenched Todd. The wind caught Hannah's curls. Her eyes teared as the wind pulled her head backwards.

'How much longer?'

'God knows. It's nee distance, really, but we're still against the tide.' Todd groaned with the effort as he lugged the oars through a broiling sea. 'Not long, I hope.'

Hannah's eyes fixed on the island. 'Still no sign of anybody, Todd.' She had to shout to make herself heard even though Todd sat only a couple of feet from her.

'That's good.'

'I don't think it is. Ry should be there, somewhere. And Milburn. It's dark now. Why's there no lights in the cottage?'

'I divvent knaa, man. Is there leccy on the island?'

'It's not the middle of the Atlantic, Todd, man. It's less than half a mile offshore. Course there's electric.'

Todd groaned again. Hannah cupped her hands and scooped out water from the floor of the boat. It was useless, of course, but she had to do something.

'I don't care what you think, we need to call this in.'

Todd downed oars. 'You mean, you haven't already?'

'No. You told me not to, remember?'

He growled as he pulled on the oars once more.

Two-hundred metres to go.

**

Ryan was vaguely aware that the noose around his neck had been loosened. He gasped for air but took in little. His

The Lighthouse Keeper

windpipe remained constricted by the pressure it had been under.

He felt the rope knot around his waist instead and, as if in a dream, imagined himself floating upwards, arms and legs hanging downwards like pipe cleaners.

It was only when The Lighthouse Keeper opened the external door and Ryan became engulfed in a torrent of cold air, he made sense of what was happening.

He was being hauled up towards the exit.

Ryan felt his head, his arms, his legs batter against the doorframe as The Lighthouse Keeper dragged him through the narrow gap onto the gallery.

The gallery began to rotate like a carousel. Ryan's vision swam. Blackness again threatened his consciousness. His eyelids fluttered.

Until they snapped wide open at the words of The Lighthouse Keeper.

'It's time you heard how my story ends,' Ahmed Nuri said.

**

They abandoned the rowing boat the second it crashed against the outermost ridge of St Mary's Island.

Hannah and Todd triple-jumped from rock to rock. Hannah slipped on the algae rich surface. Todd hauled her to feet and dragged her ashore, her feet scrabbling for purchase.

'What now?' She rubbed her scraped and bleeding knees and elbows.

'I thought we'd do a bit of nude sunbathing. What the hell do you think we do? You call Foreskin, I find Ryan.'

Todd hunched as he sprinted towards the cottage and Hannah brought her phone to her ear.

The dense cloud overhead parted fleetingly. The moon made its first appearance of the night, shining like a spotlight on the lighthouse tower. It attracted Hannah's eye. Drew her gaze upwards.

She saw the four figures atop the gallery. Her phone slipped from her fingers and splashed into a rockpool.

'Toddd!'

**

'Mother left me outside the Social Services office, the bitch. 'It won't be long. I love you, son,' *she lied. She never came back for me.*

Two weeks later, I worked out where she was. Uncle Jed had an allotment. A glorified shed, really. They sometimes left me outside. 'Water Uncle Jed's plants for him,' *she'd tell me, while they locked the door and did whatever they did.*

And that's where I found her, two weeks after she died, with Uncle Jed's gun next to her. Her pale, white flesh had gained some colour; a sort of blackened purple which made her more beautiful than the ugly witch had been in life.

Only one thing remained as it always had: her carrot coloured hair.

I swatted away the flies and picked up Uncle Jed's gun. Weighed it in my hands. That's when I realised mother wasn't the only one to blame. None of it would have happened without Uncle Jed.

So, I took the gun with me. It was something to remind me; something to ensure I never forgot either of them, or how they treated me.

I always wondered if the gun would ever serve any other purpose. Well, now I know the answer.

I promised you my story, Molly Uzumba, and you have it. You all have.

I wanted you all to hear it. I thought it might help you understand. I hope it has.'

He raised the barrel of the gun and released the safety catch.

**

'Wait!' Ryan yelled. 'This isn't the way you do things. You need your routine. You need your message. What satisfaction will you get from doing it this way?'

The Lighthouse Keeper

Nuri's gun swung away from Ferdie Milburn, bound and gagged to the gallery rail, and rested on Ryan.

Nuri smiled. 'Thank you. I'm grateful to you. If you hadn't spoken, I'd have pulled the trigger by now. There'd be no enjoyment in acting so swiftly.'

Nuri sniffed the air. 'Can you smell it? His fear? Ah, I could drag this moment out forever.'

Ryan's thoughts raced like a Formula One car. Beneath him, the island unfolded like a Google earth image, so tiny, so far away, yet the sound of the waves crashing against the rocks seemed so close.

Molly Uzumba sobbed alongside him. Fear convulsed her entire body. She felt urine gush down her thighs, gather in a pool at her feet.

Ahmed Nuri laughed. 'Oh dear, Molly. I wonder if you'll incorporate that into your story?'

The gun returned to Milburn, its barrel inches from the man's chest.

'You don't kill men,' Ryan shouted. 'It's not what you do.'

Again, the weapon swung away from its target.

'Tell me', Nuri said. 'When did you know it was me? Was it the address book?'

Ryan shook his head. 'No. You weren't the only schoolfriend in her book. Your story stacked up. It was the gear in the lock-up. The Clockwork Orange stuff. A colleague said you'd have had a troubled upbringing. You'd have had violence inflicted on you. She said it would have affected you, deeply.'

He was buying time now. Hoping against hope Todd Robson might disobey Danskin's instruction and arrive over the clifftop with the cavalry.

'Still doesn't explain how you knew it was me. I'm intrigued.'

'The memorabilia reflected a taste for violence. And, your boiler suit was cloaked in red paint.'

Nuri barked out a laugh. 'At least you didn't think it was blood. Did you? Oh, come on – tell me you didn't?'

'No, I knew it was paint.'

'And you knew the paint belonged to me, how?'

Ryan needed to spin the story out but wasn't in a position to refuse to answer a direct question.

'We knew you were an artist, remember. I'd seen your work. When I spoke to Sally's guardian, we were looking for a man called Keith. Not fifteen minutes ago, it dawned on me. Lesley Moffat's speech affliction meant she wasn't calling you Keith at all. She was saying 'Keif'.'

'And that led you to me how, exactly?'

'The mural on your apartment wall when I interviewed you over Chelsea Birch. It was signed '*Keifer*'. That's your pseudonym, isn't it?'

'Bravo. If I didn't have this thing in my hands, I'd applaud you.' Nuri waved the gun in the air.

'Can I ask you something?' Ryan asked quietly. 'I know you killed Chelsea Birch. I know she shared your 'interest', shall we call it? That's how you met. But how did you manage your alibi? Dozens of people confirmed you were on-line, as you claimed to be.'

Nuri laughed again. 'Simple. I WAS online. I asked a couple of questions early on, just so people knew I was there. Then, again at the end. In between, well, I just stayed logged on. Have you ever held a zoom seminar with hundreds of people? If you remain quiet, the camera won't pick up the fact you're not there. Not everyone's feed can appear on the screen. There isn't room. I simply stayed quiet, stayed logged in, and went to kill Chelsea Birch.'

Ryan had to hand it to him, he was good.

'Why kill them? Why play games with them?'

'Because I could. Why else? With Chelsea, it was easy. She'd rebuffed me. I asked her out, and she didn't reply. I didn't like that. I give the orders to others. She knew me, so she easy.'

'Why the messages?'

'Again, Chelsea was accidental. I just happened to send her an anonymous message and it struck me I could do it again. Simples.'

'And Cheryl?'

His face twisted. 'Because I didn't like her. I sent the message to her to wind her up. She made the mistake of responding. I wasn't having that. She had to go.'

Ryan sensed Nuri got pleasure from talking about his exploits. He pressed on.

'The others?'

'Because they looked like Mother. Prettier, most of them, but they all had that goddamn awful coloured hair.'

Ryan glanced inland. The lights of passing vehicles raced by like gloworms but none veered towards the car park. The cavalry weren't coming.

'Tell me about Ferdie Milburn.'

Milburn's eyes widened and he made muffled noises beneath his gag.

Nuri's lips curled in a sneer. 'I loved one woman. Sally Moffat, or LeRoux as I first knew her. There'd never be another like her. She understood pain. She understood suffering. We'd both experienced it, Alone, and together.'

'Tell me what happened.'

Milburn shook his head, frantically.

'Ah yes. We're coming to the juicy bit, Molly. Are you taking notes?'

Molly cowered away.

'It seems I wasn't enough for her. I'd treated her to a day out up the coast. Turns out, behind my back, she made plans with the skipper of the tosspot of a boat we were on. How brazen was that? Right in front of my eyes. Trouble is, I found out.'

'How?'

'Social media. That's why I like it SOOO much.'

'And then what?'

'I found out the toerag also attended the beacons on Amble Marina harbour. When Sally and I watched the film, and she began singing that horrid song about marrying a lighthouse keeper, I killed her, and vowed to kill him, too.'

He waved the gun in Milburn's face. 'I mean, look at him. He must be twenty years older. Perhaps that's what attracted her to him. She went for those types, you know, Haswell and all.'

The cliffs above St Mary's Island remained deserted. Ryan knew there was no hope for any of them.

'They say fortune smiles on the brave. Well, it certainly smiled on me,' Nuri continued. 'On a wet day, I was sitting on a bench outside The Fat Ox. Lo and behold, who should sit next to me but good old Ferdinand Milburn. That's when I knew the moment was close. This moment. Except, he recognised me, too, and the snivelling wretch buggered off, but I knew he'd be back.'

He buried the gun beneath Milburn's chin.

'And now, this is my moment.'

**

'Toddd!' Hannah screamed from below.

Nuri took his eyes from Milburn. Looked down towards the source of the cry.

Ryan had one chance, and this was it. He had no weapon. Only what was in his pockets. His hand shot inside his jacket. Reached for his phone. Prepared to hurl at Nuri.

It was the wrong pocket.

His fingers curled around another object, its ridged and sharp edges biting his fingertips.

As Nuri turned back towards them, Doris Jarrod's old engagement ring hit him smack between the eyes and rebounded to Ryan's feet.

The Lighthouse Keeper rocked unsteadily on his feet as he swung the gun round in a wide arc.

Three wild, rapid-fire shots rang out.

The Lighthouse Keeper

Hannah gasped at the sound. Through a swirling cloud of startled and screeching seabirds, Hannah saw a figure somersault from the gallery towards the rocks below.

'Noooo!'

Todd dashed from the cottage. Looked towards Hannah. Followed her line of vision, and sprinted towards the lighthouse.

**

It seemed to take forever. Finally, after a lifetime of waiting, Hannah saw the door of St Mary's lighthouse opened.

Todd emerged, grim-faced.

Hannah wept.

The door opened again.

Ryan emerged, bloodied; an arm hanging limply by his side.

Hannah began breathing again. She sprinted to him. Hurled herself at him.

'I thought you'd gone.'

'You divvent get rid of me that easily. It's just me arm. I'll live.'

'Ferdie?'

He shook his head.

'Molly Uzumba's up there. Pretty shaken up she is.'

'So, it was The Lighthouse Keeper who fell. I thought it was you, Ry. I thought it was bloody-well you.'

Her fists pummelled against his chest.

'No. Once The Lighthouse Keeper knew he'd got his revenge, he turned the gun on himself. He's gone, Hannah. It's over.'

'Thank God.'

Ryan moaned. Seemed to sway. He let go of his winged arm and slid his hand beneath his jacket.

'Ry?' Hannah asked. 'Ry? You ok?

He slumped to his knees on the rocky island, his hand clutched against his chest.

'No. Ryan. No; please no.'

Slowly, he withdrew his hand.

Hannah closed her eyes. She couldn't bear to see Ryan's lovely, damaged, scarred hands dripping with his own blood.

Hannah,' he said.

She opened her eyes. 'Yes?'

'Hannah Graves: will you marry me?'

In his hands, his lovely, damaged, scarred hands, he held his grandmother's antique engagement ring.

****

Author's note:

Thank you for taking the time to read *The Lighthouse Keeper* - it means a lot to me.

If you enjoyed this, the third Ryan Jarrod novel, please tell your family, friends, and colleagues. Word of mouth is an author's best friend so the more people who know, the greater my appreciation.

I welcome reviews of your experience, either on Amazon or Goodreads. Alternatively, you can 'Rate' the book after you finish reading on most Kindle devices, if you'd prefer.

If you'd like to be among the first to hear news about the next book in the series, or to discover release dates in advance, you can follow me by:

Clicking the 'Follow' button on my Amazon book's page
https://www.amazon.co.uk/Colin-Youngman/e/B01H9CNHQK%3Fref=dbs_a_mng_rwt_scns_share

OR

Liking/ following me on:
Facebook: @colin.youngman.author
Twitter - @seewhy59

Thanks again for your interest in my work.

Colin

About the author:

Colin had his first written work published at the age of 9 when a contribution to children's comic *Sparky* brought him the rich rewards of a 10/- Postal Order and a transistor radio.

He was smitten by the writing bug and has gone on to have his work feature in publications for young adults, sports magazines, national newspapers, and travel guides before he moved to his first love: fiction.

Colin previously worked as a senior executive in the public sector. He lives in Northumberland, north-east England, and is an avid supporter of Newcastle United (don't laugh), a keen follower of Durham County Cricket Club, and has a family interest in the City of Newcastle Gymnastics Academy.

You can read his other work (e-book and paperback) exclusive to Amazon:

The Girl On The Quay *(Ryan Jarrod Book Two)*
The Angel Falls *(Ryan Jarrod Book One)*

The Doom Brae Witch
Alley Rat
DEAD Heat

Twists*

(*An anthology)

****

Printed in Great Britain
by Amazon